giraffe people

JiLL MaLONE

Ann Arbor
2013

Bywater Books

Copyright © 2013 Jill Malone

Bywater Books First Edition: May 2013

Printed in the United States of America
on acid-free paper.

Cover designer: Bonnie Liss (Phoenix Graphics)

Bywater Books
PO Box 3671
Ann Arbor MI 48106-3671
www.bywaterbooks.com

ISBN: 978-1-61294-039-7

This novel is a work of fiction. Although parts of the plot
were inspired by actual events, all characters and events
described by the author are fictitious. No resemblance
to real persons, dead or alive, is intended.

For Mary & Gavin, the finest of families.

Acknowledgements

I'm grateful to the U.S. Army for 18 years of military bases and unlikely friendships; I'd never have made it to Hawaii without you.

Thanks to Erin Culver, Shelly Wilson, Bett Norris, Mary Malone, Kelly Smith, and Caroline Curtis for your tireless support and encouragement.

Fort Monmouth, I loved you more than I realized at the time.

Fall 1990

Lachrymose. Meaning unknown. Pretty sure it's an adjective.

I want *lachrymose* to mean sad. I feel sad when I say it. In the white space, along the margin of the bulletin, I write the word, next to my name. Variations on my name. I've been doing this during church services since I learned to write. Nicole. Nic. Nicci. Cole. It's sort of like my version of the American flag on the moon. I'm here. I'm right here.

Dr. Black is giving the sermon this morning. He's an ass in real life—as a human, I mean—but his sermons are amazing. He's funny and clever and charismatic, and you feel like being a Christian is the most courageous thing you can do, the way he talks about it. His kids are terrified of sex, and weird about their bodies. The older girl asked me if I had hair, you know, down there, and I thought, Are you a freak to ask that? Of course I have hair there; I'm fifteen. Haven't you read any books about this? Some people have written books on the subject: hair down there, and when you get it. Jeremy says mine is darker than he expected.

The kids on this army base, Fort Monmouth in New Jersey, are all fuck-ups. The worst kids of any base I've ever lived. We've all heard rumors about the German bases, how the kids there are worse, drinking in bars at 16, sick on drugs, pissing the German police off, but I've lived in Germany, and those kids were nothing to these kids. The chaplain school is here at Fort Monmouth. My dad runs it. Our neighborhood is all chaplains' families, and on the other side of the base, in the lower ranks' housing, are more chaplains' families. We're living on a post where three-quarters of the people are ministers or their families. Can you imagine anything worse?

Last month, Stacy Masteller jumped off the roof of their house and broke her ankle. She was wasted. David Kirk told his folks he was going to spend the night at Jeremy's house, but he actually went to New York to see Metallica, and then dropped acid and ended up in the emergency room. They're making things harder for the rest of us.

Alicia leans over and asks if today's Communion.

"Yeah," I say.

She knows, she just likes to talk during the sermon so she won't have to listen. This is new, me being able to sit wherever I want during the service. Mom said she knows I'll make wise choices. Really, Mom is talking about my name. She wants me to start going by Nicole. She says I'm not a kid anymore, and Cole sounds juvenile, and boyish. Meghan told me that Mom even talked to her about it—encouraged Meghan to mention what a cool name Nicole was, and how, when she was a kid, she'd gone by Meg, but she wasn't a kid anymore, and how a name could reflect that. Meghan told the story like my mom was this great comedian, like the whole thing was a routine or something.

"Why do you keep writing 'lachrymose'?" Alicia asks.

"It's on this week's list."

"You're still doing those lists?"

"Every week."

"God, your parents are totally freaking out," she says. "I thought you only had to do them over the summer."

"Meghan said she thought they were helping both of us. My parents agreed with her."

"Did you tell them you have eight classes, and field hockey, and friends, and don't want to have a nervous breakdown until you're a junior?"

"We negotiated."

She looks at me, her crazy fro tidier today, because it's Sunday. Alicia is taller than I am—she's six feet with hearty freckles across her cheeks and nose, light black skin, and glasses she's always pushing back into place. "They're going to let you date." She says this like they're going to let me skydive.

I nod. "One date for every list."

"Oh, girl," she says in that mmm-syrup voice. "You're in trouble now."

The truth is the lists have nothing to do with it. Two weeks ago, my dad took me to McDonald's and ordered fries and said, "I don't want Kelly sleeping over anymore."

"Why?"

"Listen, Cole." He sucked his Diet Coke for a long time before he said, "I don't like it, and that's final."

I had no idea what he was talking about, like what? But the way he said it was actually scary. I was glad to be in the middle of McDonald's with people around. He said it like each word choked him. And then he said he and Mom have decided I can date Jeremy after all.

We hear the ushers called to the front of the sanctuary, and know that the sermon is over. In a few minutes, we'll have grape juice and wafers and Alicia will ruin the holy meditation with some inanity about Ms. Overhead and her preoccupation with science fiction. Alicia worries that our literature class reads too much genre fiction, which will make it harder for us to get into a good college. They made all the incoming sophomores read Ayn Rand's *Anthem* this summer. If they'd bothered to read the book themselves, my mother said, they'd have realized how ironic the assignment was.

"Maybe they meant to be ironic," I told her.

"This is a book about rebelling against authority and being an individual, and they made it required reading for teenagers in public school. It's insane."

I liked the book. It had a sex scene and everything. My mother read it too, so we could discuss it before I had to write my paper, but she never said anything else about it.

Meghan's eighteen, and just missed getting into West Point. Instead of going to Princeton, on an ROTC scholarship, she enrolled in West Point Prep (in military lingo, United States Military Preparatory School, or USMAPS), to try to qualify for entrance to West Point next fall.

She's our cadet, my family sponsors her—she refers to us as her patrons—which just means we invite her for meals, and outings, and take her shopping, and watch her play intramural rugby. Like me, she's good at Science and English, and thinks Math is a stupid alien language that's as cruel and unfathomable as corsets and hoop skirts. Actually, she said foot binding, but when I looked foot binding up, I decided Math was a little less painful.

On Sundays, she comes for lunch at one-thirty, and then we work on the vocabulary list, and then we play some soccer at the parade ground two blocks over. My brothers, Nate and Nigel, like to tag along with us for the soccer. We usually play boys against girls and kick their sorry butts. For a while, I invited Kelly to play with us, but she says Meghan gives her a migraine. I'm like totally forbidden from mentioning anything about Meghan when Kelly's around.

Meghan is scary athletic. She's 5'6" and blond and curvy, and looks like a cheerleader who is going to be all Queen of Sarcasm, but she's fast, and aggressive, and has a big surprising laugh that you hear all the time when you're around her. And she's cool. Nate is seventeen, and totally in love with her. It's embarrassing, and kind of incestuous. I mean, it's like she's our cousin or something; otherwise, why would a cool 18-year-old hang out with a bunch of kids?

Nigel and Nate and I have the exact body of our dad: stooped, long-legged, with a narrow chest and flat feet. We're like giraffe people. Instead of his olive complexion and black hair, we're brown haired, like Mom, with her huge, darkly blue eyes, and bled-out Irish skin. Nate's thicker these days, sturdy and athletic, whereas Nigel has a distance-runner's spare frame. I'll never be curvy, but at least I'm not scrawny anymore.

I haven't finished my vocabulary list. I forgot to write definitions and parts of speech for half the words, including *lachrymose*. So while everyone else is chatting and taking their time with the lemon-peppered chicken, salad, and scalloped potatoes, I'm all shovel and gulp. Meghan knows. I can tell because she keeps ducking her head to wipe her mouth so no one will see her grinning.

Given to weeping. That's the definition of *lachrymose*. I am like a vocabulary black belt. (I considered boredom too, but my instincts said sad.) Mathematics makes me feel extremely lachrymose. We're nearly through the list when my parents announce they're taking my brothers to the PX to buy new cleats.

"How was your date last night?" Meghan asks, once they've gone. "More compelling than the vocabulary list?"

Jeremy's a senior this year, and the punter for our shitty football team. His dad's a chaplain too—he teaches at the chaplain school, so I guess my dad's his boss. That's weird. I've never really thought about that before. Anyway, Jeremy gets the whole "my dad is a minister and in the Army and we are freaks in every way" thing. So that's a way we can relate. His mom is Pentecostal, and so creepy. Jeremy says they used to speak in tongues at his old church, when they were stationed in Georgia. He's totally lying.

I watch Pepper stand up on the windowsill and bark at the squirrels on the exterior ledge. Mom leaves peanuts on the window ledge for them. It's like she's deliberately torturing the dog.

"Come on," Meghan says. "We'll take Pepper for a walk, and you can tell me about the date."

"It was nice," I say as Pepper drags me to the oak trees across the street.

"Don't say nice."

"Sorry. It was tense and atmospheric."

"How? What did you do?"

"Miniature golf, and Burger King. I had the chicken sandwich."

"Fun."

"It was OK. Jeremy drives, and that's cool. His mom lets him borrow the car whenever."

"Ah."

I like how she says that. *Ah*. Like a detective deducting some clue. "We went for a drive after golf."

Pepper takes a shit, and I have to scoop it up with a plastic bag. It's warm and squishy. I love that dog, but really.

7

Meghan's hair—curly and bobbed—is not long enough to pull into a ponytail. She told me she doesn't even comb it; she just showers and smoothes it down with her fingers. How does she play rugby with her hair in her face? I have this urge to tuck it behind her ears.

"You guys just drove around?" Meghan asks.

"Yeah, for a while."

"And then?"

Jeremy and my dad made a deal. Jeremy talks about it like this blood oath. He vowed he wouldn't sleep with me. Since I wasn't there, I don't know what my dad actually said, but according to Jeremy, it was entirely about penetration. About there not being any. With me. Ever.

"Yeah, then we stopped driving around." I look at Pepper, choking herself to reach the squirrel in the grass. Pepper's optimistic. I almost let her try for it. "He wanted to eat me, and at first I said no, because Kelly said oral is just a ruse to get me to beg for more, but he kept kissing me, and I wanted him to, and so I said yes, and he did, and it was kind of . . ." Meghan looks at me, and I'm not sure how to describe it. "Uneven, I guess."

"Uneven?"

"Yeah, uneven. It felt good sometimes, and then didn't. And then I just wanted to go home, and finish my History essay."

Meghan laughs, and puts her arm around me. She always knows how to be totally supportive.

Spendthrift. You've used this word on at least three lists. Enough already. It means prodigal. Noun or adjective.

There's a guy in our Biology class that we call Bangs. I think Kelly started that. If a politician could draw the perfect campaign daughter—preppy and stylish, pretty without being devastating, appealing and witty, slender but not too tall—Kelly Paulson would be that picture. Unless you knew her really well.

In middle school, she and I played basketball together, but she hung out with the rich kids, so we never talked. Last year, we had four classes together—including gym, and I learned that Kelly's ruthless. I've never met anyone who gets me into more trouble. When Principal Gregg told us we'd be suspended if he found a scrap of proof that we'd set off the cherry bombs in the quad, Kelly told him the next time he pulled us out of Algebra, she'd call her parents and have them make a formal complaint to the superintendent of schools. He actually twitched. Then he told us to consider it a verbal warning, and to go back to class.

Kelly thinks Jeremy is lame, and I should date Bangs instead. "He's got one of those long skinny dicks. I can tell." She whispers this to me, but it's a carrying whisper, and the girls at the lab table in front of us glance back.

"Why don't you date him?"

"Because," she says, "he's yours. He wants you like you want him."

Bangs is a skater. His head is shaved, except for his bangs, which are so long that they reach his chin and cover his entire face most of the time. He slouches, so it's hard to tell for sure, but I think he's over six feet tall. He always wears dark jeans and torn t-shirts, and has thin strips of leather tied around his forearms. We have Graphic Arts and Biology together, and second lunch—not that I eat lunch with him, I've just noticed that he has second lunch too. He sketches in charcoal, and carries his skateboard everywhere. His backpack has ANARCHY sewn across the top in red thread.

Kelly has been trying to get him to ask me out since freshman year, but he won't speak to her. No matter what she says, he just sits there, grinning. It makes her crazy.

"I have a new plan, and it's going to work," she told me at lunch.

"Plan for what?"

"Bangs," she said. "This afternoon, everything changes."

I don't argue with Kelly anymore. We split my fruit roll-up, and I tried to ignore my unease.

At the end of Biology, she tells me not to wait for her, that she'll see me in the locker room before the game.

Jeremy meets me in the hallway outside the gym with a bag of Reese's. "Hi," he says.

"Hi."

"I made you a tape." He hands it to me. "Cure singles."

"Thanks."

"Good luck at the game."

"Thanks."

"OK. Bye." He pecks me on the lips and hurries away.

We play a home game against Long Branch today. They suck at field hockey, and Coach told us she's going to play second string for most of the second half. In the locker room, Diofelli comes out of her office, and stands at the end of the bench by my locker: "How's the groin today?"

Diofelli is our assistant coach, and one of the P.E. teachers. Last spring, she called me into her office and yelled at me for twenty minutes because I played three varsity sports, but stood around in gym like some Barbie in heels. As a letterman, I'm now exempt from gym, and get study hall instead. Still, Diofelli could be an enforcer for the mob. She is a woman you do not sass, even if she comes into the locker room while you're changing and asks you about your groin.

I shrug.

"Extra stretches before the game," she says.

"OK, Coach."

"And you jog around the field while the other girls run sprints."

"OK, Coach."

"Good luck, Peters."

Kelly comes in behind Diofelli and winks at me, licking her lips. I grab my socks and shin guards and finish suiting up.

"She wants you to patch her wound," Kelly says, as she stuffs her bag into her locker, "with your tongue."

"Please stop saying that."

Kelly laughs, and pulls her shirt over her head. I want to ask what she's planning, but Coach calls us to the field, and I file out with the others.

At Monmouth Regional, field hockey is more popular than any other girls' sport—including basketball, and last year we were fourth in state. I'd never even heard of it, until my friends called me the summer before our freshman year to try-out. No one told me about the skirts.

The skirts wrap, with two buttons at the waist, and fall just below your panty line. If we wore these skirts to school, we'd be sent home, but on the field, they're our uniform. When coach handed them out, I put mine on and announced I'd quit first. Dana Myers told us to wear black shorts underneath and quit whining.

Field hockey: twenty girls in short skirts, with clublike sticks, shin guards, mouth guards, cleats, and a hard rubber ball; two goalkeepers in thick pads, and facemasks; same rules and positions as soccer.

The glare is wicked this afternoon, and we smear black under our eyes so we look even more incongruous as we take shots on the goal. Our head coach, LaMonte, a black woman with a gap in her front teeth and short, thick limbs, reminds me to jog the field while the others run sprints. They're babying me, but a jog instead of sprints is just fine.

During the huddle, I see Meghan, sitting on the top row of the bleachers, between my mom and Nigel. She waves to me.

On their second play, Long Branch scores on us. Their sweeper, a dense-legged black girl, hits into me after the goal, and raises a single index finger. Gloaters suck. I officially hate

11

this girl. Jamie and Dana, our co-captains, call Shield, and no one looks at me. Behind me, I can feel Kelly and Renee tense. Dana passes the ball to Jamie, and I am gone. Down the field, certain they will get me the ball before I pass the fullbacks. Their sweeper yells my number. I hear it, like a chant, as I run. When I break right, I run harder, and the ball bounds down the line, so that I'm chasing it now, stick cocked. I slap left and score.

We take the ball from them and score off a corner. And then the sweeper takes a swing at me with her stick, and gets carded. After I score off the penalty, I start getting shoulders and sticks from all of them. Just before the half, they take me down. Three of them, I think, but mostly I'm practicing tuck and roll. Before I'm up, I hear Renee and Kelly, and get to my feet grinning. My team is kicking some Long Branch ass in a plaid-skirted brawl.

We go out for subs, and then to Carvels after for ice-cream sandwiches. Dad, still in his uniform, arrived just in time to see the fight. He stood on the sidelines shaking his head.

"Are all your games like that?" Meghan asks. She's eating cookies and cream like she doesn't know cookies and cream is completely gross.

"Someone always tries to cripple Cole," Nigel says. He never misses any of my games. The other girls love him. Kelly calls the house sometimes just to talk to him. "Even Ocean, and they suck."

"Don't say suck," Mom says automatically. She hands us bottled waters.

"Man," Meghan says, "and I thought rugby was fierce."

Indefatigable. Hard to figure. (And ugly to pronounce.) Jeremy is indefatigable about dating.

We have Graphic Arts after homeroom. Kelly and Leisha and I trek from one end of school to the other, and occasionally make it before the bell rings. This corridor houses the photography studio, printing presses, and shop, and reeks of chemicals, dye, and metal shavings. None of the windows open, and the fans are just fancy holes. This morning Kelly has a cut to the right of her eye, and two of her fingers are taped. She and Renee and three Long Branch girls were red-carded.

"Today," Mr. Pang tells us, "we're going to pair up and take photos around campus."

Mr. Pang's hair parts exactly down the middle; his nails are long and, yes, I think it's true, manicured. He has a wispy, hint of a mustache, and this great chuckle laugh that he throws around all the time like we're the most amusing people he has ever met.

Now he calls random pairings and gives each couple a 35mm camera and a hall pass. I get paired with Bangs. Kelly gets the senior with the droopy eye.

Bangs hands me the camera, and stalks beside me. He is much bigger when you're close to him. We walk into the quad, and down one of the side paths toward the baseball field. It's October, sunny, but my jacket feels good. He's bare armed.

With the camera rested against my thigh, I pause and look around the field. It's empty out here: just grass and dirt and diamond. Beside me, Bangs slouches, kicks at the grass with his Vans.

I point to the cyclone fence behind home. "Want to climb?"

He stares at me, before he walks to the fence. I don't see him move and then he's halfway up, scaling like a Ranger.

"Wait," I call. I run to the other side of the fence, and wish I had nerve enough to ask him to hang upside down. Instead, I climb onto the dugout and from this angle catch Bangs on the fence, as well as the line to first base. He tosses his bangs back, and I get aspects of these tosses—flicks of his mane. The light is low and clear and I can see the mole on his cheek.

I shoot half the roll—him on the fence, and running the bases, and sitting cross-legged on the pitcher's mound—before I pass the camera to him. Through the viewfinder, he scours the landscape, and then says, still looking through the camera, "I saw your game yesterday."

I don't know what to say, or even if it's true, but I turn toward him, listening.

"Wish I'd got some photos of that," he says. He lowers the camera, grins at me.

We have eight classes at Monmouth, but only seven a day, so every day you drop a different class. Today we drop Geometry, and I climb the stairs to English after Graphic Arts to wait in the hallway with Kate and Alicia. Ms. Overhead locks the door between classes so she can masturbate without interruption.

Jeremy waves from across the hall, and then comes over to us. "Hi there," he says to Alicia and Kate.

They smile at him.

"Walk me to class?" he asks me. He has European History now, two classrooms from mine.

I step away with him, and he leans in quickly to kiss me, pressing a folded note into the front pocket of my jeans. "I heard they tried to stampede you yesterday."

I wonder where he heard about it, and how accurate the telling was.

"Five goals?" he grins.

I nod.

"Wish I'd been there."

Jeremy is black-haired, with dark blue eyes, and pale skin. He's broad shouldered and taller than I am, but he isn't greedy about space. It's easy to stand with him like this in the hallway. Can I

14

read the letter now, or should I wait? I'm still trying to decide when the bell rings.

After Ms. Overhead picks readers for the fourth act of *Hamlet*, and doesn't choose me, I unfold Jeremy's letter.

> Dear Cole:
> About Saturday night in the car. I really want to be with you, but I don't want to miss the trip either. I talked to Mike, and he said, we just get this one opportunity and we should savor it. That's what he said: savor it. You know Mike. I hope it's all right that I talked to him about it. I just thought I needed some guidance. When I'm around you, I don't always think straight.
> Want a ride home after practice?
> Jeremy

OK, the thing I told Meghan about Jeremy and oral, not entirely accurate. The truth is, I asked Jeremy to. Begged. Cajoled. Pressured. I'm tired of being this girl. Me. I'm tired of being me. For a little while, I want to be someone else. Another kind of girl: a little less in my head, a little more in my body. Present. I want to be present.

Mike, Jeremy's older brother, is a sophomore at Penn State. Their dad made them come home for Evening Prayer. He forbade Halloween, sleepovers, PG-13 movies, television. In high school, Mike fronted a metal band, and his parents threatened to send him to a therapist. Before Jeremy, Mike used to make me mixed Cure tapes. He kissed me once, late on a Sunday night at the parade ground. I don't even remember why I was outdoors, but I saw him at the war memorial and he called to me. Savor. Yes, I want to be savored. Devoured and consumed.

Ms. Overhead says my name. I look up.

"Well, Cole?" she says. "What's your position on Hamlet?"

"He's a jackass."

The class turns toward me, awake all at once. Alicia has her hand over her mouth.

"Care to expound on that?" Ms. Overhead says.

"What kind of guy doesn't look behind a curtain before he stabs someone? And he's so mean to Ophelia. Ophelia's pretty unrealistic—I mean, why is she mad, exactly—but that's no reason to ignore her, and speak in code like a jackass. So her father manipulated her, his did too. Hamlet is a wishy-washy brat."

I don't want to see Jeremy anymore. The bell rings and I leave before anyone can say anything.

We practice until 6. Drills mostly, and sprints. Today, Coach makes me do half the sprints, and then sends me to jog around the field for the rest of practice.

Bangs is propped beside the gym door, holding his board by a truck as though it were a briefcase. I pause in front of him, and he scoops his hair behind his ear.

"Your number," he says. "I need it, to call you."

He copies it down on the title page of our Biology text. In Sharpie.

Turns out *indefatigable* means tireless. That's not what I thought, and kind of disappointing. Doesn't it sound like it should mean hard to figure? My father is indefatigable about my salvation. Well, everybody's, but his stance on mine is particularly relevant to me. No offense.

At night, usually around ten, Dad goes for a walk through the neighborhoods. He says during night walks his mind wanders and comes back sleepy. Sometimes I go with him. In fact, when we moved here, and were still living in temporary housing, we walked through this very neighborhood, and Dad said it looked like a ghetto. The houses are all three-story brick duplexes, but instead of being divided down the middle, they're divided by floor. One family gets the ground floor, and a maid's room; the other family gets the second floor and a maid's room. In every backyard, metal trashcans, and laundry lines.

I don't think Dad's happy here. His stepfather and aunt died two years ago, and afterward his mother had a nervous breakdown, and still calls late at night crying, and his current job is administrative, and he suddenly has three alien teenagers living in the house with him. And Nate got caught with a girl in his room in August. Later, when I'm thirty and have a kid of my own, I'll have more sympathy for my father during this assignment, but right now I'm fifteen and I think he's a dick who's having an affair with his secretary. It's the way he says her name: *Miss Jensen*, like it's whipped cream.

Tonight, he calls on the intercom to ask if I want to walk with him. (I live in the maid's room on the third floor and have my own bathroom—Nate's punishment for getting caught with a girl was to swap rooms with me.) Bangs hasn't called yet, but waiting is lame, so I agree. Dad tells me to wear a hat.

And he's right; the wind is indefatigable through the streets, and our clothes. The yards smell like mucky leaves and have toys and bikes and skateboards tossed on them because no one worries about thieves. And I want my mind to wander down the alleyway, and out the gate and through civilian streets, and come back braver. I think of Jeremy in the car on the drive home after practice, chattering away like it's not over, like he doesn't know.

"How's Leroy?" Dad asks.

Leroy teaches me guitar. He's an old black guy with one of his front teeth missing, and he plays blues like you've never heard. This one song *Walking the Dog*, well, you can't breathe when he plays it. Dad's asking because he can hear me playing even from two floors below, and guitar is a safe subject for both of us.

"He thinks I'm not practicing my scales enough."

Dad winks at me, and we keep walking. Of course I don't practice my scales enough. I don't practice anything enough.

We pass the metal bus stop, painted white now to cover the graffiti where Kiki Stewart and I wrote the names of every couple we knew with black marker. This is our last year in Jersey. Dad knows it'll be Alaska or Hawaii for his final assignment, and we'd all prefer Alaska. We should know in the spring where we're going.

I played Leroy one of my songs at our last lesson. He kept his eyes closed while I sang, and when I finished, he asked me to play it again. I'd never played for anybody before. It felt kind of sacred.

The Barnes' dog is baying. The lights are on in every room of the General's quarters. He has a really ugly daughter. She's the same year as Nate, and has a crush on him. Pepper is tugging against my dad. Partly I'm eager like that. Like Pepper. I want to pull against everything. I want to strain. I think maybe I do.

Resilient. I love this word. It's reptilian! Resilient means recovers readily; buoyant. Adjective.

Sunday afternoon, Meghan and I go over the vocabulary list at the dining table after lunch. Mom and Dad are napping, and the boys are playing Sega.

"Where are you?" she asks.

"What?"

"Where are you? You're not here. Not at this table, in this room."

"I played some of my songs for Leroy. He thinks they're good."

"What songs?"

"You know, for the guitar."

"You write songs?" She says this like I've admitted eating babies.

"Yeah."

"Will you play one for me?"

I can't decide if she's teasing me. So I shrug.

"Will you?" she insists.

"If you want," I say, and shrug again. Ophelia bugs me. She went crazy all of a sudden, didn't she? Boys. Jeremy came over last night and we watched a video—he loves Hitchcock, so we watched *Spellbound.* Gregory Peck is gorgeous. In the movie, he's crazy in that hard to understand way that Ophelia is. Like convenient-to-the-plot kind of crazy. Before he left, Jeremy kissed me in the kitchen. He grabbed my shoulders and kissed me hard, and when he let me go I felt like I was filled with helium.

"Now?" Meghan asks.

"What?"

"Will you play a song for me now?"

"My guitar is upstairs," I say.

She stands, and I do too. I still don't know if she's teasing me, but I lead her upstairs, and unlock the door to my room and then we stand there just inside. She's never been in here before, I'm pretty sure. She sits on the bed and looks at me.

"I'm ready," she says.

I get my guitar and sit on the floor and tune it. By the second

19

verse, I'm OK. I just don't look at her, keep my head down, and sing. When I finish I wipe my hands on my jeans.

"You wrote that?"

I look up now and she isn't teasing me. I nod.

"Do you have more?"

I play another. And another after that. I don't know how long we're up there, but I play and play and it stops feeling weird that I'm not alone. When I look at her, at last, her face is tense. Only for a moment, though, and then she grins at me.

"You're a surprising person, Cole."

"Am I?"

"Yes."

I want to ask why she looked tense, but I don't know how, and she's been so nice about everything that I grin back at her like I'm not worried. "You know *Hamlet*?" I ask.

She nods, still grinning.

"What's the deal with Ophelia? I don't get it. Her arc and everything."

"She loses everyone she loves all at once."

"Well, it does sound kind of harsh when you say it like that."

"Let's go for a walk," she says, helping me to my feet. "I'm wild to be doing something."

I follow her down the stairs and on the last staircase, she stops, turns in front of me so abruptly that I nearly slam into her, and says, "Thank you for playing for me."

"Sure." And there it is again. I'm entirely helium.

I babysit for the Thorns a lot of Sunday and Tuesday nights. Usually the kids are already in pajamas, and I just play with them for a while, read stories, and then put them to bed. Afterward, I finish my homework or watch MTV or whatever until the Thorns get back around ten. Tonight Karen wakes up crying. She and Annie sleep in the same room, so I get her and bring her into the living room with me. Karen is ten months old with a big, almost hairless head and huge brown eyes; she's the happiest kid I've ever met. She'd rather be laughing than anything else.

I sit on the couch with her and she looks at me for a while, then she rests her head on my chest and falls asleep. No kid ever slept on my chest before. It's kind of amazing to hear her breathe and feel her heart and the weight of her. I don't move for a long time. When the ginger cat comes and sits on my leg, her purring synchs with Karen's and they both hum against me. Exponentially more interesting than Geometry theorems.

When I get home, I stop in the kitchen for some water and find a note that Christian called. By the time I get upstairs, and ready for bed and everything, it's nearly eleven, but Christian has his own line in his room, so I call anyway.

"It's Cole," I say.

"Hey."

It doesn't sound like Christian. The voice is raspy.

"I hope it's not too late to call. I just got back from the Thorns."

"Who are the Thorns?"

Now I know it isn't Christian. "I babysit for them."

"Oh."

"What are you doing?" I still have no idea who this is, but he's talking like he knows me, and I can figure this out if he keeps going.

"I skated all day at Hand's place. Now I'm playing guitar and talking to you."

It's Bangs. I forgot he had a real name. "What kind of guitar?"

"A Gibson electric. I just got a wah pedal."

"What do you play?"

"You know, whatever. I can play some Metallica."

"Who's Hand?" I ask.

"Oh," he says. I can hear the wah pedal cry. I want to see his guitar, the way he holds it. "We call him Mr. Hand, but that's not really his name. He has a skate shop in Asbury Park—it's this crazy warehouse, and he built some ramps in the back. Pretty sonic."

"Mr. Hand?"

"Yeah, it's about this bumper sticker on his car. *I'd rather be masturbating.*"

21

I blush. I feel it. And I realize he was stalling, trying not to tell me.

"Is that guy your boyfriend?" he asks.

"What guy?"

"The one with the black hair. The football player."

"I don't know."

"He seems like your boyfriend."

I don't know what to say. His guitar cries in one long wail, and we both listen.

Every week, Meghan designs thirty-word vocabulary lists; I define each word, give parts of speech in my answer, and we go over the whole thing together. If I do five a day, I get a day off every week. *Inimitable.* It means matchless. We're going to be inimitable against Freehold this afternoon. We have three more games left this season; our last is the day before Halloween.

My parents bought Nate a Toyota this summer, and they pay for his insurance since he drives Nigel and me to school every day. We pick Doug up too, and the four of us in Nate's hatchback are snug with our school bags and my field hockey gear. Doug and Nate play soccer in the spring, and the rest of the year they smoke pot and talk about brewing their own beer and try to convince girls they're different from other guys.

"Hey, Cole," Doug says after he adjusts the radio to more bass than the car can take, until the windows rattle. "Did you get Allison's number for me?"

"I told you. She has a boyfriend."

"So?"

"So she's not giving you her fucking number."

"Oh, you said a naughty word. I'm telling your mom." He screws around and glares at me. Doug is brown-haired and brown-eyed and has a sweet face that he thinks gives him a disadvantage with girls. "Who's her boyfriend?"

"That dude Jay."

"The baseball guy?" Doug asks, scowling.

"Yeah."

"Oh shit." He glances at my brother. "I hate that fucking dude. He dated Tina last year, and even after he dumped her, she still talks about him like he pisses diamonds." Doug turns back to me. "Look, Cole, if anything changes, I want her number. You'll keep me informed, right?"

"Count on me."

"Excellent." He turns back around, and switches the station. "Dude, when are you going to get some decent speakers?"

Bangs is in the parking lot, popping ollies beside the opened rear doors of a two-toned brown van. Two other guys sit inside the van on plush brown swivel seats. All three of them have the same haircut. One says something and Bangs turns to stare at me.

"Hey," he says.

"Hey," I say.

"Well, well," Doug says behind me.

Bangs kicks his board up and falls in with us without a word to the guys in the van. Tied around his waist is a torn plaid shirt.

"Let me have that." He takes my gym bag and throws it over his shoulder.

"I'm Doug," Doug says.

"Christian."

Doug sneers at me. "Have a moral day, kids."

"Prick," I whisper to his back.

Bangs walks me to my locker. "Those guys were your brothers?" And suddenly I feel bad for not introducing him.

"Yeah, the quiet ones were Nate and Nigel. Nate's taller."

"Cool." He stuffs my bag into my locker. "See you later."

"OK."

Perched in the chair of her desk like a preening bird, Kelly regards me. "He what?"

"Last night he called, and we talked for like an hour."

"I am the god of all things." She says it louder. "I'm the god of all things. Say it."

"You're the god of all things."

"I really am. I made this happen." She's wearing a silk vest and a skirt. She looks like she's going to temp as a secretary. No one else I know dresses like this for high school. "You two are my responsibility."

I'm worried when she says this. It's kind of crazy, right? Kind of mad scientist? But the bell rings, and we have to jet, and I don't have time to analyze the variety of ways I should be troubled.

In Graphic Arts, Bangs and I process our best shots from the roll at the baseball diamond. He picks a close-up of me—and crops out everything but my hair and face. We shot in black and white and I look like a refugee in a windstorm. For my own part, I pick a shot of him on the fence, defiant, his fingers linked through the cyclone, and one of them missing a nail. I've never been able to look at him like this before. To take him in. His eyes are fierce, his nose Roman, his lips fuller than a boy's should be.

When I take the photograph out of the fixer, I'm reluctant to hang it up. Then he's against me in the dark room, pressed to my back, and just for a second instead of the chemicals, I smell him: oatmeal and soap and cinnamon gum.

My mom still makes my lunch. Every day I get a brown bag with a peanut butter and jelly sandwich, white cheese popcorn, pretzels, frosted animal crackers, a fruit roll-up, raw carrots, and a box of raisins. Once, when she was going to visit my grandparents for three weeks, she bagged everything but our sandwiches, and left it all—including extra paper bags—in baskets with each of our names marked on them with freezer tape. She thinks we're inept and would starve without her.

Joe is sitting at our table with Matt and Christian Sorrentino (the other Christian—not Bangs) when Kelly and I arrive. Joe wears red Converse all the time—even to gym—and bleaches his hair, and then rats it like Robert Smith. He is The Cure's biggest fan. I had a crush on him all freshman year. He only ever teases me.

"Well," Joe says, "who's going to get red-carded this afternoon?"

"My money's on Kelly," Matt says between bites of pizza.

Kelly ignores them, and eats some of my popcorn.

"What happened to the football player?" Joe asks me.

"What?"

"I saw you this morning in the parking lot."

"So?"

"So, what happened to the football player?" Finally he stops staring at me, and looks, instead, at Kelly. "Wasn't the skater your little project?"

"What's a matter, Joe," Kelly says, "missed another window?"

"You know, Kelly." Joe stands and looks down at her. "I hope I'm around when she dumps you. That'll really be something."

He leaves without saying more, and we all look at Kelly. Something happened, but no one's sure what. Was he talking about me dumping Kelly?

"What was that?" Christian Sorrentino asks. He's having Mountain Dew for lunch again.

"You know Joe," Kelly says. "All drama all the time."

Matt and Christian look at me, and then let it go and ask about our Spanish homework.

I have study hall with Jeremy. We sit at the smallest table by the Biographies. He hands me a note as soon as I arrive, and watches me while I read it.

Cole:
Doug said you had something important to tell
me. It's probably better if you write it. Ms.

Adams already yelled at Lollipop for talking.

Doug is a wicked fuck. I read the note a few more times, and then write a response—

Do you talk to other girls—I mean on the phone or whatever?

He takes the note and reads through it and then looks up at me. He has three lines across his forehead, and a divot between his eyes.

Sure. Girls in my study group.

It is not right that he's worried. It's not right that anyone knew before he did, or that he should feel bad about any of it.

I talk to another boy. Not about school. He asked if you were my boyfriend and I said I didn't know.

He reads the note and does not look up for a long time. I'm supposed to be working on my Biology homework. It seems disrespectful, somehow, to do Biology homework now.

Do you want him to be your boyfriend?

I am so tired now. Just holding my pen exhausts me. I read the question again and again.

"What are you two working on?" Ms. Adams asks. I am so grateful to see her, hovering there, wringing her hands and glaring at us.

"Biology," I say, and then I am, with half the period still to go, and a vigilant Ms. Adams checking alternative pursuits.

When the bell rings, Jeremy asks if I'll come over to his place tonight. He has the maid's room in their quarters, and a saltwater fish tank and a waterbed. It's Mike's old room, and I

26

have only ever been there with groups of kids during the day. We promised, when they let us date, that we'd never visit one another's room.

"OK," I say. "I'll come over after my parents go to bed."

I score three goals against Freehold, and have to sit out the entire second half of the game to rest my groin. We win by six. Nigel and I make it back to the base in time to catch the last ten minutes of Meghan's rugby game. A heavy girl with breasts like a prison matron gets her nose broken and there's blood across her face, and both hands, and her shirt and several of her teammates. I wish I had never seen so much blood, and the way they are painted with it. They stuff cotton up her nose, and she goes right back in.

"Mom and Dad ordered pizza," I tell Meghan, after they have won. "Do you want to come over? Dad said he'll drive you back to the dorm after."

She agrees, and drags her grey Army sweats on before we all set off.

"What's happened? Why do you look so grim?" Meghan asks me. "Is it the Hamlet paper?"

"She gave me an A–."

"She really does hate you."

"I know, right. How about your Calculus quiz?"

"B. Calculus is nefarious."

"It's so totally nefarious! Way to dominate the language!" I give her a high five.

"You two have gotten really weird," Nigel says.

Meghan laughs and links her arm through his. From the street, the house lights warm us, and our appetites stir; desperate, striving aches.

Straight after dinner, Meghan leaves. She has piles of home-work, and so do I. By ten-thirty, I finish the bulk of it, and take the stairs down from my room to the wooden back door, which

I unlock, and open easily, and then the horrible screen door, and finally I'm in the backyard. Nate's bedroom light is the only one still on.

At Jeremy's, every light is off in the entire building—four sets of families—and I wonder if he fell asleep, if I'm risking getting caught for nothing. I find the backdoor unlocked, slip my shoes off to climb four flights to his room, and let myself in.

In sweatpants and a white t-shirt, he's sprawled on the floor reading his History text. He stands when I come in and we both hold our breath. Illicit. Just standing in his room is illicit. Even his clothes seem illicit. A table light, the blue glow of the fish tank, and a boy in the half dark, intent and watchful. Then we hear a door. All the interior doors are metal, and close with a heavy click.

I'm on the far side of his bed, and flat on my stomach when his bedroom door opens.

"Hey, son. I thought you'd still be up." His father closes the door and moves deeper into the room. I can hear him approach me. "I've brought you a little snack."

"Thanks."

"Hungry, weren't you?"

"Yes."

"What are you working on?"

"History. Another three chapters."

"Then I won't keep you. The hot chocolate should help."

"Yes."

"Well." He moves away, and the door opens again. "Well. Good night, then. Not too late, if you please."

"No."

"Night, son."

"Night."

Even from the floor, my heart's a mouthy snitch, calling through the corridors of the building, shouting to his father. I've clawed my palms in my panic. They bleed from little half moons.

Jeremy crouches beside me. "I'm sorry. He never does that. I'm so sorry. I've locked it now."

28

"I thought he knew."

He smiles, pale and breathless as I am. "I did too."

And then he kisses me. Like the kiss from the kitchen, hard and urgent, and I can't breathe, and I'm crying and we haven't even done anything, not really, but I'm terrified. All at once, I'm terrified.

Both of us gasping, he goes on kissing me. His arms cradle me, his hands inside my shirt, and a different urgency comes, one that makes me forget his father stood in this room with us moments before. He presses his knee between my legs, and we roll once. I understand, at last, about Eden: how you could make a soul out of nothing but breath.

When I wake, we're spooled, in our clothes, and still on the floor. My arm underneath him is asleep, and tingling, but I've never been this warm. Against the window shade, the night presses like a face, and I know I should get up; I should leave him and get home. His breathing is deep and languid and mine.

I peel away from him, and sneak out; the red glow of his bedside clock reads 3:23.

Pedantic. Ostentatious in one's learning. Adjective. Ms. Overhead is pedantic about everything, even stuff that has nothing to do with English.

My mother has taken up woodworking. Every morning, she puts on overalls and a flannel shirt, and goes to the basement to build benches and ornate shelves with hooks, and freestanding cabinets. She belongs to a sort of club that meets once a month to review one another's work. Before one of these meetings, she's stressed, bitchy, and dangerous.

While I'm pouring cereal, I hear her moving below me, and can feel her absorption, her intensity. It's distracting.

"What?" Nigel says, paused in the doorway. And then he hears too, and shakes his head. "She went down there at like 5. She should hang a hammock and then she can just live in the basement." He places an empty bowl on the counter for me to fill with cereal. "I ran this morning."

"How far?"

"Four miles."

"What time did you get up?"

"Five."

"How's that less crazy than Mom?"

"I don't wear overalls."

We eat at the kitchen table. He reads a *Peanuts* book from the seventies, while I finish my Geometry. At 8, Nate will run in, yelling about how he's hungry and we're going to be late, and why doesn't anyone wake him. Until then, I'll write theorems and think of Jeremy's breathing, and the burn of him against me when I woke. The eerie gurgle of the fish tank and the way he kissed my face and held me like he was going to lift me up and run from the building. Like the whole place might come down around us.

Geometry is the most painful thing I know. When I learned

about the Inquisition, I imagined them making you solve Geometry problems in little cells for months. That would be so maniacal and wicked. Mr. Henderson uses an overhead projector, and sits at a stool and mumbles his lesson. He has pockmarks and weird moles by his eyelids and totally got stuffed into lockers and garbage cans when he was my age. He's nice, but in that *Please don't look at me, I'm hideous and shy and just interacting with you hurts me* kind of way. So, asking for clarification, not an easy thing.

"Cole," he says, glancing at me and then back at his slide. "Would you like to show us your solution for problem 28?"

I walk up to the board and write my theorem. Being left-handed, even writing on the board is a chore. This problem, I'm pretty sure I've done right. I didn't get a chance to check with Ian before class. Ian likes to wear old bowling shirts he found at Goodwill, and has that blond hair that's actually white, and keeps telling me I'll never understand Geometry until I learn to play pool.

"Good job, Cole." Mr. Henderson calls on mouse-girl to solve for 32. She is wearing her coat. She does this a lot, and I don't understand it. Maybe she sneaks outside between classes to smoke.

I am going to get a B in this class. It's going to wreck my GPA. The brown van sat in the parking lot, shut up and empty, this morning. We dropped Graphic Arts, so I haven't seen Bangs yet. I don't even know if he's at school.

Joe tosses a note onto my desk.

We have a gig Saturday night—a house party. Any chance you could come?

I wear my skeptical face.

You think my parents are going to let me go to a house party?

I toss the note back.

They don't have to know it's a house party. Tell

31

**them you're going to the movies. Trevor and I will
pick you up.**

Trevor has long, lank black hair, and wears leather vests without
a shirt underneath. I smile at him, and write back:

Joe, my parents don't find you guys reassuring. They think
you listen to metal and tear the heads off puppies and play
Dungeons and Dragons and sacrifice virgins.

Is that a no?

he writes back.

No. It isn't. Give me a couple of days to figure something out.
Can I bring a friend?

He's all grin when he hands me his response.

Sure, anyone who isn't Kelly.

In the hallway, before English, I tell Alicia about the house party.
"I remember," she says, "when we all spent Saturday night at
the roller rink."
"We were twelve."
"Yes."
"Do you want to go with me?" I ask.
"Oh no. I am not participating in more of your misadventures.
Last time, that party at John Rafferty's house, my parents
grounded me for two weeks. And it was a boring party."
Every party I had ever been to was boring. People standing
in the same groups they kept at school, talking about class and
each other.
"But this party has a band."

"Girl, you know they just play three chords and holler. Ask Stella, or Kelly; they love courting trouble, just like you."

Bangs comes over to our table at lunch and sits beside me. Christian Sorrentino and Matt Cabrese both stare at him, and then at me. Kelly introduces everyone, and Bangs nods at them.

"What are you doing Saturday?" he asks me.

"I don't know."

"A friend of mine's having a party. There'll be bands and everything."

"Bands?" I ask.

"Yeah, we're playing."

"You're in a band?"

"Sure."

"What kind of music do you play?"

"All kinds." He looks at Kelly. "You two should come."

Without checking with me, Kelly says, "We'll be there."

After practice on Friday, Renee and I head over to the football field to watch the second half of the game against Red Bank. Her boyfriend, Dwayne, plays fullback. Football bores me—and, of course, we're losing—but the games make excellent crowd watching.

"That girl's wearing Saran Wrap," Renee says. We look at her for a while. "She must be cold."

It's interesting how many teachers come to football games. Most of them bring their spouses like this is a date. Coach Robins—our varsity soccer coach—waves me over.

"Hey, Coach."

"I'm glad to see you, Peters. Saves me having to track you down." Coach Robins is a stretched, muscular man with forty spiked hairs on his head. He seems painfully old to me, but is probably fifty-five. "I saw your game Thursday. You've pulled your groin again, haven't you?"

How is it proper, this conversation? I nod.

"I thought so. Listen, I've had an idea." And he explains to me about taking a brace for my hamstring, and folding it in half, and tucking it into my groin. "A little extra support. I think it'll save you straining the damn thing over and over."

"OK, Coach."

"Don't 'OK, Coach' me like a twit. I want your guarantee."

"OK, Coach—I promise." You have to humor adults. They can totally fuck with your life.

"Good, Peters. Now get lost. I'm trying to watch football."

Renee and I have eaten four chili dogs, and three bags of chips, and a box of licorice, and have shared a beer that some chicks we play ball with smuggled in. We were the only freshmen to letter in three varsity sports last year. They happened to be the same three varsity sports. I've known Renee since seventh grade, when she weighed forty pounds more, and had buckteeth.

"Y'all going to the party after?" she asks.

"No."

"I don't know why I keep asking," she says, and then groans as they sack our quarterback. "Does your boy do it right there in the car, or does he wait until he gets you home?" Renee and Dwayne have been having sex since she was a freshman, and she assumes the same for the rest of us, no matter how we protest.

"It's not like that," I say.

"Uh huh. Whatever you say, baby."

Twenty minutes after the game ends, Jeremy comes out with his duffel, and puts an arm around me. "I wasn't sure you'd come," he says.

"I wanted to see you. Since I can't tomorrow."

"Oh, right." His enthusiasm almost falters. "I'll bet you're hungry."

"Starved," I say.

"Chicken wings?"

The wings are so hot that they burn our fingertips. We're

34

exclaiming, and biting into them all the same, orange sauce across our mouths.

"There's beer," he says, and grabs two cans from the cooler behind my seat. We're parked across from the bowling alley, in a turnaround shielded by greenery and another brick memorial commemorating some battle someplace. The MPs won't check out here for another three hours.

The interior of his mother's white Honda is plush and blue and spotless. My family doesn't have vehicles like this. My father's van didn't run when he bought it—he had to tow it home before he could work on the engine and sort the problem out. He always sorts the problem out, and the vehicles always look like they have problems to be sorted.

I want to ask if Jeremy is sick of losing. Game after game, and they never win. Can't find a way to manage it, though, without sounding like a vainglorious ass.

"I missed you," he says, "when I woke."

"You wouldn't budge. I practically had to throw you off me to get home. You're heavier than you look."

He grins, and hands me another wing. "I don't remember falling asleep. You were crying, and I was kissing you, and then I woke up alone on the floor."

"Irascible" means hot-tempered, and I wonder, as he's nibbling at a wing bone, how temperate Jeremy is. Would he be mad if he knew I was going to a party tomorrow night, and that I'd been invited by two different boys? Would he disapprove that I'd lied to my parents, that Kelly's mother had called and convinced them we were going to take the train into the city to see a play, and that she had their permission to drop me off back home Sunday afternoon? (Apparently, her mom had to promise we'd sleep in separate rooms.) Was it terrible, that after all this trouble, I didn't even want to go? Would, in fact, have preferred another Saturday night of miniature golf and Burger King, than this elaborate charade? I didn't want Jeremy to know, or Meghan. I didn't want to tell either of them how I'd schemed.

"Beer?" He hands one to me, and then, as he fiddles with

35

the radio, he says softly, "I could get used to kissing you to sleep."

More *ware*house party than the usual house variety. Kelly's mother pulls up to BOARD The Skate Shop in Asbury Park, and waves to the two fellows at the door (they must weigh four hundred pounds apiece, but they wave back and grin friendly gold teeth).

"Ladies," one says, and holds the door open for us. This chivalry crap is all down to Kelly. Tonight she's wrapped in a blue dress that glitters, and rounds places on her that never seemed round before. When I showed up at her house wearing jeans and a t-shirt, Kelly said all the stuff I didn't know had really started to annoy her, and now I'm freezing in borrowed clothes: a short black skirt, and a green V-neck cashmere sweater that somehow manages to give me cleavage.

Inside, decks line the walls—the visual interspersed with photos of famous skaters, and sick tricks, and ads for Vans and Independent, and cardboard signs with "THE MANAGEMENT RESERVES THE RIGHT TO BEAT SHOPLIFTERS DOWN." Behind display cases are wheels, trucks, grip tape, and punk cassettes. Racks of magazines lead into the clothing section of the store: sweatshirts, t-shirts, and thick pants, and an entire corner of rubber-soled shoes. A dude sits on the glass counter beside a cash register and leers at us. Four girls in the corner, by the shoes, giggle something and stare. Everyone else wears jeans and sweatshirts. Fucking Kelly.

Almost like an alcove, the store is just a foyer for the building, and once we walk beneath the rolling gate, we're inside the warehouse with its Keyhole Bowl Ramp, half-pipe ramp, and the makeshift stage that towers above the room. The place is dirty in that way that smells—like an old refrigerator—and crowds of kids move in and out of the rumble. That's right, rumble: my ears hurt, and I'm grateful to be wearing Kelly's clothes because they're going to need torching when we get out of here. On the stage, four skinny boys dressed in black play with their heads bowed, distortion bursting from their amps. Bangs isn't one of them, and Joe's band doesn't suck like this.

"I know that guy," Kelly says, pointing. I follow her gesture, and realize, with horror, that I know that guy too. "Isn't that your brother?"

I cannot say yes, because that would mean that I accept it: Nate is here too, and I am so dead.

"How'd he manage that?" Kelly asks.

And then I realize that Kelly's right, and Nate must have plotted as well, that we have mutually assured destruction, and so are both safe. He's standing by the bowl, with Doug and a couple of skanky girls with streaks of white bleached into their hair, watching a guy with a Fu Manchu mustache skate.

"Your brother looks good," she says.

"What?" I say, but then Bangs joins us, grinning at our outfits.

"Kind of formal," he says. His jeans have holes in the knees, and his t-shirt proclaims *Armed Resistance* and has a stick figure holding a guitar out like a sword.

"When do you play?" I ask, so he'll stop staring at me.

"10:30."

"You skate these?" People could die here: high entries, and hard surfaces. No one's wearing a helmet or pads.

"Yeah, I had a couple runs earlier. Pretty sonic." He unwinds his sweatshirt from his waist, and hands it to me. "Put this on." I think he's as embarrassed of my clothes as I am, until he adds, "You're cold." It might just be shock that has me shivering, but I put the sweatshirt (Independent Truck Company with the sweet red logo) on anyway, and am grateful for the camouflage.

I've just realized that Kelly's gone when Joe slams into me— he's wearing Army surplus boots and jeans so tight his balls must ache. He has dyed his hair black, that deep, fake black that makes people look like they've been bled.

"Oh, Cole," he says. "I didn't see you." And then he sees Bangs, and takes a step back from me.

"This is Christian," I say. "Christian, Joe."

"Hey, man," Bangs says.

Joe takes out a cigarette, and looks at it. "Our singer is no-showing."

I don't think this grammar works. How do you no-showing? "What will you do?" I ask. "Have someone else sing?"

"Sure," Joe says. "I'll sing. That should clear out half the place at least."

"What do you guys play, *Just Like Heaven* and *Fascination Street*, or just classics like *Killing an Arab*?"

"Don't be funny, Cole, it isn't helping."

"You totally play *Just Like Heaven*, don't you?" I insist.

"Yes," he hisses.

"Do you have a set list?"

"Why?" he asks.

"Just let me see it." He hands the set list over: U2, The Cure, The Ramones, The Clash. God, I want to hug the guy. He's so predictable. "I know all these songs."

Joe stares at me. "To play, or to sing?"

"Either."

He looks at Bangs, then back at me. "You got a guitar in your pocket, by any chance?"

"You can use mine," Bangs says to me.

Joe tucks his cigarette behind his left ear. "Well, I guess it couldn't be worse than dropping out, right?"

In their band, Doggy Life, Joe plays bass, Trevor drums, and Ernie—a slim poetic kid with acne—rips lead guitar. Their lead singers change every gig. I can't even remember the name of the last couple guys. Jason? When Joe tells them that I'm going to sing with them tonight, they cock their heads like Pepper when you ask her some question that doesn't include the word treat or walk, and then Trevor says, "Chick singers are bitchin'."

We're all backstage (in a hallway that stretches the length of the building), and Trevor's got a six-pack of Budweiser on his amp. He graduated last year, and looks like Mr. Metal in his leather vest, with his lank black hair, and giant pirate skull belt buckle. He's a big dude, who spent lunch periods flicking anyone unlucky enough to sit nearby.

"You look different from last year," he tells me. "You want a beer?"

Bangs brings his Gibson—red and pristine—and a little amp into the hallway, and sets them up for me. After a couple of strums, I already feel rotten about playing such an instrument in this shithole.

"It's pretty," I say, and mean the sound, and the guitar. I'm nervous, like before a cross-country race. Nervous as a kind of palpable energy: my stomach wonky, my head light.

Joe kneels between us. "OK, so it's Super Sock Monkey Puppets, and then us. You've sung into a microphone before, right?"

I nod.

"This'll be fine. You've seen us play a bunch of times. You know how we work."

I know these guys can all play, and that no one who ever stood up with them could sing. Joe grabs his bass, and waves Ernie over, and the three of us play a couple of Cure songs. Ernie stops watching my fingers after five measures, but Joe keeps his eyes on my left hand, nodding along in tempo, but also in a way I find encouraging.

On stage, the place is hot; the lights make everything except the kids closest to stage just a bunch of random noise. If Bangs hadn't lent me his guitar, I couldn't have done this, not with only the mic stand to hide behind.

Joe introduces us, and then we roar into *Judy Is a Punk* like we've rehearsed the damn thing, our guitars rapid fire, and the drum kicking up against the bass, and I see kids leaping around the floor in front of us. Over the drum, I can't hear myself sing, but it can't matter. These kids are crazy—they're flinging into each other like they're on bungee ropes; for them, the lyrics are the least of it. I think so, anyway, until I see several of them singing along to the chorus. And that's when I stop feeling like I'm going to vomit, and start singing like I wrote these songs, and mean them.

When we play *Just Like Heaven* I hear girls start screaming, and the invisible crowd shifts on the floor beyond us. Under the lights, we could be alone, the four of us. Ernie, his shoulders hunched, his hair covering his face, is resonant, and pure, stationary except for his gliding fingers. Joe bounces all over the fucking place, and rushes up to scream random lines at the crowd from the stage's edge. I keep hitting my teeth against the microphone, and finally grab it when I belt the lyrics, and let the guitar hang against me like I'm a tired rocker. Trevor drums the current beneath us, the one the kids keep diving into. We are so cool. No one has ever been as cool as the four of us, on this stage, with this wailing crowd.

Joe drives me home after. We won first prize—I didn't even know it was a competition, but we got $50 when the crowd cheered loudest for us at the end of the night. Bangs' band, Slim and None, won second place, and $25.

Kelly left with my brother; anyway that's what Doug said. He said it with a smirk, in this tone meant to antagonize me. I have no idea if they saw us play, or what, and I don't mean to be all stage actress, but she is dead to me. My brother, for real? That is so wrong, and gross, and not OK with me. Bangs isn't old enough to drive, and caught a ride to this party with his crew, who are headed to another party afterwards, so I was kind of screwed until Joe offered to take me home.

Bangs walked me to Joe's car, and said watching me play was even better than watching girls fight over me. He told me to keep his sweatshirt.

Joe turns the heater on high, and hands me his scarf. "Man, we're lucky you came tonight."

I'd thought Bangs might kiss me. When he played, he had a little bounce during the chorus, and the rest of the time he just thrashed his head in this furious, whiplash way that was rhythmic and punk and weirdly angelic.

Joe and Trevor and Ernie want me to be in their band. "Jesus, just imagine what we could sound like if we practiced," Ernie said, and grinned. He looked like a completely different person when he grinned, not meek at all.

"How's a girl like you sing like that?" Trevor asked.

"What does that even mean?" I said.

But Joe had already steered me toward the car, and I never heard Trevor's explanation.

"A girl like me?" I ask Joe now.

He glances at me, and then lights his cigarette. "You want one?" he asks.

I nod, and he lights another, hands it over.

"Have you ever noticed anything about our front men?" he asks.

"Besides the fact that they can't sing?"

"Yeah, besides that."

I think about them, the four or five that I have seen play with Doggy Life. They're kind of blah, and interchangeable. "They're ordinary," I say.

"Not one of them had presence. Not fucking one. They just stood up there mumbling into the mic, and no one cared. The audience got bored."

"Yeah, and?" He's totally dodging the question.

"You walked on stage tonight, and they were all watching you. From the first number, they were absolutely fixated. It was wild. The whole crowd just kinda tuned into your frequency."

I flick ash into the tray. An old Police album plays on his crappy tape deck. Maybe none of this even happened. The bands, and the funky warehouse, and Bangs' guitar, and Joe driving me back home because Kelly ran off with my brother. Trevor had called me a virgin. I felt it. He'd meant I was too fucking good and pedestrian to be something else on stage. Too virginal to be provocative, that's what he'd meant. That's what Joe is trying to explain now, walking deep into the woods to avoid the road.

I stub the cigarette out, and stare into the darkness. In seventh grade, we took a field trip to the factory where they print the *Asbury*

Park Press. The tour guy said they used enough paper every year to go around the earth a bunch of times. That just crushed me—wrapping the world in newspaper, like you were going to put it in a box.

At the gate, the MP checks my ID card, and waves us through. Joe parks out front, and kills the engine, but I'm already out. "Thanks, Joe. See you Monday." I toss his scarf onto the seat, and close the door.

The triumph all spoiled: the lights burning into me on stage, Bangs' guitar heavy against my body, the kids singing along. I tiptoe up the stairs in my bare feet. In the morning, they'll leave for church and never think to look for me. Just another sneak creeping home.

Watershed. A drainage area. My life is a watershed. Noun. But as an adjective, *watershed* means an important point of transition, like the night I first played with Doggy Life (not to make everything about me, but anyway).

I never get to sleep in. On Saturdays, I have to be at my guitar lesson with Leroy by ten, and school days are worse, and Sunday school begins at nine. When I wake up the morning after the warehouse party, I can't believe it's nearly 10:30.

The maid's room only has a tub, though my dad rigged up an extension-nozzle-thing that drips a little when I'm in a hurry, but this morning I run the bath, and scrub and dunk a bunch of times until the smell of cigarettes is gone. Then I put a damp washcloth over my eyes like the light hurts me, and soak and think. The summer before freshman year, my parents sent me to a basketball camp in June, and then in July I went on this outdoor adventure called Allegheny Outback. Mom asked me if I'd be interested in rafting and canoeing and camping for a couple of weeks, and I said yes, and she signed me up. That was all I knew about the camp when I got dropped at Tim Fitzgerald's one Saturday morning.

Tim's dad put our bags in the minivan, and told me to take shotgun. He said we'd drive to Pennsylvania with the windows down because the air conditioner wasted a lot of gas. He was kind of a funny guy, but friendly, and had thinning blond hair and squinty eyes just like Tim. Anyway, Tim climbed into the van, and another kid that never said a complete sentence to anyone the entire trip—he was the kind of shy kid that goes bright red and trembles all over if you even look at him—and then Jeremy climbed in.

Tim's dad drove us to White Sulphur Springs, this retreat center in Pennsylvania, and told us interesting stories about his Ranger training, and what it had been like to drive a tank along the East German border, and the time he went to Latin America to meet with a missionary who got killed that same year by agitators. When we stopped for lunch, he told the shy kid to take shotgun, and I ended up on the bench seat with Jeremy.

We didn't talk at all in the car. Not one little exchange. When we got to the center, there were three other girls, and six more boys. We spent the first night in cabins just down the road from the retreat center, and we cooked dinner, and sat around the campfire talking. There were only two seniors, and they seemed pretty upset about that, like the rest of us were infants. I didn't know that first night what a great trip we'd have. Those were some of the nicest kids I ever met. No one bickered or bitched or ragged on anybody else. They were all competent kids, handy and confident, and easy to talk to. We had two college counselors, this small blond with a bunch of freckles who told the girls she had extra pads if we needed them, and her twin, a guy a little taller than she was, who smiled a lot. The outback leader was in his thirties and had a beard, and looked exactly like a disciple. He spoke in a quiet, solemn voice, and always said Christ in this way that indicated to me he was new to Christianity. He'd probably been wild ages ago when he was a kid.

After we had devotionals and breakfast the next morning, we did some trust exercises: falling backward off a ledge into the arms of the other campers, leaping onto a rope from one platform to swing across to another platform where a kid would grab onto you to make sure you didn't plunge to your death, that kind of thing. Late in the afternoon, we canoed to another campsite and slept in tents, and rock climbed, and rappelled, and hiked and fished.

Jeremy asked to be my partner the fourth day for our rock climbing and rappelling adventure. At the time, I was disappointed because this sweet Puerto Rican kid, Sean, had canoed to the island with me, and we'd been partners ever since, but Jeremy asked me first, so he spotted me while I climbed along this rock ledge, and then I spotted him. I really just stood below him, and walked along with my arms out, and hoped he wouldn't fall backward and crush me. He climbed faster than anyone else, and when the leader saw him, he asked Jeremy if he wanted to climb a higher face. Then we stood and watched Jeremy climb all the way to the top of this sheer wall. He was like Spiderman. He went up so fast it looked simple, but nobody else could climb ten feet up this wall. The rest of us had to walk up the trail on the backside in order to rappel down the face.

That night at dinner, Jeremy and I cooked chili for everyone, and he talked to me like we'd been buddies for years. And that's how it was from then on. After the trip, when I started high school, before Jeremy or Nate could drive and we all had to take the bus, we'd get to school forty-five minutes early and Jeremy would sit beside me in the hallway and we'd do our homework, or talk about movies, or talk about nothing at all.

In the hot bath, I think about Jeremy scaling that wall. I didn't know then how it would be. That day, watching from below, I admired him: the skill of the only boy who could manage the ascent.

I've just climbed out when someone knocks on the door. Why I answer wearing nothing but a robe I cannot explain, especially since the robe will not stay closed, but I do. I open the door without even asking who it is.

Jeremy opens his mouth, then takes me in, and closes his mouth again without saying anything.

"Hey," I say, and step behind the door like it's a shield.

"Hey," he says. "I was hoping you'd be here."

"I am," I say. I have no idea why I say this. Coming from the bath, I know I look splotchy and drowned. Why did I open the door?

"Do you want to get some pizza at Carmellini's?" he asks.

Carmellini's is a little place just outside the post, maybe an eight-minute walk. I ought to invite him in, standing in the hallway is terrible, and the neighbors will hear us.

"Come in," I say, and open the door wider. "It'll just take a sec to get dressed." I haven't even made the bed, and the room still smells a little like cigarettes. Classy.

I pull the covers up on the bed, and then grab some clothes from the dresser. He stands just inside the door and looks around. The furniture is mostly this ancient stuff my mother had in her room when she was a kid, but the desk and rocker are oak and simple and not hideous.

After I blow-dry my hair, I feel all right again, and like myself in my jeans and t-shirt.

"Did you have fun last night with Kelly?" Jeremy asks, crouched beside my acoustic guitar with his hand stretched out like he might touch the neck.

I pull him up to kiss him, and he hugs me afterward, and smells my hair. "Strawberries," he whispers.

Kids are loose everywhere. Nearly noon on a Sunday, and you hear them screaming up and down the street. Trees and the stone pillar of every doorway are tagged with a corny yellow bow. At Sunday school in September, they handed out a bunch of names of deployed soldiers for us to send care packages to. My soldier is an atheist. I sent him a bunch of Milky Ways and Starbursts and a *National Geographic* magazine and a letter saying that I hope God watches over him even though he doesn't believe in God because if God doesn't watch over him, and he's killed, he'll go to hell. He wrote me back right away to thank me for the Milky Ways—they're his favorite—and to say that he doesn't believe that hell exists, but he appreciates that I hope God watches over him. For a heathen, he sounds pretty nice; he even said that I'm right and Geometry is pure evil. This time I sent Strawberry Bubblicious and Apple Jolly Ranchers and a book of *Calvin & Hobbes* and some photographs of grass. He said he's sick of looking at sand.

Here in Jersey it's a beautiful fall day with piled leaves and corny bows and cracks in the asphalt and Jeremy and I walk side by side, our arms touching. He's wearing a red sweatshirt and jeans and has his hands in his pockets. Because we aren't in some endless desert, or the woods of Pennsylvania, because it's wholly improbable, the two of us alone like this at midday on Sunday, I tell him about the party—about playing with Joe's band, about Kelly and my brother, about the lies I told, and Joe having to bring me home after I got ditched.

He orders a pepperoni pizza, and while we're waiting, I finish the story. He hasn't said anything since I started. We're drinking vanilla shakes. Jeremy has an appetite just like mine.

"I wish I'd heard you," he says finally.

"Why would Kelly go off with my brother?" I ask.

"Maybe she was mad."

"At me?"

"Maybe. Or maybe she just wanted to. Maybe she wasn't thinking too much about it."

He means maybe she didn't do it deliberately, but he doesn't know Kelly like I do. He doesn't know that she calculates everything she does.

"You remember that day at camp when we rappelled down the cliff?" I ask.

"Sure."

"Why did you ask to be my partner?"

"Don't you know?"

I shake my head. His red sweatshirt makes his eyes bluer. His eyebrows stand at attention, like he combs them straight up.

"Do you remember the day we met?" he asks.

"A pickup game," I say. "We were playing football."

"I'd watched you from my window. You were better than most of the boys."

I shrug.

"On my first play," he says, "you tackled me so hard I fumbled, do you remember?"

I laugh. He's smiling and it seems OK to laugh. Jeremy always answers questions this way. I don't remember tackling him. I remember the game. Doug put his hand down my pants when he tackled me, and then tried to pretend he hadn't. On the next play, Nate kneed Doug in the balls, and left him on the ground without apologizing or anything. We all just stood around waiting for him to get up, and then Jeremy came over and asked if he could play.

A guy brings the pizza out. It's one of those colossal thin crust pizzas: beautiful and steaming.

"It's hot," he tells us.

47

"We're dating, right?" Jeremy says after he finishes the first slice. "I don't have to be your boyfriend. I mean, we don't have to be all serious or anything." He shovels another piece onto each of our plates. "Next time you play I'd like to be there. I'd really like to see you play."

Beleaguered. Beset, harassed. I'm going to use this word all the time. I'm going to beleaguer everyone with this word. (Beset is pretty cool too.) Verb.

My History teacher totally killed people, like as an assassin for the CIA, or black ops, or whatever. Some U.S. agency employed Mrs. Brooks to take people out. I know it. She's this tiny lady— five feet tops—with severe short blond hair, expensive sweater/ slacks combos, and one of those plastic chalk holders that she knocks against her desk when she calls roll.

In her classroom, her desk is on a platform above us, and behind her desk is another, higher platform the length of the chalkboard that Joe says was specially constructed for her. I have her for History of Asia. We've been studying the Boxer Uprising, and really China has just been so wholly screwed for ages.

Mrs. Brooks is linking influences (she loves to link influences) when Jay Edwards raises his hand. We all stare at him. Jay pitches for our baseball team, and is flawless. He's the only senior in our History class, sits next to me, and grins all the time like life is the most fun ever. Since Allison started dating him, he has come to every field hockey game, and usually brings a bunch of other baseball players. He makes me feel a little swoony, I have to say.

Brooks beams at him, "Yes, Jay?"

"Is this going to be on the test?"

"Yes, Jay."

"As an essay?"

She winks at him before turning back to the chalkboard.

"I kind of agree with them," Jay says.

Brooks twists around, her arm poised to write. "Agree with whom?"

"The Fist guys."

She nods. "Tell me more."

"Their country got hijacked. What were they supposed to do?"

"A lot of their rage was directed at their own countrymen."

"Yeah, but they thought they'd been corrupted, you know, by

49

foreign influence. In a way, that was worse than being foreign."

My parents would say they were martyred. Those Christians. In fact, they'd say Christians in China are still being martyred. Dad could give you statistics.

The bell rings.

"The exam is Monday," Brooks calls. "Cole, good luck this afternoon."

Jay grins at me. "Everybody's watching. No pressure."

Yeah, no pressure: Regional finals against Wall; if we lose this one, we're out. I wish I could barf, then I'd feel better. Since the game begins at 2 p.m. today, I'm excused from my last class. I'm tempted to flee. I can't explain why, but I just want out of here.

My whole Kelly-is-dead-to-me thing kind of misfired. On Monday, during homeroom, *she* ignored *me*. She came in and started talking to Leisha, and it was like I didn't exist. Same thing in Graphic Arts, and then, during lunch, she didn't show at our table. A couple of times, in the hallway, I've seen her holding hands with Nate. (He's had warts on his fingers since he was seven!) Now I catch rides to school with Jeremy, and sit with Bangs in Biology, and eat lunch with Joe, and big fucking deal because she's totally unaffected. The party was five days ago and I don't recognize my life anymore.

In the locker room, Diofelli comes up to me, shaking her head. "Now you're wearing a brace? Why didn't you say you'd pulled it again?"

"No, Coach Robins had this idea about using a thigh brace." She stands there watching me fold the brace over itself, before I yank it up to my groin.

"How's that working out for you?" she asks, skeptical, her forehead pinched.

"I think I baby it less."

"Well, that's something." She shakes her head again. "Look, Peters, just relax out there, can ya? You've been tense as hell all week."

I'm down the first play. Smeared with mud and slow to rise. No whistle from the refs, though two girls slammed into me, one with her stick, both of them laughing. My shots on goal are wide and sloppy. Behind me, the crowd groans when I miss. The bleachers are full of bullies—Wall brought as many fans as we did, and our cheerleaders rile them.

While rain sloshes down on our white home jerseys and our carefully hair-sprayed bangs, and some artful makeup jobs, Katy and Dana parrot-call the plays, shout to the halfbacks for support, try to keep us focused in this mess of a field with these goddam Amazon girls determined to trample us.

The next time they tackle me, I get a stick in my back, and the heavier one says, "Stay down." I hear the whistle on the play, but I haven't moved yet. The mud is thick and slippery and clinging to me like little hands. Renee helps me up in time to watch the ref present each girl with a yellow card. Is it terrible that part of me wants to be injured enough to stay down? To be carried off the field? To rest in the nurses' station until this lousy game is over?

And if my groin gives, I could get out of basketball too: safe on account of injury, available to play in a band instead. Several times, I drop without any assistance; we all do. We look like crazy, skirted swamp people.

No one scores during regular play, or the first shoot-out. Play is so rough that seven girls get carded; two with reds have to leave the field. Wall scores twice in the second shoot-out. Though my first shot went wide, like all my attempts this game, my second smacks the goalie in the shoulder and drops in front of the goal. We lose 2–0.

I can't actually say what the worst thing about losing is. Everybody came to the game: Jeremy, Meghan, Bangs, Joe, my entire family. Is it worse having witnesses, or getting trampled into the mud, or playing in a sad, rotten way? Or is losing to Wall, and being out of the tournament the worst part? It's all bad. The last field hockey game I'd ever play at this school, and I totally sucked ass.

In the locker room, I take longer than I need to pull sweats on, and stow my uniform in a plastic bag. I don't even bother to scrub the mud off; it's in my hair and I'll probably need some kind of chisel. Over the roar of hair dryers, I hear the seniors crying.

51

Nobody has blamed me, but we all know this is my fault: the first game all season I didn't score.

Jennifer's wearing a red lace bra under her white home shirt. She looks like a soggy underwear model as she's peeling off her jersey. My mother would never countenance a red lace bra. Not under any circumstances, not even when I'm a junior.

Down the row from me, Kelly sorts through her locker, her head bowed, bruises on her thighs from one of the girls who got red-carded. She won't look at me. Tragedy in every direction.

In the parking lot, they're all standing around our green van, except Nate. Jeremy, Bangs, and Joe are with Meghan by the mounted spare tire.

Mom says, "Oh Cole," in that irritating, forlorn way.

But I only half hear because Meghan walks toward me with a big grin, and winks, "You've got a little something all over your face." And I'm laughing and hugging her and the game's just another thing that happened, like Kelly at the party. And more than anything, I'm super-hungry.

Muse. To ruminate or wonder at. Verb. Also, an inspirational chick, like from the Greek. Then it's a noun.

Meghan and I have taken control of the couches in the sunroom. Usually the boys dominate this room to play Sega, but not today. It's cold as fuck, though, with all the windows, and I'm starting to feel a little empty about our victory.

You know how everyone from Norway always wears sweaters, even when they're fishing, or whatever, they have these really beautiful sweaters on? Meghan is just like that with the knitted sweaters. Hers are in greens and blues, knitted by her mother, and they fit her perfectly like maybe her mom knitted them right to her. Today she's wearing one with a rolled collar, and rolled wrists in a sea-foam green that makes her hair seem even blonder.

"Muse," she says. Her socked feet on the armrest, she's propped on four of my mother's throw pillows.

"OK, are you kidding me with this one?" I tell her the definitions, and the parts of speech.

"In my entire class of twenty-five, nobody put anything but noun. We got a long lecture about thoroughness."

"Oh?" I raise my eyebrows in an effort not to gloat.

"I don't think I've ever heard it used as a verb," she says.

"Let me muse on that."

She flings her pen at me. "You're adorable. Maybe that's why three cute boys waited for you after the game."

I blush, and watch sunlight glint off the crystal figurines on the windowsill. Pepper sleeps with her head tucked against my thigh. In the summer, when I first met Meghan, I asked if she had a boyfriend, and she told me she never dated. She didn't have time for dating. Her saying that made me feel less serious somehow.

"Hey," she says now.

I look at her.

"I'm not judging," she says.

And suddenly, without preamble, I tell her about the party at

Board, and playing with Joe's band, and all the phone calls with Bangs, and how Jeremy is almost painfully sweet.

"They want you to join the band rather than play basketball?"

"There's no way to do both. Practice and gigs and school, I can't do all that and basketball too."

"Which would you rather do?"

"Play in the band."

"This seems really straightforward, then."

"Really?" I say. "How do you figure?"

"Just tell your parents you'd rather be in a band."

So, the truth is, when she makes this statement, the first thing I realize is that I've never considered telling my parents I'd rather be in a band. I've spent a lot of time trying to decide how to sneak out to practice and gigs—study dates, babysitting, drama club—but it never occurred to me to be frank.

"You think my parents will let me play in bars?"

"Well, I think you should anticipate all their objections, and have a ready solution. You know their first concern will be transportation—how will you get to the gigs and practices and home again?"

"Joe."

She nods. "He's OK with that?"

"Yeah, he offered."

"Will your parents be OK with that?"

I shrug. "They like Joe."

"What about your safety?" she asks. "How will you guarantee that?"

"What do you mean?"

"Well, you'll be playing gigs in bars at night, right?"

"With three guys," I protest.

"Teenaged boys," she says. "How would they fare in a bar fight?"

She's doing a good job of catching my parents' tone. I have no idea what to say. I try to imagine Ernie in a bar fight, or Joe. Trevor is another story, but he's the devil I know, and not the guy I figure will defend my honor, or whatever. Jeremy would, but his parents would never let him go to a bar, even as a roadie.

I hadn't really thought about playing in bars, or anything. When I first learned piano, I'd play once a month for the Protestant service at Ft. Leonard Wood. Hundreds of privates listened and applauded and grinned at the eight-year-old with her feathered bangs playing *Morning Has Broken* during the offertory.

Meghan looks me over. "What you need is a chaperone."

"You mean like an adult?"

"Something like that. Give me a few days to think it over."

Am I the only person who thinks about the tortoise and the hare when someone says *race relations*? It just sounds preposterous and archaic, like referring to someone as colored. At Monmouth Regional, there's a group of kids involved in the Back to Africa movement. They wear leather Africa medallions, and turtle-necks, and dress like geeky intellectuals. In the rap-inspired style of lettered gold rings, capped gold teeth, piled gold chains, and puffed football jackets common at our school, these kids stand out like preppies.

But they're also the kids that we all admire. They're informed and political in a way that seems conscientious and grown-up. They aren't the kids that we were told about at orientation when we were warned that Monmouth Regional had racial tensions. In the previous five years, the school has experienced a number of racial skirmishes including knifings, brawls with bats and pipes, severe beatings, and a gunshot death.

During junior high, my friends were nerds and jocks, black and white, military and civilian, and teachers bullied us worse than we bullied each other. Until our basketball game against Asbury Park, only my brothers had ever tormented me. Our team got a police escort from the bus to the gym, security guards throughout the gym during the game, and then another escort back to the bus afterward. It was surreal. I laughed about it until two girls from Asbury Park called me over during warm-ups.

"Hey," one said.

"Hey," I said back, all grins.

"What'd you say about us?"

"What?" I asked.

"My friend heard you."

I looked at the other girl. She glared at me. They were both a little smaller than I was, maybe 5'6" and wearing white sweaters. In the middle of the gym these girls played me, while our friends and family filed into the bleachers, and security guards flexed by the door.

"Heard what?" I asked. I couldn't look at the one glaring at me anymore, so I looked at the one talking.

"You called us niggers. My friend heard you."

"I never," I said.

"You called us niggers, and you best watch your back."

Now I couldn't look at her either, and so I stepped away, toward my teammates.

"We're watching you," she said.

I played the worst game of my life that day—well, until the field hockey game against Wall. Even while they were psyching me out, I knew that was the point, and it still didn't matter. I couldn't stop it from happening. Those chicks scared the holy fuck out of me, and no armed guard could change that.

After the race-wars lecture at freshman orientation, I walked through Monmouth's hallways quickly, keeping my head down when I was alone, or sticking to the right if I was with a friend. Of the three fights I saw freshman year, two involved pairs of black girls, and ended with chunks of hair strewn on the floor by the lockers, and skin under painted nails, and the other was white boys hurling each other into tables in the lunch room. We knew about the drive-bys and the gang wars. We all heard stories about turf, but even those Asbury Park girls weren't fucking with me because I was white; they were fucking with me because I was on the other team.

As a freshman, with a handful of friends my own age, I had a serious phobia about getting jumped; and on Valentine's Day, when I got stuck behind a mob of kids and heard shouting, I'd started to search for another route to the gym when a girl on the edge of the crowd said, "What the fuck you looking at?"

I kept backing up, when someone grabbed me.

"I said, *What the fuck you looking at?*"

Before I could respond, another arm came around me, and a familiar voice said, "Bitch, who you addressing?"

"Oh I—" the girl began.

"Oh you nothing. Get your ass out the way."

Propelling me through the crowd—past some girl screaming in an incomprehensible register at her baffled, frightened boyfriend—we arrived at the locker room, and I finally glanced up at Jayna, one of my basketball teammates. If she hadn't looked so fierce, I might have cried with relief. The girl in the hallway outweighed me by a hundred pounds, and had two friends flanking her.

"Thanks," I breathed.

"Hate that bitch," she said, shaking her head. "I'm a talk to somebody 'bout her. Tired of that bitch." She stared at me, and then punched my shoulder. "You a'right. Don't you worry 'bout her."

"No."

She laughed, and punched me again. Jayna probably weighed 160 pounds, but she was 6' 2" and not to be underestimated. I'd seen her scrap on the court against some huge girls, and better them time and again.

After that, I stopped worrying about getting jumped, and walked through the hallways like a human. In high school, we form tribes of interest, and the girls I played ball with would have done anything for me. They'd proved it on and off the court. They were cool and beautiful and yelled my name whenever they saw me. They called me kid, and meant it kindly. It didn't matter that I was sick of playing ball, that my body was drained, that the guitar lit me up like nothing before. I played starting point guard on a team that finished fourth in the state; I owed them.

If Meghan could dream up some genius story to get my parents to let me quit basketball and join a band, maybe she could inspire another version to persuade the rest of my tribe.

Ineluctable. Not to be avoided, inescapable. Adjective. How the hell do you pronounce this word anyway? The emphasis on the third syllable sounds pretty stupid.

Nigel and I have our book bags and all our crap spread out on the dining-room table—it's oval, oak, and has these cool talons like maybe the table is really a petrified creature. If Mom isn't home—she left us a note that she'd gone grocery shopping; she won't take us anymore because she says she buys more junk food when we tag along—this is the best room for studying with two long windows and a chandelier, and the glass cabinets of china patterned with swirling blue, and the red hutch with the music boxes, and Pepper's tail thumping as she dreams.

Studying with Nigel keeps me honest: he's the quietest person I've ever met, and he keeps busy, so I never talk to him because I feel like I'd be interrupting. He's working on his Spanish, while I brainstorm ideas for our photography project. Bangs and I are paired again, and this time the assignment is to tell a story in sixteen photographs.

You know how hard it is to tell a story in sixteen photographs? Bangs thinks we should photograph some drawings and, depending on the way the photos are arranged, the art will be different, so the photographs will be an interpretation of the drawings. I guess he's thinking like an artist, and I'm thinking like an athlete. My first idea involved static shots of someone kicking a soccer ball into the goal, and my second was Nigel sprinting across the parade ground. All of it seems so common, though—pictures of artwork, pictures of athletes—same old, same old. What about staging a crime? A bank robbery in sixteen shots? Or a murder?

It's difficult to concentrate because Mom left lasagna for me to put into the oven, and, according to the timer, it'll be done in twenty minutes. Despite the spinach she insists on using, her lasagna is pretty much the most fantastic thing you'll ever eat. Even Nigel, Mr. Concentration, keeps staring at the kitchen, like he's considering a raid.

When Pepper jumps up and runs into the kitchen, we know Mom's home. We also know she's got groceries. Still, neither of us moves, not even to open the doors for her.

"Kids," she hollers from the kitchen door, "I've got groceries." And then less than a minute later, louder, "Nicole and Nigel, let's hustle." We drag into the kitchen. On her first trip, she brought four bags in. She'll stroke out carting the groceries in one day. "You two bring the rest in. I'll start unloading these. Where's your brother?" We shrug.

The entire van is full of brown bags of groceries. Whenever Mom goes to the commissary, it's like she's stockpiling goods to see us through for months. Somehow all the food seems to be gone a couple of days later.

"How was school?" she asks, when we return to the kitchen.

"Great," we mumble. "Fine." We make another trip to the van.

"Did Nate bring you home?" she asks. Whenever she sees us, Mom asks a thousand questions. She'd have been a ruthless interrogator for the military. I let Nigel answer and go back for another load. Since when do I care where Nate is?

"Last load," I say. "And, yes, I locked the van."

Mom frowns at me. "Thank you for putting the lasagna in the oven. I bought some French bread too. It's in one of these bags." There are bags everywhere. "You two clear your books off the table, and Nigel, I want you to set the table while Cole fills the water glasses. Your father will be home any minute."

By the time we've cleared our books, and set the table, Mom's unloaded the groceries and sliced the lasagna. Dad is never later than 5:15, and Nate still hasn't showed. If he doesn't make it for dinner, he is completely dead; we need prior permission to skip family meals.

Dad rides his bike to work. Like a total cornball, he'll still have his right pants leg clipped after he gets inside. When we were little, we'd wait at the door for him—back when Army uniforms were solid green—and we'd swipe his cap, and help him unlace his boots, and mob him until Mom hollered at us to give him some peace. The back for his Chaplain's pin used to stab me in the forehead whenever I wore his cap, but I loved the canvas smell, the way he'd push the cap back to kiss my nose.

Today, he arrives home wearing his dress greens. I'll say this for the Army: you'd have to be a serious raggedy-ass not to look good in dress greens. He kisses Mom and compliments the lasagna, and pets Pepper as she launches at him. Nigel and I are already seated at the table, both clutching our forks, though we know he'll change before he joins us. Mom brings a salad, and rolls her eyes when she sees us with our forks.

She spreads her napkin in her lap and says, "Cole, what's going on with you and Nate?" I shrug. "Are you fighting?" She looks at Nigel. Nigel has been a rat since birth.

"Nate's dating Kelly," Nigel says. As irritating as he is, at least Nigel doesn't editorialize.

"Your friend Kelly?" Mom asks me.

"Yes," Nigel answers.

Mom appraises me, and then looks at her watch. "And he's missing dinner." She says this like they equate: dating my friend, and missing family dinner.

Dad tells us hello, and then looks at Nate's empty chair as he reaches for our hands. "Where's Nate?"

"We don't know," my mother says. She's using her ominous voice. Nate is so dead.

"Nigel," Dad says, and Nigel says the prayer. His prayers are even shorter than mine, so that we're holding our plates out to be served a moment later. The cheese has to be cut between pieces. The lasagna tastes so good that I decide not to mention all the giant raw mushrooms in the salad.

"Anything exciting happen today?" Dad asks.

We take turns answering—Mom reports that the water in the kitchen sink and basement laundry was brown again; they've had the engineers out twice, and both times the engineers said the pipes are just old, and nothing to worry about. Nigel has a Chess Club competition on Thursday after school. He tends to win these, he reminds us now. And then I tell them about my photography project, and how I'm stuck. That's seriously the most exciting thing I can think of.

"What about an instructional story?" Dad says. "Shots of a paper plane being folded, and then flown."

"Or a fist fight?" Nigel offers. "Before, during, and after. The final shot could be of a kid with a black eye and a bloody nose."

Mom scowls at him, and I decide not to mention my ideas about bank robbery, or car crashes. As though I have a stuntman or stage handy, my ideas seem to lend themselves to short films rather than photography.

"What about taking photos of actors doing a scene from a play?" Dad asks. "A story within a story kind of thing. You could photograph something famous—like the death scene in *Romeo and Juliet*."

Actors from the drama club would eat this up, especially if I let them do it in modern dress: Romeo as a skate punk, and Juliet in her Guess jeans. Not until I picture Romeo dropping in, his momentum kicking through his hair, his body crouched, then up again in that deceptively laggard way, does it occur to me that Bangs skating some sick trick is the ultimate story.

"When is this project due?" Mom asks.

"The day before Thanksgiving break."

"Which reminds me," Mom says, "Meghan's parents are going to stay with us over Thanksgiving." She doesn't even have to finish; I know I'm about to be chucked from my room. "Cole, I'm going to put them in your room, and you'll be staying with Meghan."

"What?" I say, startled.

"Her roommate is going home for break, and we thought you'd enjoy staying with Meghan a little more than sleeping on the fold-out in the sunroom."

I nearly squeak, "What?" again, but stop myself in time. I get to sleep over at Meghan's dorm room like we're buds or whatever. That is utterly cool.

Dad snickers, and then says, "If you'd rather sleep in the sunroom—"

61

"Oh no, Meghan's dorm. Please."

"I hope they bring presents," Nigel says.

"What?" Mom glares at him.

"Her parents," Nigel says, inured to her displeasure. "I hope they bring us presents."

Since I approve of presents, I decide to help Nigel out: "Dad, what's with the dress greens?"

"Oh," Dad says pleasantly, "the highest-ranking female chaplain in the military visited the school today. I hosted her meet-and-greets."

"How highest-ranking?" Nigel asks.

"Two-star general," Dad says.

A female chaplain? I've never even seen one. "What was she like?" I ask. This is how it'll be next year, when Nate's away at college; just four of us at dinner.

"Quite a speaker," Dad says. That's code for *she's a liberal.*

Mom tells me to run check the freezer. She has bought an ice-cream cake for our dessert—strawberry with vanilla cake— my favorite. Even as I carry it back to the table with dessert plates and a knife, I know that none of this is real. The evening's earnest, and friendly, the way things become when we remember them, from some distance.

Later in the evening, when I call Bangs, he tries to talk me out of using him as the subject of our photo-story. "How about a buddy of mine—Jake? Otherwise, you'll get stuck taking all the shots."

"I don't mind taking the photos, if you don't mind doing the tricks."

"What kind of tricks?"

"What can you do?"

"Are you thinking ramp, or street skating?"

"Which would give us better photos?"

I hear the guitar in the background, strummed into a rapid

heartbeat. Then the sound cuts out. "Well," he says, "riding stairs could be pretty sonic."

When they were kids, my brothers used to skate down staircases on these fat Nash boards. Awkward, and ridiculous, and so not what I have in mind. "Stairs?" I say, like I'm thinking it over.

"Yeah, if we do like three flights, and I catch the rail, that'd give you a bunch of shots."

"Catch the rail?" I repeat.

"Yeah, you know, skate down the metal railing on a bunch of stairs. I know just the place, actually. We found this staircase near the courthouse that's perfect."

"Oh," I say, imagining us cuffed, and tossed into the back of some dirty police cruiser by a fat dude whose undershirt shows. Through the phone a note whinnies. "Yeah," I say, "that sounds good."

After I hang up, I wonder if he'll wear a helmet and pads, if I'll get a photo of some horrific accident, asphalt burns and a board rocketing into the street. Why not have the drama kids stage a death scene? Why not be satisfied with something artful and clever? From the alcove, my radio plays the countdown, and an ugly old lamp streaks the ceiling with light, and the radiator clunks like a misstep, and I can't possibly work on Geometry when I've got all this in my head.

Crouched at the base of the upper staircase, with a ridiculously expensive camera that I'm terrified about damaging—like professional photographers, for magazines or whatever, would love to use this camera, and when I opened the black-leather case and saw one of the lenses for this thing, I figured Bangs must have stolen it—anyway, I take a bunch of shots but the shutter is so fast, that I fuck them up; I'm over-anticipating him. From this vantage, Bangs seems to hop effortlessly onto the lower half of the railing and coast the first flight, before another slap-hop from the pavement onto the second railing.

He has made me wear a helmet that covers my ears, though he isn't wearing one, or pads for that matter, and before his first run down the railing, I tried to squirm out of this whole thing; he's going to be killed doing this. He's wearing jeans, and a black sweatshirt, his hands red with cold, and the wind pushing through the evergreens to our right. Even with my leather jacket and wool scarf and this stupid helmet, my hands ache when I advance the film.

I feel guilty doing this—even as a spectator. And if he dies, or has a gruesome accident and is paralyzed, and I'm prosecuted for murder, or as an accessory to daredevilry or whatever, then it'll serve me right. But I hope he doesn't get paralyzed. He looks like a sugar glider: fast and fearless and soaring.

Somehow, each run, he catches the same spot of the rail, though his board changes positions—he might catch the rail with the center of his board, or either end, and sometimes he turns the board around with his hands, and sometimes he shifts his legs and rides backward. I shoot from his approach, and his descent, from beneath him, and above. We work our way down the stairs, and then I climb the cement base of the streetlamp, midway down the staircases, and shoot several descents. I'm finally starting to relax, when suddenly the board shoots away, and he skids to a halt on his ass.

"Are you OK?" I run to him.

"Sure," he says, grinning. He chases down his board, and then walks up the staircase as easily as he has every other time. He's not even winded. Mine is the heart racing, mine the uncontrollable pulse.

"I'm hungry," he says.

I nod. "Me too."

"There's a good sub shop two blocks from here." His face is chapped, and the way he's smirking at me, I kind of want to punch him. "That helmet," he says, "makes your head look humongous."

I haven't even closed the front door when I hear Mom call from the kitchen, "How was the photo shoot?"

"It was OK," I say.

"Don't say *OK*," Meghan says from the dining room, where she's setting the table.

"OK," I submit. "The camera had such a fast shutter that I mistimed about half a roll of film."

Mom brings in the CorningWare dishes of green beans and pork chops. The applesauce is already on the table—she makes it herself, so the first serving is always warm. "What does that mean?" she asks. "Will you have to do the whole thing over?"

"Not the whole thing," I say, and try not to be irritated that she thinks I'm an idiot. "We'll have to do another shoot, but in class tomorrow, we'll be able to tell how well the others turned out."

"What are you photographing?" Meghan asks.

I've already debated this one in my head, and have decided that it's better to be honest about the shoot, though maybe not about the location and the trick. So I say, "A skater. We're telling the story of a skate trick."

"What's the trick?" Nigel asks from behind me.

"A rail slide."

"Who's the skater?" he asks. Paused beside me in his socks, I realize that he's catching me up; another year and this kid will be taller than I am. He'll never be a big, broad guy like Nate, but his skinniness makes him seem even taller, and his baby-face pudge is gone.

I turn to face him, and I can't tell what he's up to, why he's asking. "Christian," I say.

Then he sits at the table, and puts his napkin in his lap, and says, "Are we eating?"

Since I've already had a sub, I only eat one pork chop, and a couple of servings of green beans and applesauce.

"So," Meghan says to me, while Nigel clears the plates, "I've got one for you: *exsanguinate*."

"To make pale," I guess.

"Oh, that's a good guess," she says. "You're thinking of sanguine as ruddy, right?" I nod. "But think of it as blood."

Bloodless would just be another way to pale, wouldn't it?

Unless, and then I have a weird shift in my belly. "Without blood," I say.

"Out of it, yes."

"I'm glad," Dad says, "that I've just eaten pork chops."

"Exsanguinate," I say. "Exsanguinate." It's a round word in the mouth.

Nigel serves us bowls of chocolate pudding.

"It's a new recipe," Mom says. "I have no idea how it'll be."

Rich, creamy, delicious, and gone much too quickly, I think. Nate excuses himself the moment he's done. My parents grounded him for a week—no Sega, no television, and no phone privileges—for missing family dinner. Nigel told me Nate and Dad were shouting, and Nate only got one week because Mom intervened.

"Well," Meghan says, and looks to either end of the table at each of my parents. "As I said on the phone, I've designated myself the negotiator here." She glances at me. I have no idea what she's planning. Until this moment, I didn't even know that she'd phoned my parents. "Cole has been approached to play guitar, and sing lead in a band."

I close my eyes for just a moment, and hear that word again, exsanguinate. I think maybe my blood has drained away.

"For Doggy Life?" Nigel asks.

We all stare at him. Nigel has a gift, really. It comes from being the quietest person. He sits, observes, and you forget he's even there until he speaks.

"Yes," I say.

Nigel looks at my father. "They're really good." How does he know this? "Doggy Life is Joe's band." He looks at my mother. "Joe came to Cole's field hockey games."

"What kind of band?" Dad asks.

"They play pop songs," Meghan says, "but I think, if Cole joins, they'll play some originals too."

Oh god. She can't seriously be doing this.

"Originals?" Dad asks.

"Cole writes songs," Meghan says. "Very good songs. If she

66

joins the band, she'll have practices two to three times a week, as well as gigs, and she won't have time to play basketball." My mother has yet to speak. We all know that the ultimate decision will be my father's, but if my mother disapproves, whatever Meghan is proposing dies on the table.

"Cole would like to join the band," Meghan continues. "She knows her teammates, and probably her school, will be disappointed, but she has an opportunity here, with the band, and she's excited about this opportunity." Meghan turns to my mother. "I don't want you to worry about her being at gigs, and so I'd like to volunteer to chaperone. My parents are bringing my car up when they come for Thanksgiving; I'll be able to drive Cole to gigs, and practices. I can study there as well as in the dorm—better maybe."

"You want to quit basketball," my dad asks me, "and play in a rock band?"

"Yes," I say.

"You're fifteen," my mother says, which is a totally absurd argument; I'll be sixteen in three weeks.

"Dad played in a dance band in junior high," Nigel says. "He didn't get home sometimes until four in the morning."

Mom looks at Nigel like he's a traitor. The dance band thing is true, though, and we all know it. Dad played trumpet in a dance band from junior high through high school. Nobody mentions he also played basketball that entire time, and that one didn't exclude the other, not even Dad.

Pragmatic. Practical. Adjective. The archaic definition is meddlesome, isn't that weird?

The photos of Bangs are fucking glorious. In one, the camera is practically underneath him, and he's crouched, with a hand on his board, well above the railing like he has just been fired into the air. Seven of the photos are mistimed, and a couple are soft, but there's one where his body is fully extended, with one arm raised above his head as though he's hailing a taxi, and the board just beyond his feet and it's the most striking of these shots, almost balletic.

"These are good," he says, viewing our negatives. "I wasn't sure there'd be a story, but there is. It's like this impossible trick." He points out three negatives, which might be successive in terms of time lapse, though they were shot from three different runs, three different vantages. "It's like this slow-motion lie."

Bangs and I pick twenty negatives to print, to allow even more flexibility with the final order of the story. We work through lunch and after school, and hang the final shots during class the next morning. The entire class is working on this project, and we're all squeezed into the darkroom to try to get the photographs printed before the weekend, as we still need to assemble them, and presentations are on Tuesday.

After Spanish on Friday—Senor Fernandez (he wears a suit jacket all the time, and is really old and distinguished) assigned us two chapters of homework, but promised we'd be spared any over Thanksgiving break—I rush to the lab to pick up our prints; afterward, I'll meet Bangs, and his buddies with the van, to catch a ride to his house to finish our project. The classroom is empty, but in the darkroom, I find Kelly looking at our photos—once they dry, they're taken off the line, and set aside in a tub. She glances at me, and then goes back to examining the photos.

"These are so good," she says. She hasn't spoken to me in three weeks.

"Thanks."

"They're almost choreographed, like a dance or something."

A dance; so she sees ballet too. It's the focus of his athleticism—the concentrated power—that makes his skating reminiscent of dance. His grace on a wheeled board is improbable, if you've met the slouching boy around school.

She hands the photographs to me. "Have a good weekend," she says.

"Sure," I say, tucking the prints into a portfolio. "You too."

Even off base, yellow bows are everywhere—like somebody wrapped all the trees in Jersey. In the two-toned brown van, with three boys besides Bangs and me, nobody says anything. Seriously. We're in the van long enough to drive to Woodmere, and nobody speaks. This suburb of Colonials with siding and patches of lawn has traffic in every direction, but aside from honking horns, an indistinct recording of Smiths' singles is pretty much the only sound in the van.

We pull into a wide, paved driveway, in front of a two-car garage, and Bangs slides the van door shut after we're out. He doesn't say thanks, or wave.

"Do I make them nervous?" I ask.

"What?"

"They're so quiet."

He nods, pulls a key from the long metal chain around his neck, and unlocks the garage door without taking the chain off. Inside: skis, a black Mercedes, a tricked-out silver dirt bike, and several small wooden ramps piled along the farthest wall. Now, in this garage, I realize that Bangs didn't steal that camera equipment; he's rich.

"My sister's home," he says, opening a door that leads into the kitchen. "She remembers you."

She remembers me? I didn't even know he had a sister.

The kitchen is tiled and cold. "Split a pizza with me?" he asks. I nod. He preheats the oven, then leads me through the kitchen, down a long hallway to a sunken great room, and then up two flights to another hallway, and finally to a closed door with a giant hand painted on it—the hand is palm out, and so detailed that the lines and veins are evident.

While he stashes his board and bag in the corner, I pace his room. On the wall opposite the door, characters from *Alice in Wonderland* are painted around a boxing ring where Alice and the Mad Hatter, in boxing gloves, are poised on tiptoes. On the wall by his bed, Marvel characters skate a ramp—Rogue is inverted, and smirking; some chick engulfed in flames maneuvers a hand plant. Above his closet, a snake twists in glimmers of purple and green.

The room itself is cluttered with two amps, an electric and acoustic guitar, four pedals, two mic stands, two wooden stools, a love seat, a double bed, a television and Sega console with games piled on the floor, and a computer on the desk by the window. On the bed he has fishing line, and clips, and black poster board.

"I was thinking," he says, "we should make a mobile." He points to the bed, and I try to follow his idea. "You know, like those things they hang above cribs." I nod. "We'll mount the photographs on the poster board, and then use the clips and fishing line to hang them so they revolve. They'll tell a bunch of different stories, you know, at the same time."

"Mount them back to back?" I ask.

"Yeah. Yeah, exactly."

I cannot use scissors to cut a straight line. If I glue something, you can tell: the glue bubbles at the edges, and ridges underneath like shifting plates. So, pretty much, I hand Bangs the photographs, and encourage him while he puts the whole thing together. We take breaks to eat pizza, and play a little guitar. I've been excused from family dinner, though I need to be back before seven to babysit for the Thorns.

The door to his bedroom is closed, and locked, and I would be killed if I tried anything like that with a boy in my room. We're on the floor, in our socks, the project spread in front of us—and from the stuff in his room, he could be any boy, Nigel or Nate or Doug, with the same crap they all seem to have; no

70

one else is as austere as Jeremy, but his dad's Lutheran—when it occurs to me that I'm having a good time. That I'm not tense or worried, or, and it takes me longer to understand this, excited. I'm not excited to be alone in a room with Bangs. I'm too comfortable to be turned on. We could be buddies. Maybe we are buddies. And as soon as I think this, I want to laugh, and I want to go straight to Jeremy's, and tell him that I understand, that he's the one that makes me feel sick and nauseated, and that I really like that he doesn't have so much shit in his room, and talks when you're in the car with him, and that when it finally happens, one night in my room, I want him to be the one. I want him to be the one who changes me.

The knock against the door freaks me out—I actually spring up and glance around like maybe I'm going to leap through the window. Then a girl's voice calls, "Christian?"

He opens the door to a girl I recognize instantly—the straight blonded-brown hippie hair, the long gypsy skirt, the bangles, and the black Mary Janes: Gabby, last year's president of our Amnesty International Club.

"Hey, Cole," she says as she hugs me. "I haven't seen you in a while." She's a small, cuter version of her brother. He seems almost painfully gaunt, like a whippet, next to her. But they have the same upturned tip of the nose, the same freckles, the same mischievous expressions. As they stand side by side, the resemblance is startling.

"I'm on my way to class," she says to me, "and I thought I'd offer you a ride home if you're done with your project." She looks at the project now, spread out on the floor, and admires it warmly. Everything about this girl is earnest and heartfelt. There were rumors that she and the black-haired girl she hung out with all during high school were witches. On warm days, they both walked through school barefoot, their shoes rested on the pile of books they carried like a baking sheet of cookies straight from the oven.

"Sure," I say. "It's not like I'm helping much anyway."

"You took all the photos," Bangs says.

He carries my bag down, and I'm trying to imagine Gabby driving a Mercedes, but I really can't. I never guessed either of these kids came from privilege.

71

Instead of heading toward the garage, we detour through the great room, and out the front door. She drives an old red Volkswagen bug with dings all over it.

"See you Monday," Bangs says.

And then his sister drives me away in her bug, chattering about her classes at Brookdale Community College, and careening all over the road like traffic signs are really just guidelines.

Erudite. Learned or scholarly. Adjective. One of the synonyms is *sapient,* which, frankly, is a much cooler word, with a much cooler definition: having great wisdom and discernment.

After my guitar lesson Saturday morning, I finish reading this short story that Overhead assigned, *The Short Happy Life of Francis Macomber,* and I have to say that Hemingway is kind of dirty and mean. We're supposed to be thinking about irony while we read it. Overhead is in love with irony.

Last night at the Thorns, I finished both chapters for Spanish, and the take-home quiz for Geometry, and after I write my response to Hemingway, I'll have History and Biology chapters to read and respond to, and the Spontaneous Speech on Monday to worry about—a three-minute impromptu speech on a subject we're handed on our way to the podium. Three minutes! I can look like an idiot in half that time. Jeremy is coming for me this afternoon at two; we're going to see a movie, and have dinner, and, in the note he gave me yesterday, he promised a surprise.

This morning Leroy taught me a sweet lick. He's trying to make me play lead, but I'm really a rhythm girl. Lead is hard to play while you're singing. After I'd played the notes a bunch of times, and could do it without looking, I noticed Leroy had his eyes closed, and his head cocked, and nodded along with me like he could feel it. He's a reverent guy, Leroy. Sometimes, when I'm with him, I think I've never really heard music, anyway not like he hears. It shudders through him, like Karen Thorn when she's laughing, like maybe he's made of it: composed of music.

This old spiritual we sing on communion Sundays, *Let Us Break Bread Together,* has the same kind of reverence. The song's so plaintive that my heart hurts when I sing it. Eventually, Leroy echoed the lick back to me, varying the rhythm, and then the key, and I echoed his variations and it was call and response, and improvisation, and then this crazy fast challenge. And he's singing, "Come on. Come on now." I get a little high, playing with Leroy, a little rapturous.

On the wall, the intercom beeps, and Dad says, "Cole?"

I hop up to answer.

"Can you come down for a minute?"

What's the point in protesting? He's in the kitchen, leaned against the counter, with a giant mug of hot chocolate held in both hands like an offering. In the narrow room, between the oven and the counter, we're about two feet apart. Over his shoulder, a stained-glass cardinal hangs in the window, and beyond the cardinal, rainfall.

"I just heated some water," he tells me, "if you want something hot."

I shake my head. His eyes are weak, and he's still in his robe, though it's after noon, and Dad never lounges.

"Are you sick?" I ask.

"Just tired."

More like ragged, I think. He sets the hot chocolate on the counter, and rubs at his face. Last year, Mom bought this robe for Dad to wear in the hospital after his hernia operation. When he got home he had to walk up and down the hallway like seven million times, squeaking every floorboard in that cheesy horror movie way, and when I complained about the squeaking he totally tore my head off, and I officially hate this robe. I'm angry just looking at it.

"Listen, Cole, your mother and I have decided to let you try the band thing."

Without considering, I launch at him. I can't remember the last time I kissed my dad, but I'm so excited, I kiss him a couple of times, and jump up and down, and maybe shriek too.

He has a startled smile on his face, and pats my arm in that *take it easy* way he does with Pepper, before picking up his mug and sipping from it. "Bands have complicated dynamics some-times. This'll be a different stress from basketball, but it'll still be a stress." He examines my face as if to trace his argument in my expression. "Basketball isn't your only gift, I know that. But it's a gift that would pay for college."

"I don't want to play basketball in college." I'm worried, suddenly, that he's going to refuse to let me quit after all. "Or high school."

"Well," he says, and it's more a gesture than a word.

I'm trying to decide if a handshake is appropriate when he says, "And Cole, church and Sunday school are non-negotiable." This has never occurred to me, I mean, to negotiate them. "Sure," I say.

"Fair warning," he says. "No matter how late you're out Saturday night, you'll be up and ready for Sunday school."

No matter how late I'm out Saturday night? "Absolutely," I say. Nod and back away. Just nod and back away. "For sure."

♫ ♫ ♫

If a guy called you up, and suggested a picnic in his mom's car, in the parking lot of a community college, in the middle of a rainstorm as a prelude to a double feature of Alfred Hitchcock's *Psycho* and *Vertigo*, you might refuse—find it a little too suggestive of the sociopath dating manual or something—but you'd be so wrong. *Psycho* is a comedy: a really black one, yes, full of camp—that knowing cheesiness—but a comedy nonetheless, and a film that changed film. (The announcer guy said it was the first time a toilet bowl had been flushed on film.) And sitting in the Brookdale auditorium, eating Red Vines and bagels with cream cheese, we laughed with a bunch of junior college nerds, from the ridiculous opening scene with the blinds and the weirdly formal illicitness right through to the light-bulb-pitching reveal and the not-gonna-hurt-a-fly leer. How cool is the skeleton on the swivel chair?

Vertigo wasn't as fun; obsession is creepy. You kind of hate to see James Stewart as a lunatic. The colors of the film—announcer guy kept saying palette—are so striking that sometimes I would forget about the actors and just admire the sets.

"Old Hitch likes blondes," Jeremy says as he climbs back into the car with our slices of pepperoni pizza.

Drizzle now, instead of rain, but it drops bead on his letterman jacket. "And circular resolution," I say.

75

Jeremy shrugs, "That's just good storytelling, isn't it? Good stories resolve on themselves. But *Psycho*, with the money misdirection, that's pure genius."

"It'd be hard to argue that Hitchcock isn't clever."

He grins at me. Neither of us mentions the sexual tone of the films. We picked it up, of course, but that's as far as we'll carry it. I have so much to say that I can't think of anything.

Headlights graze us as we drive. Tires on the wet road, and a funky band on the radio, and I'm sleepy now from food and pleasure, and this boy humming beside me.

"Do you like this?" he asks, meaning the song.

"I like this one. They're kind of all over the place."

"Red Hot Chili Peppers," he says. "Mike made me a tape."

It's only ten, but Jeremy drives back to the base, and then, amazingly, parks his mother's car at the end of the street, several blocks from their house, and looks at me. "Are you ready for your surprise?"

"Yes."

He jumps out of the car and runs around to my side to take my hand. "Follow me," he says, and then we sprint through the alleyway, across our yard, and up the stairs to the back door of my building. "Quietly," he says, when I hesitate.

I sneak us inside—someone's moving in the kitchen as we creep past, but the kitchen door never opens—and up the stairs, and into my room. In the dark of the room, I can smell us: the wet of his jacket, and my hair, and the mud on our shoes, and we're tangled and kissing, and he lifts me toward him in that way that makes me breathless. Even as the ache becomes unbearable, I realize that something is different; something in my room is different.

"Wait," I gasp. His breathing labors as well, as I stagger back and throw the light switch. The guitar is propped on a stand by my acoustic. I approach it with my hand out as though it were a suspicious dog. "A Fender," I say. On my knees now, supplicating, I pull the guitar into my lap and run my fingers over the fret board, the green and white belly, the new strings.

"Do you like it?" he asks.

I nod.

"Mike says Fenders are good guitars." I look up at Jeremy, at his beaming face. "You only have an acoustic, and I thought, you know, with the band and all, that you'd need an electric."

"Nigel told you." It comes out like I have laryngitis.

"Yes," Jeremy says. "I told him I'd got you a guitar, for your birthday, but if your parents decided to let you play in the band to let me know right away." He shrugs. "You'd need it sooner."

He bought me a guitar for my birthday: a weird, green, electric guitar. And sneaked it into my room. He kneels beside me now.

"Will you play me something?" he asks.

Without an amp, I can't play much he'd hear, and then I realize that he knows this. He grins at me, whispers, "In the closet."

An amp and cord. It's too much, of course. Jeremy bags groceries at the commissary, and bought me an electric guitar and an amp for my birthday (which is still nearly three weeks away).

"Jeremy," I say, and I know already that I'm going to cry and ruin everything. He's so excited and has surprised me with these beautiful, thoughtful gifts and I'm going to ruin everything by crying.

I plug the amp and guitar in. Test and tune, and the tears are down my face—coming no matter how hard I wipe them away—and I play the first song I can think of.

> It's Thursday in a week that never changes,
> Colder now than I remember then.
> I still see you across the kitchen table.
> When I left I wanted to be wrong.
>
> I understand I was lying to the waiter
> When I said, I meant to love you better.
> In the kitchen, light has finally faded
> Convince me we meant no harm.
>
> Yes you rant
> And oh you rave

The shameful way we behave.
Drag my hair across your face.
You're not my love. You're not my love.

Years later you will say our palms were empty,
That love was not the game we played.
Maybe we just had too much to carry,
I've got blisters from the boy I couldn't hold,

I fought that car all down the highway
Wanting every town to turn around
And for you to be waiting at the window
Oh so anxious that I had really gone.

Jeremy laughs when I finish playing. (It's a fast song, even when I'm not nervous.) "Figures you'd play something tortured."

"I love this guitar," I say. Like Overhead loves irony. Like old Hitch loves blondes. I love it proprietarily.

"It's a little used," he says. "You can see some nicks around the pickup. But Mike called some of his old band mates, and one of them said he didn't even want this guitar in his basement anymore. I guess the green kind of freaked him out."

Jeremy kisses me again, his lips soft as the guitar's nylon strings.

Ephemeral. Short-lived; transitory. Adjective and noun. I hope my midnight curfew is ephemeral.

Meghan and I are almost through our vocabulary list Sunday afternoon, when Nate bursts into the sunroom, and tells us to hop to. "We're going to the gym for some 3-on-3."

Never mind that I've just been granted a reprieve from basketball, and still have Biology reading to do, and a new-to-me guitar to practice (Joe told me our first practice is tomorrow after school)—and Nate and I have been pretending Nigel's our only sibling, Meghan and I both jump up and follow him.

"I need to get my high tops from the dorm," Meghan says.

"You girls are going with Jeremy," Nate directs. "He'll swing by the dorm, and then you'll meet up with us at the gym."

Jeremy's standing in the foyer, grinning. "How about the three of us against your dad and brothers?"

"Oh yes," I say.

"Suicide's a choice," Nate hollers after us.

At the gym, the side baskets have all been lowered, allowing four additional half-court games. Sweaty, grasping bodies, squeaky shoes, balls rocketing out of bounds, the sweet sound of swish, and for a second, I miss this game.

Nate sinks a jump shot as we arrive, and blows on his fingers. "Last chance, Jeremy," he calls. "Stick with those two and it's gonna be ugly."

Jeremy winks at me, before dropping into leg stretches. We're playing with a boy's ball because life is just like that. Meghan nails a couple from the outside, and I start thinking we should play for money.

Nate ought to guard Jeremy, but takes me instead, and makes a point of leaning back whenever I have the ball, like he's going to give me plenty of space to make my move. None of us has ever played ball with Meghan, and so Nigel doesn't know she'll drive in, fake, and cross over for a left hook. (My dad thinks the hook shot is maybe the finest in the sport, and applauds even as Nate harangues Nigel for pitiful defense.) We will destroy these chumps.

Jeremy and I handle the rebounds while Meghan steals into the paint for a short jumper, or hands the ball off for Jeremy to power up. Nate forgoes the casual defense, and starts fouling, hard and sloppy. Dad reprimands him a couple of times, and then Jeremy drills Nate in the chest and sends him sprawling.

"Time out," Nate yells, and walks off the court.

"Meghan," Dad says, passing her the ball, "what a touch you have!"

Dad handed me a basketball for the first time when I was six. Even with a granny shot, I couldn't heave that thing anywhere near the basket. Thrilled, fanatical, he encouraged me, and played the showman: dribbling figure eights between his legs, spinning the ball on his finger, and finally, lifting me as I lifted the ball, to push it over the rim with an exultant shout.

We pass the ball around and take shots as they occur to us, until we hear multiple voices calling to Meghan. Suddenly five boys wearing grey ARMY t-shirts mob her, and demand that we play a full-court game. The cadets razz her (like Doug with me) and she murmurs to us that we cannot lose as we take possession.

And that's how the thrill comes back to me. The sprint and pass, the darting shot, the pleasure of firing a worn leather ball in an arc that touches nothing but net. Meghan plays point, and Dad and Jeremy post up, and Nigel is everywhere, irritating the hell out of two guys yelling *Switch!* all through the plays. Sometimes the ball is a kite that you guide on the wind, and sometimes it's your conscience meandering around, and sometimes the ball is your child tucked against you.

We play best of three (first to twenty-one), and when Nate finally returns from his time-out, we have a much-needed sub, one whose aggressiveness we now appreciate since we benefit from it. Meghan gets her wish; we win both games, and the cadets seem to enjoy losing to her. They call for a rematch, even as we pull on our warm-ups.

That night, I plug my green electric into the little amp and play the lick Leroy taught me, and dream of a new kind of kite conscience child.

♫ ♫ ♫

The garage has brown carpet spread down the center, and a stage they've built from wood, the assembled drum kit, along with the mic stands and amplifiers, and a space heater mounted from the ceiling and glowing orange.

"Who's this dude?" Trevor asks when he sees Jeremy.

"Jeremy," I say.

"A different guy every time, huh?" he says. He drains his Budweiser, and opens another. "I see how it is."

Joe points at my case. "Bust out the Strat." I hand over my Fender, and Joe nods. "Groovy. Play me something."

I fuck about with a few progressions, and then, something Ernie's strumming in the background catches my attention. "That's Red Hot Chili Peppers," I tell him.

"You're right," he says. "*Pretty Little Ditty.*"

"You know the lyric?" I ask. "To write out?"

He nods.

"We should play that one," I say.

Jeremy writes out the lyric while Ernie teaches us the song. He demonstrates the rhythm for Trevor and we begin, in a hesitant way, to follow him through the song. Just the music, the first few times, until I turn the mic to face them, and sing as though to myself, and they're nodding along, Ernie with a maniacal grin, and Joe with a cigarette dangling from his mouth like he's modeling rock and roll, and Trevor watching Joe for changes.

"You singing Anthony Kiedis," Trevor says after we've played it a dozen times, "gives me a funny feeling right here." He looks at his lap.

"I'll bet it's just a little funny," I say into the microphone.

He laughs loudest of all of them, and gives me a couple of high hat taps.

"I knew you were a dirty girl!"

81

"Dude," Joe says, "how about this?" And he plays Concrete Blonde's *Tomorrow, Wendy*, and even as I'm singing it, convinced I'm going to hell, Ernie and Joe dance with their instruments, and Trevor flourishes his sticks, and pushes us a little faster until we've rewritten the song as a fast number, more taunt than lamentation.

Half a dozen songs played with varying rhythms and bridges—Ernie and Joe harmonizing and adding random solos with extra measures—and I get so I can sing without smacking my mouth into the mic. The boys hop and thrash and trill like displaying birds, until I groove with them, high on this thing we unleash, set roaring.

"I think we should play Saturday," Joe says as we pack up. "Practice every afternoon this week, and then play a gig Saturday at Board."

"Thursday's Thanksgiving," I say.

"Shit," he says. "Well, Friday we'll just go longer."

"Board hosts weekly gigs now?" I ask.

"Just started," Ernie says. "Saturday nights—$2 cover."

"Crap money," Trevor says. "I'll look around for something better, maybe Ichabod's. They said we could play a weeknight last time I checked. Something tells me they'll give us a weekend pretty fucking quick."

"Same time tomorrow?" Joe asks. They all look at me.

"Tomorrow," I agree, and follow my roadie to the car.

♫ ♫ ♫

Do you know about Elizabeth Bishop's poems? The one about how dirty everything is, and how somebody loves us all—*The Filling Station*—we're reading today in Overhead's class. The language throughout the poem is conversational and knowing—*a certain color*—and witty—*high-strung automobiles*—and I read it over and over and love it a little more each go.

Do you ever feel like you've exposed a secret when you read something you love? Like you've discovered a reality that, for whatever reason, had been kept from you? I think maybe the point of art is that it's intimate, and steps across time, and feels like revelation, and that I'm different simply because I've experienced it.

We have half a dozen poems to read while Overhead does her nails, and, I don't know about the rest of the class, but this poem is making me stupidly sentimental. Like, I keep thinking about my mom and her endless barrage of questions, and how she packs our lunches and includes a napkin, and the track meet in seventh grade when those two girls knocked me down during the half mile, and I chased after them and kicked their fucking asses—won the race by twelve seconds—and then noticed my arms and legs were burned and bleeding from the track and had little black pieces of gravel in them, and my mother cleaned the burns and patched me up and said that night at dinner it was the first time I hadn't complained about her coming to a meet. You know, junk like that.

"Cole," Overhead says. "Have you read the poems?"

"Yes," I say.

She smirks, crosses her arms, and leans against the blackboard. Overhead is Veronica Lake if Veronica Lake were in her sixties with a bad complexion and a habit of sucking her teeth.

"And what do you think of them?" she asks.

"Elizabeth Bishop makes it seem easy—accessible—like maybe she wrote this entire poem from the car while they filled her tank. At first it even sounds like she's judging them, but the narrator's voice is so specific that it's almost making fun of itself. And by the last line, the poem's something else again. Suddenly it's about a mother."

Her mouth is a little "O" for a moment, and then she gets all smarmy again. "Very intricately stated, Cole." Backhand.

"What is the deal," Alicia says, "with Emily Dickinson and bees?"

"What's the deal," Sarah scoffs, "with Emily Dickinson at all?"

And they're off. Arguing the merits of a dead chick who liked dashes, not even acknowledging the whispered *esso-so-so-so* of

83

Bishop's final lines. Love is a deliberate act, isn't it? Love like that, anyway: nurturing love.

Tonya makes a long point about line breaks, in reference to William Carlos Williams, that I don't follow at all. I love his wheelbarrow poem. How it's concrete and abstract in this perfect mix: *so much depends . . . beside the white chickens.*

"Over the break, you will write a poem," Overhead announces. "You may choose to write a sonnet, or a free-verse poem with at least four stanzas. Choose your subject. Also, I want you to read Steinbeck's *The Chrysanthemums* and write a response." The bell rings, and she calls to us over her shoulder, "Be good."

"Stupid Emily Dickinson," Alicia says, heaving her bag over her shoulder. "Bunch of nonsense."

"Very intricately stated," I mutter.

Alicia grins at me. "Lisa told me that the senior seminar Overhead teaches is fantastic, and they all love her. She said Overhead jokes with them and everything."

"Right," I say. "She just hates us because we're underclassmen."

She switches her bag to the opposite shoulder with a grunt. "They know we only get two days off for Thanksgiving, right? They're assigning homework like we're on break for a week."

The hallway is a torpedo crossed with a bathroom: the walls, tiled in this ridiculous blue and tan pattern, seem to slope a little tighter as you walk toward the windows by the staircase. Alicia strolls along with me to the office, though she hadn't said she's coming, and I haven't asked her to. She knows about the letters in my backpack.

Coaches. Dear Coaches. I couldn't get behind either of these greetings.

Really, if I weren't a jackass, I'd just phone them, or even go to tryouts to explain in person about not playing this year. Instead, I wrote a letter.

Last year, Coach Hoskins and Coach Henry sat in my living room and persuaded me to play ball. A building year, they said. On this little magnetic board they showed me plays, and talked about my teammates, and their goals for all of us. Hoskins had a winning record at some private boys' school I'd never heard of. His hair parted down the middle in silver halves, and he wore a huge gold ring like a wrestler.

Henry, black and intense, spent a lot of time nodding and wiping the corners of his mouth. I think he was the reason I finally agreed. He wasn't coaxing me, or bullying me, or anything. Just sitting there all thoughtful and determined. It was kind of touching.

So I wrote a letter. If I were Elizabeth Bishop, maybe I could make them see. Explain about the Violent Femmes, and how Bangs tabbed me out a couple of their songs, and the kind of wild joy I feel when I play those songs on my pistachio guitar. I wish I could explain about the wild joy.

I wish I could tell my coaches that I'm grateful for the season I played for them. My dad always says the invocation at graduations, and school events and stuff. I never know if he volunteers to do it, or if some school official or teacher contacts him. As much as the whole thing embarrasses me—all the kids hissing *Is this guy your dad? What's an invocation? Your dad's going to pray?*—the truth is that I love his blessing. I love that he rests his hand on my forehead to bless me. I love the words. I wish I could tell my coaches how they blessed me.

"Do you want me to put the letters in their boxes?" Alicia asks. I nod.

She takes the letters from me, and disappears into the office. I know they'll be angry. Disappointed. I don't blame them. And I'm sorry. Sorry to be less than they hoped for. Sorry to want something else so badly.

"It's done," Alicia says. She's looking at the frail shaft of light through the smudged glass doors. Tipped to the right by her backpack, her eyes puffy behind her glasses, her hair chaotic. "Vacation, my ass. I'm so tired of high school. Stand up there and call Emily Dickinson a genius? We are lied to every single day."

The warning bell rings and the both of us take off running, terrified of arriving late for our next class.

Diaphanous. Sheer and light; almost completely transparent or translucent. Adjective. (Kind of girly, this word.)

Meghan's dorm room is spare, like imminent military inspection with the potential of KP Duty kind of spare. The surfaces are clear and dust-free. On her half: a desk with two lamps; a bed tortured into pristine smoothness; a footlocker; a stereo; a metal chair; and a bookcase. The other side is exactly the same except the roommate has photographs on her bookcase rather than books. The closet slider-doors are closed, but I know anything behind those doors is as crisp and orderly as the rest of the room.

Though I've been here before, I never noticed how naked the room felt on previous visits. Somehow I imagined us watching movies, and running around swathed in brightly striped comforters. They don't even have a television on this floor; it's downstairs in the rec room with the foosball table.

"Those sheets on Regina's bed are mine, and they're clean." Meghan sits down on her own bed, and smiles at me. "Why do you look so terrified?"

"What?" I say, and carry my guitar and duffel to Regina's side of the room. I'm afraid to touch anything.

"Relax," she says. "We're officially on vacation in the dorms: no inspections, no demerits."

No demerits! "Oh," I say, "good." My guitar fits perfectly under the bed.

"Are you hungry?"

"Yes." No one ever really needs to ask me that.

"How do you feel about Chinese?"

"Good. I feel good about it." She laughs at me, when I add, "Sweet and sour pork," without looking at the menu.

"Fried rice or plain?"

"Fried."

"You're so easy," she says. "Regina studies the damn thing for twenty minutes and then orders the Kung Pao Chicken every time. The phone's at the end of the hallway; I'll be right back."

Money, I think, after she's gone. I have like $6 on me. God, I might as well be Nate, the master of gosh-I-forgot-to-bring-my-wallet-but-I'll-totally-pay-you-back.

"Twenty minutes," she tells me from the doorway. "Foosball?"

"Sure," I say. I think I'm sweating. I feel a little ill actually. How come I never think of these things beforehand? Why didn't I bring cash with me?

"What's the matter?"

"I have $6." It's the kind of statement that should be tagged: *said the child.*

"What?" she says. And then, "Oh, your dad gave me money for dinner." She crosses the room, all the way to Regina's side, and reaches her hand out to help me off the bed. "Since my parents don't get in until late, we'll have dinner here, and then meet up with everyone tomorrow morning for pancakes."

Of course she knows more about what's going on than I do. "Cool," I say, like I haven't been freaking for the last five minutes. "Are you any good at foosball?"

"I'm alright," she says, and I know she's going to kick my ass.

And she does. In the rec room, a girl in blue Army sweats sits cross-legged on the couch with a bag of Oreos, and CNN blaring from the television. She murmurs, "Hey," and then ignores us completely. Once the Chinese arrives, we eat it here, lounged on the windowsills, looking down at the tight little courtyard and the men's dorm across the quad.

"How many people stayed for Thanksgiving?" I ask.

"Eight in this dorm," Meghan says. "I don't know about the boys."

"It's so quiet." Whatever she ordered is so fucking hot that my lips are burning. Unfortunately, it's also delicious, and I keep eating anyway.

We play best of seven, and I lose every game. She's good, and fast, and has a murderous focus. While we've been here, the CNN headlines have repeated three times, but the girl on the couch keeps watching.

"Saddam's psychotic," she says. She's not actually speaking to us, but not to herself either. Maybe she's telling the television. "We're going to invade."

"You think so?" Meghan asks.

The girl looks up at us, bites a black cookie, and nods. "Totally."

♫ ♫ ♫

"Play me something," Meghan says. Her hair's finally long enough for a ponytail, and she's wearing a blue mask for her pores.

I brought my acoustic, and tune it now from Regina's bed. The mattress is so firm that it's kind of like sitting on a bench. Somehow playing for a girl in a blue mask is easier than playing for a girl without one.

I play *Add It Up* by the Violent Femmes, modulating my voice so no one on the floor can complain about the noise. Even though she's wearing a mask, I keep my eyes on the linoleum squares of the floor, and am doubly shocked when I hear applause. There are two more girls in the doorway of the room applauding with Meghan.

"I love that song," one says. "Do you know more?"

I play *Gone Daddy Gone,* and then some Cure, and Clash, and U2, and they're all on Meghan's bed now, leaned against the wall, their socked feet tapping air. Every time I finish a song, they're already calling for more. I'm nearing the end of my repertoire when Meghan tells me to play one of my own.

"Fast or slow?" I say, stalling for time.

"Both," the other girl says.

I play the fast, angry one first, and then the plaintive one, and this is the weirdest audience I've ever had. One of the girls is lighting matches and holding them in the air during the slow song, and Meghan still has that mask on her face though it's cracked and freaky now, and the other girl is eating gummi bears, and keeps tossing them to me between songs.

In the end, they're ecstatic and assure me that I hardly seemed nervous at all; and I learn they're both named Heather (Heather Longhair and Heather Shorthair) and know all about me from Meghan's stories, and have been anxious to meet me. After Meghan scrubs her face—"This stuff is actually starting to hurt. I think my skin may be bleeding."—we find ourselves back in the rec room playing foosball again. On the same couch in the same position, the girl is still watching CNN, and still eating Oreos—and must be sick of both.

"How old are you?" Heather Shorthair asks me.

"I'll be sixteen in two weeks."

"Sixteen?" They say this like maybe I made it up. Everyone but me is in grey Army sweats, and elastic-banded ponytails—even Heather Shorthair has one, high up, Pebblesesque.

"God, I thought you were at least a senior," Heather Shorthair says.

"For sure," Heather Longhair contributes.

Meghan scores while they're busy being incredulous.

"Shi-it!" they cry.

And then, Heather Longhair says, "Sixteen was the longest year of my life. I'd decided to be a virgin until I turned seventeen, and it was just crazy hard—those last five months especially. So, like the last night before my birthday, I had sex in the back of this blue station wagon on a blanket at midnight, and thought it was really romantic."

They're all laughing when the girl on the couch says, "Finger fucking doesn't count, but maybe she had one of those plastic dicks." She says this like she's talking to the television again.

Someone at the foosball table—I can't tell whom—mutters, "Latent."

But Heather Longhair says, "Which did your dad use, his fingers or his dick?"

And the girl is over the couch, and shrieking, when Meghan and Heather Shorthair grab her arms and throw her back onto the couch. The girl comes at them again, crying this time, and so pissed that she has two veins running down her forehead to her nose which look as though they might rupture.

This time when they throw her back on the couch, she twists off, pitching the Oreos' bag onto the floor, and sprints from the room.

I don't exactly get what has happened, but I know it's bad. Meghan, her chest expanding in that concentrated deep way like when the doctor listens to your breathing, turns to the Heathers. "She's hateful. We all agree on that." She looks at Heather Longhair. "And she can ruin your career. You'll help her do it if you carry on like that."

Neither Heather says anything; they're both breathing as heavily as Meghan, and Longhair has glassy eyes.

♫ ♫ ♫

Mr. Pang loved our photo-story. Bangs tied the fishing lure to a pipe on the ceiling, and it draped and spun like a proper mobile, and the whole class went on and on about how cool it was. I tell Meghan about our exhibition as we walk across the quad toward the tree-lined sidewalk. The wind blows leaves in that scrabbling way that always makes me jumpy, and even the streetlamps throw sinister shadows, and I'm chattering too fast from nervousness and because Meghan isn't talking at all.

The girl with the Oreos said *she*. *Maybe* she *had one of those plastic dicks.*

Meghan's mad, or anyway, she's imitating a bulldozer, and I'm taking extra steps to keep pace. I'm hungry again, and worried that she'll be exasperated if I tell her, after the fight and drama and everything, that I'm hungry. I should have brought some snacks in my duffel. I never think to bring snacks, or money, apparently. Oreo-girl insinuated Heather Longhair is a lesbian, didn't she? Pretty much called her a lesbian. Meghan said Oreo-girl could ruin Heather's career. What'd she mean by that? If Meghan weren't one notch below postal, I'd ask her.

Finally, I make myself stop talking, and sprint-walk beside her through the cold night, the stars a jumbled crowd above us. All the buildings on this end of post are administrative: several stories tall, red-bricked, with neat lawns and tidy courtyards. All the military order of rectangles and pruned shrubbery.

"I want this at any price," she says. She might be saying this to me, although I haven't any idea what she means. "But is that right?" she says, and looks at me. Her face obscured by dark. "Do I want this at any price?"

"I don't know," I say.

She shakes her head, and then says, "Let's run. Can you?" And takes off before I answer. Now I'm chasing after her—aware, all at once, that I'm wearing my Converse rather than my running shoes. Why didn't I think to wear my running shoes? It's like I'm never prepared for anything.

Ruse. A trick, stratagem, or artifice. Noun. This word makes me think of pirates, and the crafty methods they use to lure ships—the whole, look-we're-flying-a-flag-from-a-nation-at-peace-with-you thing—but also, the word's kind of old-fashioned sounding, isn't it? I mean, am I going to tell Kelly that I don't appreciate her ruses, or whatever? Please stop with the ruses, because they're obvious and immature? I think not.

Meghan practically has to beat me awake Thanksgiving morning. For a hard, unrelenting surface, Regina's bed swallowed me whole.

"You have fifteen minutes to shower and dress," she says, after a second pillow blow. "Nate's coming for us."

Hair still dripping when I climb into the backseat, I'm thankful to be going home to familiar people, to be sitting in the back of a familiar car, to see Nate's stupid letterman's jacket with the tear along the right sleeve. I'm thankful that Meghan has stopped twitching and asking weird questions. I'm thankful to be leaving the dorm, and its drama behind me, even though we'll be back again tonight.

"Your parents aren't down yet," Nate says by way of greeting. "But I saw your sweet little ride parked in front of the house. Figures the prom queen would have a convertible."

"Is he kidding?" I ask.

"I was the Homecoming Queen," Meghan says.

"About the convertible?" I clarify. It's like I'm speaking Braille to these people.

"I have a VW Rabbit."

I know cars like I know geometry. "And it's a convertible?"

"Yes," she says.

"I can't believe you left that car behind," Nate says. "Why would you do a thing like that? Isn't helping me pick up girls important to you?"

"Why, Nate," she laughs, "do you need help?"

♫ ♫ ♫

When I meet Meghan's parents, I know exactly how my mother is going to describe them when she phones her own mother this afternoon: Mutt and Jeff. I have no idea who Mutt and Jeff actually are, but from context I can tell you that one is itty-bitty and the other is not. Meghan's dad is a short dude with an impressive gut—he was a Master Sergeant with two tours of Vietnam—and has that deep, I-pop-men's-heads-right-off-their-bodies voice, and her mom is spindly and Southern genteel. They drove up from Georgia, in separate cars, to bring Meghan her Rabbit.

By the time we get to the house, the table's laid with bacon and pancakes, scrambled eggs and small glasses of juice, and real and fake maple syrup (Nigel will only use Aunt Jemima).

It's not that I'm bored so much as exhausted. I need days of sleep to recover. Meghan's dad tells mildly inappropriate stories about his tenure in the military, and his therapy clients in Georgia. He's rosy and has a joyous laugh and this tendency to look you in the eye and nod in this serious, confidential way that's completely disarming.

He's the one who proposes Scrabble. I am lame at Scrabble. The board, I just don't see it. It's a private humiliation for me, how bad I am, like not getting chess or crosswords. My mother and Meghan's mother take their coffee into the kitchen to work on the next meal. I stretch on the couch, and admire the ineffectual fire snapping in the grate behind the glass doors.

I thought staying in the dorm with Meghan would be the coolest thing ever, and now I don't even want to go back. She's mad at me, and I don't know why. I don't understand what I've done. It's like Kelly all over again. As I think this, the doorbell rings.

Nate runs through, calling, "I've got it."

Kelly comes into the living room, wearing a long dark skirt with her grey cashmere sweater, and holding a huge box of chocolates, and a bottle of sparkling apple cider. She waves quickly at me before Nate leads her through the dining room and into the kitchen, and introduces her, ceremoniously, to Meghan's parents, while Mom asks if she'd like something hot to drink, or maybe a warmed-up pancake.

Why didn't I know Kelly was coming for Thanksgiving? What else don't I know? They have the Scrabble board out, and everyone gathers around it, trying to determine teams of two. Happily I'm spared having to play, since the teams would be uneven.

Sleep would help to pass a great deal of the day. Even as this occurs to me, I slip away. Aware, at times, of voices nearby, shudders of wood and flame, and then the doorbell again, at some distance. And then a kiss, peppermint-flavored. This is my favorite part: a peppermint kiss, and I lean into it. My eyes open in the middle of a second kiss, or possibly a third. Jeremy. I am afraid that I have dreamed him, when he pulls me toward him, and kisses me as though I have returned from a long journey.

"What are you doing here?" I ask.

"It's Thanksgiving," he says. "We're all here."

"You're wearing a tie," I say, as I sit up.

He's on his knees, beside the couch, his tie red, his collared shirt white, and his pants a navy blue. In a tie, he's doubly gorgeous: older, somehow, more civilized.

"You're not playing Scrabble," he says.

"No, I was sleeping." Maybe we're compelled to make obvious observations.

"How was the dorm?"

I flick my glance around as though it's a hacky sack. Apparently, I should be better dressed, and more organized, and ask questions like, "Hey, who all's coming to Thanksgiving? And what's the dress code for the meal?"

"Mike's here?" I ask, catching his voice from the sea in the next room.

"Yeah, he surprised my folks this morning."

Jeremy climbs to his feet, and places another piece of wood on the fire. Though the doors' metal handles are insanely hot, you pretty much have to be sitting on top of the fire to be warm. Still, it lends a homespun, traditional sound to the festivities.

"Do you know who else is coming?" I ask.

"No idea. Once I heard your name, I kind of stopped listening."

"You are the saccharine king."

He winks at me, and hands over a peppermint candy. "I told Mike about your gig on Saturday, and he said he'd take care of it—make sure we can go and everything. He's excited to hear you guys, especially after I told him you cover Red Hot."

"I think Meghan's mad at me." I'm so close to him when I whisper this that I can see a weird little reddish hair on his jawline that he missed when he shaved.

"Why?" he whispers back.

I shrug. "I thought it'd be like on TV, you know, the bright, overstuffed dorm room, and everyone running around in slippers eating chocolate and listening to college radio. You know, like that. But really it's just another indoctrination center for Army robots." I tell him a watered-down version of the fight in the rec room—lay blame on the instigating sugar-high of Oreo-girl—and about Meghan's weirdness, and the sprint we took afterward in the dark, how she ran until she was gasping in a kind of hoarse bark. "And this morning, she was snippy."

"Snippy?"

"For real."

Meghan's mom comes through with the huge box of chocolates Kelly brought, and offers us some. We take a little time trying to figure out which are filled with caramel or strawberry cream.

"Don't you two play Scrabble?" she asks. Her accent is comforting, warmer somehow, and more musical than the grating ax chops of east coast speech. We shake our heads, and she beams at us. "Well, don't think a thing about it. Help yourselves to another piece, go on now." We do, and she beams again, and then takes her light in to the others.

Jeremy and I have sunk into the couch, our socked feet on the coffee table, our fingers woven together. At some point, I'll need to change out of these jeans.

"Maybe she's stressed about her parents' visit," Jeremy says. "Or maybe it's just school. Mike says he has a ton of reading that he's supposed to get done over the holiday. That he really shouldn't have made the trip at all, except he needed to get away from his dorm and his roommate and all the sameness."

Sameness is what I miss most right now. I have no place to be solitary in this house; guests staying in my room, guests at every meal, Jeremy in his tie.

Roaring from the dining room, and Meghan and her father appear to have won the Scrabble contest. Sometimes, I have lousy manners. "Do you want a Snapple?" I ask Jeremy.

"Cherry?"

I come back with one for each of us. Cherry Snapple tastes fermented, like maybe it's a little alcoholic; anyway, that's what we've decided. The first time I had one was at Jeremy's house. He gave it to me, and then stood so close that my arm kept brushing against his chest. I expected sparks, flashes of blue static; and later, on the staircase, he kissed me, and the static shocked our lips.

Mike has broken away from the dining room, and hugs me now. His hair is longer than I have ever seen, nearly down to his chin, and he's wearing cords and a button-down shirt, but you can see the ridiculous insignia of his t-shirt underneath.

"Drop Your Pants?" I ask.

"It's a dry-cleaning place."

"Right," I say. "And no chance of anyone here misinterpreting it."

"Where's my Snapple?" he asks.

So I bring another. And Mike tells us about college, using the word *anticlimactic* more than could possibly be appropriate. He seems more solid than I remember; still slight, but more muscled, and the little ridge of acne on his neck is gone.

"Is there anything you like?" I ask him. He does this flippy thing with his hair, to get it out of his eyes, just like Bangs.

"I like working on the school paper. That's pretty cool. And I've started jamming with some guys. They're good. We're talking

96

about gigging. What about you, little rock star, playing shows on Saturday nights?"

"Don't get excited, it's our first."

"Second," Jeremy interjects.

"Well," I say, "sort of."

"They're rad," Jeremy says.

"Oh *rad*." Mike grins at me. "I can't wait."

"Can't wait for what?" Meghan asks, sitting on the bricked ledge that fronts the fireplace.

"Cole's gig on Saturday night."

Meghan says, "Oh," tucks her legs up, and stretches her hands in front of the glass doors. You'd think we'd all be burning up with so many bodies in the place. The rest of them file in, and take places on the floral couches, while Nate and Kelly pull the piano bench out to sit down.

"Something hot to drink?" Dad asks. We will beverage you to death in this family. He takes orders for hot chocolate and tea and vanishes.

Jeremy hasn't let go of my hand. His is sweaty now, and tucked between us, will only get sweatier. I haven't sat in this room for a while, and am surprised by the quilt samplers on the wall beyond Nigel and Meghan's dad. Cross-stitched flowers and Bible verses are my mother's standard decorating motifs, and are displayed above the piano, and on the wall behind Mike and Jeremy and me. But the two large quilt samplers on the common wall—the greens and blues and purples—are new, and kind of cool, like dappled art.

The knickknacks are all the standard shit my parents have had for ages: brass swans, and pastoral beer steins, and three little porcelain dolls dressed as Nate and Nigel and me to match a professional photo we had taken when I was six.

Nigel and Mike play a game of chess, right in the middle of us, and everyone else tries to keep some kind of conversation going. Meghan's dad asks us questions about school, and sports, and our hobbies. He's super nice, and if he'd quit staring at me so intently—with the same unwavering eye contact as Pepper employs when you're eating French fries—he'd be a little easier to talk to.

"Do you enjoy military life?" he asks the room at large. "The moves, the new schools and bases, the transitions?"

"Transitions," Mike laughs, moving his bishop. "That's the kindest way to look at it. Here kid, have a new place, a new start, and we'll stay just long enough for you to make a couple of friends, and then we'll offer you another opportunity, in another place."

"Would that be a *No* for you, then?" her dad asks.

Mike leans back, flicks his hair. "I don't know. I see the kids now, at Penn, who've never lived in a new town, and I feel, I don't know, sorry for them. They've never had a chance to know anything else, and they're still in shock. Homesick. But I went to three different high schools. That's too much transition for anybody."

"What about you, Nate?" Meghan's dad asks.

"I've just been here for high school, but I had five elementary schools, and two junior highs. I envy those kids who know all the same kids from kindergarten, but I don't want to be one of them. I think I'd get bored in one place all the time."

"So you're glad your dad's military?" he asks.

Nate's face closes instantly, and he glances at me, because in this, despite everything, we are co-conspirators. We know the military part has nothing on the chaplain part—the endless church activities: services Sunday morning and Sunday night, youth group on Wednesday evenings, and Bible school in the summers, and all the verses we've memorized, and all the prayer groups we've attended, the choirs we've sung in, the hymns and baptisms.

Her dad studies both of us. "What?" he asks.

But we cannot be disloyal. Cannot explain the weight of God, of ministry. The expectation held by every parishioner that the three of us would exemplify a spiritual perfection, an unwavering goodness, which children of ministers must certainly have.

Dad comes in with two large bowls of caramel corn, and a bunch of napkins. Meghan's mother follows with a tray of tea and hot chocolate.

After everyone has dug in, and is perched within reach of additional handfuls of caramel corn, Meghan's dad asks again, for Nate to explain himself. Nate shrugs.

"What are we talking about?" Dad asks.

Meghan's father fills him in, and Dad, interested, sips his cocoa. "Don't stop on my account."

But it is on his account. Always. Every shift we have made, every move. The arbitrary, heartless orders are always on his account.

"I'm glad I've lived on this base," Jeremy says, shifting everyone's attention. "When we moved here, my junior year, I was angry: halfway through high school, and starting all over again. But with all the chaplains' kids on this base, everyone gets how hard that is. How you're always held to a different standard. You're a subset of a subset, but you're not the only one."

Meghan's dad looks Jeremy up and down, then scrutinizes the rest of us, and, amazingly, I don't catch a reprimand in his eyes, or pity either.

"No," he tells us, one by one, and kindly, "you're not the only one."

♫ ♫ ♫

I'm full. It's a weird feeling, but I'm not sure I can eat a second piece of pie.

"You're not going to try the pumpkin?" Mom asks, holding a plate out to me.

"Well," I say. The pie looks delicious—how often do you get to eat anything with pumpkin in it? She adds a dollop of vanilla ice cream for good measure.

The kids have gathered in the living room while the adults sip coffee at the table like civilized people. They all asked for tiny little slivers of pie, and are complaining now of having no self-control.

"I don't know if her mother came," Kelly is saying. "I only know Stacy said she was on her way. She was crying. She kept saying, *Everything is over.*"

"In the nurse's office?" Nate asks.

"Yes," Kelly says.

"So it's true," Jeremy says.

I have no idea what anyone's talking about. Stacy Masteller just went through a detox program. She's been back in school for maybe a week. We all thought it was crap that she had to come back before Thanksgiving break. Seriously, she couldn't have a few days at home to prepare for everyone at school calling her a freak and a loser?

"What's true?" Nate asks Jeremy.

But Nigel is the one who answers. "Stacy's pregnant."

"How is she pregnant?" Nate asks.

"That guy from the mall," Nigel says. "That old guy with the sideburns."

"Are you serious?" Kelly asks. "She slept with that guy? He's practically thirty."

"How do you know?" I ask Nigel. Stacy Masteller has the worst luck I've ever heard of. She breaks an ankle jumping, drunk, off the roof of their quarters; she's sent to in-patient detox without any cover story at all; and now she's pregnant. She's officially mythical. You kids want to end up like Stacy Masteller? There lies the grim path to Stacy Masteller.

"We saw her," Jeremy says. "Nigel and I."

"She said that mall guy was the father," Nigel says. "She said he wouldn't even take her phone calls."

Stacy and I were friends for a month. Her mom took us to see *Pet Sematary* in the theater. It was surreal: she bought our tickets, and snacks, and everything, and then sat in a different row as though she didn't know us.

"She's a sad girl," Mike says.

"You mean like pathetic?" Nate laughs.

"No, I mean unhappy."

"And unlucky," I say. The phone rings; Mom answers and calls for me. It's Bangs.

"Happy Thanksgiving," he says.

"You too."

"I know you have a gig on Saturday night, but do you want

100

to hang out during the day? We could pick you up—Gabby and a couple of her friends, and you and me. They want to go to the shore."

"My guitar lesson ends at 11."

"So after?" he asks.

"Sure." I give him directions, just in case Gabby needs a crib sheet. I feel like a walk. Like being in the house with all these people after too much rich food is making me kind of woozy. This phone call is my chance to escape; it's an opened window.

Meghan comes into the kitchen with a stack of forks and dessert plates. She rinses them and loads the dishwasher. Maybe I should just ask why she's mad.

"Do you feel like a walk?" I ask. She doesn't look at me. Doesn't answer. I'm starting to be angry about this whole thing. Sorry I'm not psychic or whatever, but navigating your stream of consciousness is not my forte. "You know what, forget it. Just stay here and be mad. You with the silent treatment is one long stretch of boring."

And then she hugs me. It's crazy—premenstrual crazy—like there should be warning labels. She's holding on so tightly that she's pinching my neck. "I'm sorry," she says. My shirt muffles her voice.

"It's OK." I pat her back. What is Stacy Masteller doing for Thanksgiving? How do you top detox and pregnancy at 16? Her mom's really nice. She has one of those dry senses of humor, and a super-soft voice. How do you tell something like that? Hey, Mom, this sick dude with sideburns got me pregnant. Mom, you know how embarrassing rehab was, well, I think I've discovered something even harder. Mom, I can't catch a break.

Jeremy and Nigel and Mike come on the walk with Meghan and me: the five of us in the windy dark not speaking. Every house lit up and cheerful.

Indelible. OK, so this might be my favorite word ever. Permanent, indestructible, unable to be forgotten, or blotted out. Adjective.

Late Friday night, Meghan and I have books spread out on the dorm beds; *Shooting Rubberbands at the Stars* on the tape deck; and I finish Geometry and another draft of my stupid poem.

We ran five miles this morning; Meghan has the meanest kick. I beat her in a sprint the last hundred yards, but another few steps and she would have retaken me. Except for five hours practicing with Doggy Life, I just sat around and ate. They had another Scrabble championship, so at least I missed that.

My fingertips are sore. I had calluses before, but apparently they weren't enough. We practice in Joe's garage, and his mom came out with hot chocolate and brownies for us about halfway through. She's short and chubby and has a little bald spot on her crown. Heaped with whipped cream, the hot chocolate alone would have made me love her, but caramel brownies with walnuts! I kind of wanted to hug her, the brownies were so good.

"What's your poem about?" Meghan asks.

"Oh, you know, being a kid. Sort of what that means or whatever."

"Read it to me."

This is what I read:

> My barefoot granny slices
> bites of apple,
> teeth for drowning in a brown
> sugar bowl. Her sometime red hair
> piled high but not staying.
> Granny is whistling, awkward and low.
>
> White blender rumbles
> eggs into flour. On linoleum tile my shadow
> catches. My little black curled

beneath her green counter. Spoons
and saucers can wait
for a while.

Mother whisks wild—
a sound like ducks landing.
Butter in pans, bubbling
brown pools. Outside, my father
paints the deck, kneeling—a color so yellow
I hear it inside.

His coveralls blue as my granny's
whistle, his back's to the window:
the clatter of pans.
Aunt Joanie talks funerals,
Yahtzee, gardens. August scarred
in its cantaloupe way.

"Jesus," she says.

"It's corny, right?" I ask. "Granny is the most embarrassing
word I know, but it's truer, for the weirdness of it, I think."

"Let me read it."

I hand her the latest revision, and think maybe I should
have written a sonnet instead. Historical cheesiness is more
acceptable.

"Is this how you see?" she asks.

"No, it's how I remember."

"How long have you been working on this?"

"God," I say, "like days. The first couple drafts rhymed."

"Cole, this is really good."

"Good enough for Overhead to give me another A–?"

"I like *sometime red hair* best."

"Thanks," I say. I kind of want to burn the poem now. I think
she just feels bad about being a jerk before. *Granny* is seriously
the worst word. I'd rather say *penile* than *granny*. For years I just
referred to her as my grandmother unless she was present, but

then I read in this book how *granny* is commonly used in Britain, and it seemed less horrible somehow.

She hands the poem back to me. "So you're going to the beach with Bangs tomorrow?"

"Yes." And I cannot wait. I thought I'd be away the entire day—my guitar lesson, the beach, the gig—but it turns out my guitar lesson was cancelled on account of Thanksgiving break, and no one told me, so I get to have another three-hour breakfast with too many people asking too many questions. Somebody told Meghan's dad that I decided not to play basketball this year, and he's all over that. He said choosing to play in a band and writing a letter to my coaches were acts of self-affirmation. What does that even mean? This is my self. This. I'm a fan. Enough already.

"How does Jeremy feel about you hanging out with Bangs?"

"He didn't really say anything." I want to ask why she was mad before, but what if it makes her mad again? What's the point in that, really? If she's over it, then I should be over it too, right?

"I didn't expect to see Kelly on Thanksgiving," Meghan says. "Why wasn't she with her family?"

"I know, right? They've been dating a month or something, and already they're family-formal. At least she brought chocolate."

"Well, Nate seems pretty crazy about her."

"He's just tired of his hand."

"Oh my god," Meghan says, "you are so bad."

"Whatever. Nate hasn't spoken to me in weeks. It's like we live in different households." I shrug. This room has no posters, just white-painted cement walls. I'd go crazy in here all the time. No character or permanence or anything. The Army and its drones—why not make them wear fatigues to bed too? It's depressing.

"Where are the Heather-hairs tonight?" I ask.

Meghan looks busy with her books, mutters, "I don't know."

You can't count on anything. Not any place—all these stupid schools and assignments and moves and quarters and churches. Not on anyone, either—Meghan might as well be Kelly. They're as variable as everything else. It's retarded. And posters on the walls don't even matter in the end. They're just posters. Some band you're into for five minutes and then you replace them with something else.

At the end of the year, we'll move and I'll never see Jeremy again, or Bangs, or Meghan, or this school, or Jersey even. I'll never see the Jersey shore again. All the garbage, and flat grey waves, and stupid sand—it's shitty and I'll miss it anyway. I'll miss even its shittiness.

"I feel really vapid," I say. And then I start crying. It comes from nowhere, and Meghan stalls on her bed for a minute before she crosses the room and hugs me.

"Vapid, huh?" she says.

"Totally," I sob. "Totally vapid. Spiritless or prosaic. Adjective."

She starts laughing, and the sound makes me feel better. I guess that's the upside of everything being temporary. Eventually you'll feel better.

♫ ♫ ♫

Joe is a wreck. The dye totally fucked up or something and his hair went orange, so he shaved his head and now he resembles a medical experiment—his head is really small; his skin pale and sickly; and he has a crooked scar on the back of his head. I never noticed with his hair all teased.

"Stop looking at me," he says.

"Maybe a hat," I suggest, "or a bandana?"

We're backstage, waiting for our first set. With Trevor's hair pulled back, his cute pudgy face surprises me. I'm seeing these guys for the first time. Except Ernie looks exactly the same.

Bangs lent me another one of his sweatshirts, and I borrowed a short black skirt from Meghan. It's my rocker outfit. On our drive back from the shore, Bangs painted my fingernails deep purple. He blew on them and everything. It was sweet.

Jeremy comes backstage to kiss me, and has a weird tight smile.

"What's the matter?" I ask.

"Um, so they're all here," he says.

"Who?"

"Your dad, and Nigel, and Meghan and her dad."

I hit him. "Don't fuck with me. I'm nervous."

"I'm not fucking with you," he says.

"Dude," Trevor says, "your dad came to the show?"

"You're serious?" I ask Jeremy.

"Yes. They're here."

"Joe," I say, "we can't play *Tomorrow, Wendy*."

"Why not?" Trevor says.

"My dad's a minister."

Trevor frowns. "Your dad's a preacher?"

"Yes."

"And he came to our show," he says. "That's kind of wild."

"Joe—" I blurt.

"We'll play *Me and Julio down by the Schoolyard* instead." Joe looks at the other guys. "Ernie, wail out a solo, and we'll watch you for changes."

The stage lights keep me mercifully blind, and the drums batter us into *Desire* and I don't care if they're out there, judging this dirty venue or my skirt or Joe's tragic haircut or anything. Joe's bouncing on my right, and Ernie, eyes closed, head bowed, sways on my left, and I hear kids screaming from the floor beyond us. I'm rhythm girl. I'm the storyteller.

For *Just Like Heaven*, Ernie carries two intricate solos, and Joe and I dance, and Trevor hits some crazy counter beats and it's an ache through me, this music. It's this prowling animal, and I want to grip its fur and climb onto its back and ride it. I don't want to hide up here under the lights. I want to tear away this sweatshirt, and these pretty notes, and scream.

And then we play *Jane Says*. Two boys rush on stage and throw themselves into the crowd during Trevor's drum solo. A fucking mob of kids at my feet, thrashing up to us, yelling some approximation of the lyrics, and I'm singing about heroin addiction, in front of my dad, and there's no lightning.

106

Cloy. To weary by excess of food, sweetness, pleasure. Verb. Why does this word remind me of my mother?

We go out for pie after the gig. All of us. While we're loading the drum kit and amps into Trevor's van, the dads and Nigel and Meghan and Jeremy and Mike and Bangs catch up with us, and Trevor starts with the, "It's a pleasure to meet you, sir," like an utter ass, and then he suggests a diner he knows with the best pie; and Meghan's dad is all, "Pie! An excellent notion." In four vehicles we caravan to this goofy diner where the waitresses—dressed in mint-colored uniforms and pink, ruffled aprons—call everybody "sweetie."

Squeezed between Ernie and Trevor, Meghan's dad has this delighted grin. "What are your musical influences?" he asks.

Trevor has half a pie in front of him, and an entire slice of cherry in his mouth, when he grunts, "The Clash, Sex Pistols, Ramones, Dead Kennedys. You know, the classics."

"If you don't mind my saying," her dad continues, "your music is easier to listen to than your forebears."

"Forebears," Trevor repeats. "Yeah, cool."

Mike and Ernie and Bangs are talking licks and pedals. Somebody gave Nigel coffee; he and Joe sit at the end of the table spazzing out.

"Well," Meghan asks my dad, "what'd you think?"

He smoothes his mustache, says, "I enjoyed it." He sounds shell-shocked honestly; baffled maybe that his ears didn't rupture and bleed. "They seem comfortable playing together. In fact, Cole, you seem comfortable playing on stage. That's really something."

"Thanks." My cheesecake is a brick of goodness—delicious, but hard to swallow.

"The first dance we ever played," Dad says, "I remember feeling like I'd forgotten how to breathe."

"You played in a band?" Trevor asks, and they're off on dance-band history. What's with Trevor and the rapt attention?

In this *wasn't-Marilyn-Monroe-just-the-end?* dive, the fluo-

107

rescent lights color everyone a nauseating alien green. I'm disappointed. Without reason or whatever, I can't even explain why I'm disappointed; but on stage everything was piercing and bright and authentic and now, crowded into this horseshoe shaped booth with the scratchy vinyl and five hundred people gobbling pie and talking competitively, as if we're all trying to hit the highest register or whatever, I just want to crawl under the table and put my hands over my ears.

"How was the beach?" Jeremy asks.

I feel rotten about hitting him. He wears a leather jacket made of goat. It's just so wrong to make leather jackets from goats, or to look this good wearing one. "It rained the whole time, and was windy—like an arctic wind. I didn't want to get out of the car actually."

"You're a different girl," he says, "on stage."

I don't know what he means. I just want everyone to be quiet. Be quiet, and eat, so we can go. One final night of sleep on that rock bed in that white room before I can go home to my attic, my peace, my own little songs.

♫ ♫ ♫

Meghan climbs the stairs ahead of me. She hasn't said anything to me all night. Light from a skylight throws bars across her body, and my arms, as our footsteps echo. Almost there—another twenty paces to her room, and then I can drop.

At the top of the staircase, the giant metal door at her back, she turns, a step above me, and pushes my hair back from my face. Heavily, my eyes close heavily. Her fingertips are brushes, soft and light and soporific. I might dream just standing here. I might dream her face closing on mine. I might dream her mouth, her tongue, the tears on her face.

She presses hard against me, bites my lip, and I wake all at once. Like on stage, that kind of awake, where my skin seems to burn. She takes my hand and pulls me down the hallway, into her room, onto her bed, and my pants are half off.

"Please," I say. "Please." She bites my ear and I hear the rasp as she breathes into me. "Please."

And then she's inside. I swallow the entire world. I can feel planets inside me, humming. She wraps around me, lithe and dense, a secret I want to lean into. Her hair in my face. A fragrance like ash. I hold onto her as the muscles down her back and legs begin to tremble. "I'm sorry," she cries. "I'm so sorry."

♫ ♫ ♫

My bedroom smells of spiced aftershave. It's 4 in the afternoon on Sunday: the guests gone; the house practically haggard from overuse; my bathwater scalding. I've finished everything but two chapters of reading for History of Asia, and my take-home Biology quiz.

Dad let us skip church today. We had poached eggs on toast, and read from Psalms. Dad loves David: the warrior poet thing appeals to him, they're kindred in their military devotion to God.

After we'd eaten, and the grownups had refills on their coffee, Meghan's dad told Nate, "You really missed out last night. Those kids put on quite a show." The guy totally believes you can talk about anything, that by expressing your feelings you'll share and grow.

"I wish I'd gone," Mom said. "I should have drunk a pot of coffee and gone."

Meghan sits between her parents, rolling and unrolling the cuff of her sweater. She hasn't looked at me. When her mom asks if she feels OK, Meghan says she had awful dreams.

Language crushes me. These letters we put together to make sentences that are supposed to mean something. To get beneath and around something and express its girth—language is really just math after all, right? We're all trying to develop these eloquent expressions. We're all trying to solve for x. It's fucking heartbreaking.

Hours later, tucked into bed, in my flannel pajamas, with the electric blanket set to medium, I pick the phone up on the first ring, and ask, "Hello?"

"Did you finish the quiz?" Bangs asks.

"I haven't started it."

"What are you doing?" he asks.

"My atheist sent me an eighteen-page letter. He has tiny cursive and I've been reading this for forty minutes."

"What does he need eighteen pages to say?"

"It's a story about this time he and his friends went into the woods and shot at each other with air rifles, and he nailed a kid in the face, and blinded his right eye."

"Fuck," Bangs says.

"Yeah."

"What happened after he shot the kid?"

"They drove to the emergency room, and the whole group of kids waited there in these red hunting jackets. They think they're going to jail. That's as far as I've gotten."

"Read it to me," Bangs says.

I read the rest of the letter. Afterward he gives me the answers to the Biology quiz, and then I tell him I'll see him in the morning, and I turn off the light and think about my atheist in the desert writing out this story, his confession to me.

I have this dream,

he wrote,

> where I'm running through the woods in my fatigues, and these Republican Guards pop out and shoot me. They always hit my kneecaps. And then I'm in the back of a truck with Clint and Steve and they're taking me to the hospital, and I'm just a kid wearing hunting boots. At the hospital the doctors have no eyes. They're walking around with their arms straight out like zombies. I think this desert goes on until there's nothing, until you just drop off the

earth. I hate this fucking place. Say a prayer for
me, will you? Tell your god to remember, or forget,
or anyway, to spare us. I don't want to die here.

How can I intercede for him? Meghan wouldn't even look at
me. We've done this thing—is it fucking? Did she fuck me?
Whatever we did, God saw us. He might be angry. What if God
is angry?

Objurgate. To reproach or denounce vehemently; up-braid harshly; berate sharply. Verb. At first I thought you were just messing with me. Ha, ha, only a sucker would believe this is a real word. Now I'm sorry it exists in my head. Holy redundant already.

For Speech, we're going to spend the entire week in the library researching our topics for mock debate. I've been paired with the reputed genius Monica Prader, this poser who smokes with the metal kids in the parking lot, and cannot ever shut up. (She's the kind of person my mother would say talks your arm off and hollers down the hole.)

Our topic is the death penalty, with Monica and me arguing against it. We're supposed to research independently before comparing notes, but in these carrels in the farthest corner of the library by creepy books on Economics, Monica dictates while I scrawl notes. My parents support the death penalty. They're sort of wrath and judgment people. But we've already found some alarming statistics to support our position, and will annihilate Josh Tarbet and Holly Mercer with our insider information, and these totally merciless facts.

Monica closes the next to last book we've pulled, and glances at me. "I thought you were like a jock or whatever. Then Saturday night I saw you playing with Trevor's band at Board." *Trevor's* band? She turns the last book over in her hands. "I dated him for like a month freshman year. He's intense."

"Trevor?" I say.

"How is he, anyway? I haven't talked to him in like forever."

I shrug. "He delivers bread or something part-time. But he's, you know, pursuing music."

"Right. He's really good—I mean, you all were—I love Jane's Addiction."

"Thanks."

"You should totally let me know the next time you play. I'm so there." And then, before she reads another set of statistics to me, she adds, "It's almost pointless, if you think about it, debating the death penalty. I mean, if we go to war, or whatever."

My arguments against the death penalty are a page-and-a-half long already. Monica's electric blue eye shadow matches her nail polish. "Pointless?" I ask. "What do you mean?"

"Well, we'll be watching death on television like twenty-four/seven, right? We'll be putting people to death—regular people—like all the time. It just seems pointless to debate the morality of killing prisoners, doesn't it, when we'll be bombing school children?"

Last night, Nigel told me that Dad volunteered for deployment to the Middle East without talking it over with Mom, and they had some snide comments about it.

"What did his CO say," I asked Nigel, "when Dad volunteered?"

"Dad said he made this face like, *Are you intoxicated, Chaplain?* and then just shook his head."

"What's Mom mad about, then? Obviously, he's not going anywhere."

"She's probably mad that she might have been left here to deal with you and Nate by herself." At this point in the conversation, I leapt on him, and we spilled tortilla chips all over the kitchen floor.

In the library, somebody giggles and is shushed; I think of my dad killing children, my atheist throwing hand grenades into classrooms. "We don't bomb schools," I tell Monica.

"No?" She says, flipping through the book. "Ever hear of Dresden? Cambodia?"

"Ever hear of Dachau? *The Killing Fields?*"

"Greater good, right?" Monica laughs. "Why shouldn't kids die for oil? It's as good a reason as any."

"What the fuck—"

But she puts her hands up, and shakes her head. "I got us off topic. I'm sorry. Anyway, I don't want to piss you off, I'm hoping you'll do me a favor. I'm hoping you'll give Trevor my phone number, tell him I said hey, and he should call me. Will you do that for me?"

"Trevor?" Maybe this chick is some kind of diabolical genius;

I almost ask, curious what she'd answer. "You want me to give Trevor your number?"

She laughs again. "Totally."

♪ ♪ ♪

Since I'm not playing basketball this season, I'm back in gym. We're starting gymnastics: mats cover half the gym, and apparatuses the rest—we have rings, parallel bars, a vault, even that freaky pommel horse; this is serious. Last year Diofelli required two routines. Gymnastics is such bullshit, why aren't we playing basketball or something? I can do a somersault and a tripod, and that's more or less the extent of my repertoire. I almost fell off the balance beam twice last year during my routine. The whole time Diofelli kept ducking her head to her clipboard and snorting.

"Good thing you decided to be a rock star," she tells me as I wait my turn at the mat. "Otherwise you might have missed all this."

Jeremy and I have gym together, so welcome to doubly embarrassing. He can do walking handstands and back flips and everything—which is fun to witness, but the whole time I'm watching him, I worry he'll be watching me when I butcher cartwheels, and the fun kind of inverts.

Over the past few days, I've already seen four girls from the basketball team, and they've been all, "A band, for real?" but not mean or anything. In the hallway, Jayna ran up and punched me, and said Coach Henry read the letter aloud and told them he knew I'd agonized over the decision, and that he hoped we'd all support each other. I actually teared up when she said that. She hit me again, and told me I'd better come watch their games.

"All right, Peters," Diofelli says. "Amaze me."

I start with a backward roll, and keep pretty much on the mat. That's sort of the highlight of my efforts. At the end of the mat, Jeremy offers me a hand up.

"Nice," he laughs.

"Yeah, we couldn't just square dance, right? A solo routine maximizes the humiliation factor."

"Maybe I should tutor you," Jeremy says.

I look at him in his sweats and white-socked feet: his black hair frantic with static from the mat, his grin lopsided.

"How would that work?" I ask.

"We could start," he says, "with your bridge."

This statement is as forward as he has ever been, as aggressive, and if we were not in the middle of gymnastic torment—well, if we were any place else—then I could respond the way that I want to respond. Not with words. I'm tired of words, especially words like savor. "Yes," I say. And I mean that I am ready. That I am more than ready, that I am exhausted with readiness, and that I agree to know this—with him, with Jeremy—to know this.

Diofelli blows her whistle, and we stand for a minute, ignoring the whistle and the dusty, noisy room, and the kids filing from it. Then Jeremy grins, and tugs the sleeve of my shirt, and walks dutifully away.

♫ ♫ ♫

On our night walk with Pepper, Dad seems extra quiet. The streets are patched with ice, the night cloudless and stinging. He wears his parka with the hood pulled up. Short on his arms, the coat makes him seem sort of Incredible Hulk or something, suddenly too large for his clothes. We are giraffe people.

"Have you seen Stacy Masteller," he asks me, "around school at all?"

"We have Chorus together, but we haven't talked or anything. She sits with the sopranos."

"How does she seem to you?" He scrutinizes me after he asks this, and then looks away, as if my answer doesn't matter after all.

I don't really know what to tell him. Since Thanksgiving, I've tried to tell if she's pregnant—showing or glowing or running to the bathroom to barf or whatever—but she pretty much just looks miserable all the time, which is how she looked before and not really conclusive regarding the whole pregnancy thing. "Sad," I say. "She seems sad."

"Her mother came to see me. This is a hard time for them, with Dave gone."

"Where's Mr. Masteller?"

Dad stares at me, and then shakes his head. "Deployed," he says, "since September."

"Oh, right." My father thinks I'm the most self-involved person on the planet. It's his favorite refrain during his lectures, and my not knowing Stacy's father is in Saudi Arabia is so going to bite my head off. "I forgot."

"Well, Stacy hasn't forgotten."

"No," I agree, seriously. If Stacy had forgotten her dad was deployed to the Middle East, then that would certainly put me out of the running for most self-involved person on the planet.

"Cole, I know you're busy, that you have a lot going on." It's funny how he can say this with sincerity, and still make it sound like I'm not trying. "You're not the only one, though. Stacy has a lot going on too. Your brother has a lot going on." My brother? "And I'm tired of the two of you not speaking. Whatever is going on, I want it dropped. Especially if it's about Kelly."

He's mad. He's yelling at me. I stop walking—in the dark the metal slides bend like tragic figures in the empty playground. I hate this man. I hate his tirades and his random indictments and the way he's taking all his disappointment out on me. "I wish they'd let you go to the desert," I tell him. "I wish they'd sent you. Then I could be drunk and pregnant and maybe you'd worry about me for a change."

"Cole—" he yanks my arm. Even in the dark, I see his anger. "Don't you ever—"

I rear back, but I can't pull away. He's hurting me. He has hurt me. I'm wounded. Pepper barks. "Let go of me. I haven't done anything. You're yelling at me like I've done something and I haven't done anything."

"Cole—"

"Let go. Let go." I'm crying so hard that I can't breathe. And now we're struggling. Dad tries to grab both my arms, and I hear my atheist, the voice I've given him, saying, *Tell your god to remember,*

116

or forget, or anyway, to spare us. And I'm afraid. "Let go of me," I say, and I fall back in the grass, and Pepper barks again and stands between us, and then I run, in the dark, away from the park while he yells after me, my name in a roar.

I'm running the wrong direction, of course, to get to Meghan's dorm, so I cut into the alley and backtrack through the neighborhood, keeping away from the streetlights but running near the road. I have a stitch, but I'm afraid to stop, and when I get there, I know I should take some time to get control of myself and not look like a raging snot head, but I run inside, and up the skylighted staircase, and down the hallway past a girl in her pajamas, and knock on Meghan's door. And when a black girl I don't know opens the door, I fall into her arms, sobbing, and probably take six months off her life.

"Cole?" Meghan asks from somewhere behind the girl. "What's happened? Cole?" They set me on a bed, and Meghan tries to uncover my face, but I'm pretty determined to keep it buried in the bedspread, and then I hear the other girl say, "I'll get water."

"Cole? What's happened? Cole, you're scaring me."

Yes, scared. Me too. But for a while I can only cry.

After she brings my water, the girl—Regina—packs a couple of books and her bathroom kit, and tells Meghan she's going to sleep in Heather Shorthair's room. She pats my head awkwardly as though I'm some kind of sad puppy, and says she hopes I get some rest.

"I'm sorry," I manage.

"Baby," Regina says, "whatever it is, we've all been there."

So, that's my lesson for the night, right? We have a lot going on—every one of us—and we've all been there before. Why do people think it's comforting to point out that your experiences imitate everybody else's?

I drink the water. Meghan sits on the edge of the bed, with her hand on my shin, and stares at me. Regina's bedspread is mussed, and there's a book on the floor—the place almost looks trashed. "I'm sorry," I say again.

"Are you hungry?" she asks.

"Starving."

She tosses me a granola bar. "Tell me what happened."

I devour the granola bar, and tell her. No one listens like Meghan.

"Let me see your arms," she says. I take off my coat, and my sweatshirt, and pull up my sleeves. Only my right arm is bruised, and not deep or anything. I feel wrenched, but that's going away now, that feeling of being wrenched, and scared.

"I love that I'm the rotten one," I say. "I'm the one who isn't trying, and meanwhile he's prying my arm off, and being insane, and trying to wreck his marriage."

"What do you mean?"

"He's fucking his secretary," I say.

"Miss Jensen? She's sixty years old with half a dozen grandkids. What are you talking about?"

"She's sixty?" OK, so I've never actually met Miss Jensen. I figured her for thirty, with strategic makeup and clothes and dialogue. And there's the way he says her name. "For real, she's some old lady?"

"Yes," Meghan says.

"Well, anyway, he's trying to ditch us and go to war."

Meghan laughs. "Like Théoden King."

"Like who?"

"Théoden King, from *The Lord of the Rings*. He wants to die like a warrior, in battle."

"Great, so Dad wants to ditch us and die in battle. That makes me feel so much better."

"It's not about you at all, Cole. I think he just wants some meaning. Your dad doesn't enjoy being an administrator."

How does she know all this? How does she know about Miss Jensen, and what my dad doesn't enjoy? "He's told you this?" I ask.

She shrugs. "It's more an impression I have."

"You've met Miss Jensen?"

"Sure, at his office."

I've never been to his office. I don't even know which building it's in. "Is he in love with you?" I ask.

Meghan reddens, and says in a harsh, scary voice, "Don't be an ass. Your father is in love with your mother. He's not having an affair with Miss Jensen, or me, or anyone else. For a perceptive kid, you're being really stupid."

"Now you're mad at me," I say. I try to stand, but she pulls me down.

"Cole, stop. I'm not mad at you."

"This is the worst night ever," I sob. "And now I'm homeless, and your roommate thinks I'm unstable, and tomorrow I'll be sixteen, and we have to sing that hideous *Little Mermaid* song at the assembly, and my grandmother called tonight and said she got married when she was sixteen, and what kind of thing is that to tell somebody?"

She puts her arms around me and squeezes. "Which hideous *Little Mermaid* song?"

"*Part of Your World.*"

"I thought you were singing *An Unexpected Song?*"

"We're singing both. We've had to rehearse during lunch with the school band. It's ridiculous. All the songs out there and we're singing something from a cartoon."

"What time tomorrow?"

"Two," I say. "And you're not coming. It's embarrassing enough without you, thanks. Are you listening to Depeche Mode?"

"Yes, and don't change the subject. I want to come. I want to hear you."

"Since when do you like Depeche Mode?"

"It's Regina's."

"I'm still hungry."

Meghan looks around her room. "I think I have a bagel in my bag. Where's my bag?"

At some point her bag fell behind the bed, and once she digs out her bagel, she stands and tells me, "I'm going to call your parents; tell them where you are."

"I don't want to go back there."

119

"I know."

I don't even have a toothbrush. What if Dad demands Meghan bring me home? Or worse, what if he storms down here and drags me away? Cyclone dad.

Meghan comes back and hops onto the bed. "Do you want pajamas?"

"He said I could stay?" She nods. "Are you like a hypnotist or something?"

"Pajamas, toothbrush, what do you need?"

"Are we going to bed already? What time is it?"

"After eleven."

"It's practically my birthday," I say.

"Not quite yet."

By the time we're back in Meghan's room, both soaped clean and dressed in plaid flannel pajamas, it's midnight. "Happy birthday to me," I say.

She tosses a wrapped box onto her bed. "Happy birthday to you."

"What is it?"

"One way to know."

I tear the paper from the rectangular box. It's a copper bracelet—a hammered piece the width of a shoelace, with two small copper knobs that fasten to my wrist. "It's beautiful," I say.

"Do you like it?"

I nod. "Thank you."

"You can wear it in the shower and everything."

"I love it."

We're on her bed: the striped comforter warm and twisted between us, her mattress as unrelenting as Regina's all the way across the room. I lie back. Her pillow smells of tropical fruit. Under the desk lamp, my bracelet flashes.

"Any birthday plans?" Meghan asks. On her belly, beside me in the narrow bed, her head rests on her arm.

"Babysitting for the Thorns actually."

"You're babysitting on your birthday?"

"It's their anniversary," I say. "Anyway, the actual day never

120

matters; since Nigel's birthday is two days after mine we always have a joint celebration. Except this year he's going skiing with the youth group, and I've got gigs at Ichabod's and Board, so I think we're having flank steak next week or something. If I haven't been disowned."

"Somehow I doubt you've been disowned."

"I'm sixteen," I say, yawning. "I've waited forever to be sixteen."

"Why?"

"Why? What are you, a hundred and two? You don't remember? Sixteen—in practically every other state—means you can drive. In Germany you can drink in bars. And it sounds different—sixteen—like I'm not a kid anymore." I turn the light off, and roll to face her. Our knees touch in this little bed, but I can't bring myself to move. I want to ask her if we bomb kids, and if she'd volunteer to go to war, and if Jeremy was serious today on the mats.

"Do you feel different?" she asks.

"A little squished maybe."

"That's the thing about getting older," she says, "it's harder to keep the weight off."

"Hey, easy with the giving of complexes; it's my birthday."

"You're right," she says, curling around me. "You know I love you, don't you?"

"I don't know what I know," I say. "Sometimes you won't even look at me."

She rests her hand on my hip, and then sings this dirge version of Happy Birthday, which is weirdly consoling, like a lullaby. She has a pretty voice that warms the room, or perhaps tiredness warms us, or proximity. And I pray for my atheist, and for Stacy Masteller, and for forgiveness.

Soughing. To make a rushing, rustling, or murmuring sound. Verb. This is onomatopoetic, right? I actually thought it might be a violent act. You know, death by soughing.

Early on the morning of my birthday, Meghan drops me off at home, and I sneak into the kitchen to grab a banana, intending to flee upstairs, to avoid everyone. But Dad's making waffles, and when I walk in, he turns, and gives me a giant, swallowing hug. "Happy Birthday," he says. And I want to believe him, the hug and the waffles and the cheer in his voice. I want to believe.

Nigel and Mom call to me from the dining room, and I walk through to another chorus of Happy Birthday, and bacon and scrambled eggs and grapefruit juice, and presents. Presents!

From Mom and Dad: cash and a little bottle of perfume that smells citrusy and amazing. Cards with checks—my favorite kind of correspondence—from the rest of the relatives. Nigel wrapped his present in a paper sack, stapling it closed.

"Nice," I say, and then I lift out the short black skirt and can't speak.

"Meghan helped me pick it out."

I nod. It's my size and everything. "Perfect choice," I say.

"You can wear it Friday to your gig."

Maybe Meghan's bracelet works like a blessing, or a charm or something. Maybe we're all under a spell.

"You kids need to get ready for school," Mom tells us. She's deliberately not looking at the skirt. "Cole, don't forget you have your assembly today."

No, I haven't forgotten. Ms. Ruhl wants us all to wear black slacks and button-down white shirts, like waiters. For years she danced ballet professionally, and moves through the world at a different tempo from regular people. She's regal or whatever, and during our choral rehearsals, she stands at the piano and directs us with nods of her head, and sudden flicks of her arm, while she accompanies us.

Jeremy and I leave the base with plenty of time to get to school, but detour before we arrive, and sort of lose track of everything in the universe. With the passenger's seat tipped back and some keen contortion, he manages to destroy the starched smoothness of my white shirt and give me hickeys and make me beg before either of us realizes that we've missed first period.

"Please," I say again.

Idled in some parking lot, my pants are half off, and there's no one in any direction. The heater hums, and our breath, and we've fogged the windows as he pulls my shirt away. Will it happen like this? In a car, in daylight, on a school day—none of these things as I imagined.

♫ ♫ ♫

In the cafeteria, Joe and Bangs and Ernie have gathered around a large box at our table.

"You're here," Bangs says. "I worried when you weren't in Graphics."

"You have second lunch?" I ask Ernie.

"No," he says, "I'm not here."

"Oh." They're grinning at me like scheming nine-year-olds. "What's in the box?"

Bangs holds up a white t-shirt with Doggy Life printed across the chest in medieval font, then turns it around to reveal a graphic of a small ugly dog playing bass in front of two tremendous speakers.

"Oh my god," I say.

Joe throws me a shirt. "Try it on."

"Oh my god." I'm hopping now. "We're like for real with merchandise and a logo and everything." The boys resist bouncing with me, but they totally want to, they're all drunk with excitement.

"Ernie and Christian drew the graphic and printed the shirts," Joe says. "We wanted to surprise you."

"You guys!" And then I jump at them and kiss their blushing faces, convinced now that sixteen is charmed.

"You working as a caterer?" Bangs asks, pointing at my outfit.

"The assembly," I remind him.

"So you came to school for lunch and a slack afternoon of school spirit. Well plotted."

"Mostly I just wanted to miss gymnastics."

We eat hamburgers, and tater tots, and avoid the weird non-ketchup sauce. I get t-shirts for Nigel and Jeremy, and I'm not the girl I was yesterday, I don't even remember her.

♫ ♫ ♫

Annie Thorn has learned to climb. She scales the bookshelves, the kitchen counters, the furniture, even the dining table. If it were summer, I'd have her up in trees, but trapped in the house we're forced to be inventive. We link chairs with sofa cushions and ottomans, and I'm the crocodile that gets Annie if she touches ground, as well as Karen's guide on her tentative expeditions. They're squealing with delight, and occasional terror, and I tell them a story about a window in the moon and the boy who climbs down when he's bored.

We play for less than an hour before books and bed. My throat aches: the assembly and practice and December and talking half the night with Meghan. This afternoon, while we waited backstage for the guest dude to finish his routine—juggling of disparate objects, AIDS sucks and here's why, condoms condoms condoms— I told Stacy about our gig at Board.

"I've heard of you guys," she said.

"You should come."

She shifted, pulling at the collar of her shirt. "Yeah, maybe."

Then we just stood there, with nothing to say, until we marched out to sing our corny songs.

After school, I rode to practice with Joe and Ernie, and Ernie told us we should play some Creedence because no one would expect it and he'd never heard a girl sing Fogerty before.

"Which Creedence?" Joe asked.

"I was thinking, *I Put a Spell on You*," Ernie said.

"Doesn't that seem kind of obvious?" Joe asked. "What about *Have You Ever Seen the Rain?*"

"What do you think, Cole?" Ernie asked.

"Who the fuck is Creedence?" I said.

When they relayed this to Trevor, he was too stunned to tease me. "You don't know CCR? Jesus. Don't admit shit like that." He ran out to his truck and brought back *Chronicle, Volume 1.* He played the cassette, and we sat around and debated which songs to try.

"Maybe we should do *Fortunate Son,*" Ernie said. "Like crazy political, and with a girl singing, we'll confuse the fuck out of people."

Every time we played the song, the solos got longer. Ernie ripped for nearly ten minutes, while Joe and Trevor staggered and backbeat, and I started to love the song, the righteous fury of it. Afterward we tore into The Sex Pistols' *God Save the Queen,* and they're both anthemic, if you think about it; which is probably why I can't get either song out of my head, why they've merged together now: *God save the queen, I ain't no fortunate one, no-woah.*

On the Thorns' couch, MTV counting down, I reread the same sentence about Nixon opening China. Opened like a treasure chest, like a delicate conversation, like Jeremy's jeans. We couldn't, this morning in the car—he didn't have condoms—or anyway, that's what he said. And so it was grinding, and fingers, and hand jobs all round. I don't know if I came, I couldn't tell. Mostly I just had to pee really bad.

Why is it always me that pushes? Isn't it supposed to be the boy? I want to ask Jeremy if he's worried about his soul, about losing it, or if he's stressed about me; but if he answers yes to either question, then what? Yes, Cole, I'm concerned about going to hell. Yes, Cole, I think you're a freaky nymphomaniac. Or maybe he just doesn't want to.

I fall asleep on the couch, and when Mrs. Thorn wakes me it's after ten. She gives me an extra ten for my birthday, a pair of dangly purple earrings I'm totally wearing to the gig tomorrow, and a picture Annie colored of flowers or umbrellas or possibly bats. I jog the block and a half home and walk quietly upstairs, prepared to drop without changing or brushing my teeth. On my bed, I find a package wrapped in newspaper: a black Independent sweatshirt, and a card signed *Nate.*

Sartorial. Of or relating to tailors or tailoring. Adjective. The example usage in the dictionary was *sartorial splendor.* For real? Dig me and my sartorial splendor.

Advent Sundays are my favorite. Not just for the music—Scarlet Taylor singing *O Holy Night* changes you—but everyone dresses a little nicer, and the pine wreaths smell like forest, and there's the ceremonial lighting of the candles, and Chaplain Davis's sermons, and the mythic story of King Herod hunting babies, and the angel's visitation, and the crazy pageantry. Attendance rises too, which makes finding a pew where Alicia and I can talk quite challenging.

"I can't believe she made us read our poems aloud," Alicia says. "In front of everybody. She never said we'd have to read them in front of everybody."

"I've told you for months that she's evil."

"There's evil, and then there's this." Alicia's dress has a huge red sash around the belly, and she's wearing a bow in her hair. She looks like a really big five-year-old. "And she wrote 'How Romantic' in the margin of my poem. With two exclamation points. How Romantic. I hate her."

We're singing *What Child Is This? Haste, haste, to bring Him laud.* The drama is just operatic. At the pipe organ, Clarence has a furious hairdo, and a green sweater vest bright enough to guide ships.

"You seem," Alicia says, "kind of dazed. What time did you get home last night?"

"One, I think."

"How was the show?"

"Insane. We sold out of t-shirts. How crazy is that?"

"The ones with the ugly dog? Pretty crazy."

"And you know, compared to the bar, Board is almost pristine."

"What's it like at Ichabod's?" she asks.

"They had security guards in front of the stage to keep the thrashers from climbing onto the stage. And the cigarette smoke in the place was just nasty, worse maybe than the stupid drunkenness. We only played one set, but the manager wants us to have a weekly slot."

"First they're letting you date, and now they're letting you play in bars. What's happened to your parents?"

"Meghan."

"I need one of those."

"Your parents seriously won't let you come to Board?"

"Cocaine." Alicia rolls her eyes. "That was their entire argument."

"Keep them away from my parents."

"I don't think they have facts so much as raging paranoia."

Chaplain Davis stands and raises his arms in prayer. Dark skinned, with grey in his hair, and a voice of silky persuasion, his sermons appeal to character and goodness and compassion, and I'd listen with my eyes closed if Alicia could keep still. His daughter, Joselyn, is the most beautiful girl I've ever seen—a finishing school kind of girl—slender and elegant.

Last night at Board, Bangs came with his sister, and after the show she gushed, and said she'd bring all her friends to the next show. "CCR by way of The Cure," she said. "You guys are super fun. Cole, we should maybe do something wild with your hair before the show next week. Punk up your persona."

Meghan, my chauffer chaperone, nodded so vigorously at this suggestion that she practically gave herself whiplash. Jeez, how boring am I?

"Actually, I have ideas about that too," Joe said. "We're gonna print some Doggy Life tank tops, and Cole, you should wear one next show."

"Dude," Trevor said, "black t-shirts are key. They'll sell faster than the white, I guaran-fucking-tee." And then he cocked his head, and pulled the hood of my sweatshirt. "Will you feel all naked out there in just a tank top?"

"Does that worry you?" I asked.

"Yes. How about you wear the tank top and your little skirt, and Joe and Ernie and me will just wear pants. That's fair, right?"

"What?" Ernie said.

"Don't be a pussy, dude. She's the one they're looking at." Trevor promised we'd have more gigs in the next few weeks—leave it to him. Monica Prader showed backstage, and they smoked pot and had a couple beers, and Trevor was just ridiculously giddy.

The interior of the post chapel reminds me of Noah's Ark: imagine the hull of a great ship inverted—the beams and pews solid, creaky wood; the length of the sanctuary suitable to pairs of every creature. If the ship were grounded, and rolled, and had stained glass windows depicting the Stations of the Cross and the Ascension, it would be this room exactly—cold, massive, and buzzing with the pipe organ, and the PA system, and the resounding choruses.

Honorable Joseph, his faithfulness, his devotion to Mary, Chaplain Davis asks us to emulate Joseph's trust in God. A visit from an angel would certainly make faith easier though, wouldn't it; clear up those pesky questions about whether or not God exists, or has a plan, or gives a fuck.

"Did Jeremy go last night?" Alicia asks.

"No. He has some project for English that's due Monday. His parents said he couldn't go unless he finished."

"Not quite as decisive an argument as cocaine, but they have another week to think of something better. Oh, God, that reminds me, what has Nate told you about Doug?"

"What about him?" I don't mention that Nate and I are still speechless.

"Doug and David Kirk and that new kid with the earrings broke into the general's house and raided his bar. They got so wasted that they passed out in the general's study. One of them even got sick on the carpet, or a potted plant, or something. They are so busted."

"When did this happen?"

"Friday night—I heard yesterday at swim practice. The general called the MPs and they put the boys in handcuffs and everything."

"I wonder why Nate wasn't with them," I say, as we rise for the final hymn. In all probability, Kelly saved my brother from collective boy stupidity; and for the first time, I'm grateful that she's dating him.

After the service, Alicia and I have more cookies, and punch, and she tells me that her soldier asked her to send him some skin mags.

"He did not," I say.

"He did. Skin mags. For real. He wrote it in caps, and underlined it three times."

"Gross. What will you do?"

"Oh, I sent him a *National Geographic*. It's got some saggy indigenous people in it. That's as close as I'm going."

"I'm sending my atheist a Doggy Life t-shirt and a bunch of candy and playing cards and a photo that Bangs took of me in the fall. He wanted to know what I look like."

"I'll bet he did."

"Hey, they're not all perverts."

"You mean they're not all as open about their perversions."

No, I think, I'm surrounded by irritatingly honorable men.

♫ ♫ ♫

Sunday night, dejected, Creedence blaring from my tape player in a futile attempt at inspiration, I review Geometry for the exam, and the inevitable B that will result. A protractor is emblematic: the discomfort unending.

Three taps at the door.

"Who is it?"

"Me," says Jeremy.

I check my watch as he slips inside. "It's so late."

"I had to see you." Maybe I look worried, because he adds, "Everyone's asleep."

"Then I should turn this down." I lower the volume, and try to relax. Did he bring nervousness with him?

"Cole," he says, "come sit down." I clear away the math from the bed, and sit beside him. "You're unhappy with me." He's had a haircut since I saw him Friday. No jacket, dressed in pajamas and his slippers, he came impetuously. "And I think I know why."

"Do you?"

"Yes," he says. "You think I'm stalling."

"Is that what I think?"

"Yes."

"Stalling? Are you sure?" Anger is the blood pushing through me—the cells and tissue and synapses. I am anger. "Not afraid or uninterested or like sickened, right? I think you're stalling."

"Sickened? Uninterested?" He shifts on the bed so that he's facing me, and puts his hands on my elbows. "Why would you say that?"

"Why? Oh, I don't know. Maybe because you let me beg—I was begging you—and you just wouldn't. Have I been unclear? Is that the problem? Do you not get that I want you to fuck me?"

"Jesus, Cole. I sat in your living room and promised our parents I wouldn't. I gave my word. If they had any idea the stuff we've done—any of it—they'd never let me see you again."

"Like how you get off every time no matter what? You figure they'd disapprove of that too, huh?" But now I want to cry. There's rejection, and then there's a dialogue about rejection, and the dialogue is way more painful. I stand, and cross the room. "Forget it. I don't even know why you're here."

"You don't know why I'm here? Really? You don't know?"

"Oh my god, Jeremy, enough. I've got Geometry brain, and I just don't care. You don't want to have sex, that's fine already. Whatever. I don't care."

"No, obviously not."

And then he's gone and there's only the heavy, empty click of the door.

Pergola. This sounds like math, but it's an arbor of trelliswork on columns used to train vines, which actually is weirder than math. Noun.

Since I'm all about the bright side, I'll tell you that catching the 7:15 bus on Monday morning means that I don't have to see Jeremy at all. I couldn't deal with asking Nate for a ride, so I got up at 6, and ran out to wait with everybody else. Stacy Masteller has her black jean jacket on, and must be freezing her ass off. She nods at me, and then we all stand silently, looking for the bus.

The bus picks up the officers' kids first, and then the enlisted kids, and then makes three stops to pick up eight civilian kids. Stacy and I sit across from one another three-quarters of the way back. Once the enlisted kids climb on, the decibel level rises, and some bastard in the back starts flicking Skittles around.

And another example of bright-side thinking: by the time I get to school, I have an extra forty-five minutes to study Geometry. I'm going to get a higher B on this test than I got on the last test. For real.

During our mock debate, Holly Mercer and Josh Tarbet open their pro-death penalty arguments by saying that life is valuable, and therefore, anyone who takes a life should forfeit his own. Although I am not a reputed genius, I see a great black hole in their logic. Monica Prader and I decimate them. Midway through, they break form to holler at us, they are so frazzled.

Monica Prader argues surprisingly eloquently. I'm glad to be on her side; her rigorous logic terrifies me a little, each argument a thrusting knife. She high-fives me once we're back in our seats—a preposterous gesture from poser metal girl, but points for effort.

See, I'll catch the bus, and B my way through Geometry, and mock debate, and stare at slides through microscopes, and no one will know. No one will guess what it costs me. No one will know that I wanted to hide under the bench in the locker room, that I came to those tumbling mats like aristocrats went to the guillotine.

♫ ♫ ♫

The boys are silly this afternoon. While we're tuning our instruments in Joe's garage, I tell them about our birthday dinner. "Our birthdays were last week, so no presents or anything. It's this joint dinner for Nigel and me and we'll have flank steak and crab and salad and bread and shit, and everybody wants you guys to come."

"Your dad loves us," Trevor says. He's unaccountably pleased with this thought, and beams at me.

"Well, he's only met you the once."

"Tomorrow?" Joe asks.

"Yeah," I say, "around 5."

They nod.

"So." I adjust the microphone, and avoid looking at any of them. "I want to play you guys something." When no one objects, I tear into it, the song driven by furious guitar:

> I finally get it now
> You were leaving anyhow
> There's nothing I can say or do
> Another bout of scream and shout
> You're packed and moving out
> Well, hooray, hooray for you
>
> You lecture from the door
> I've heard it all before
> And you'll never convince me
> There's no convincing me
>
> I'm brave enough
> Brave enough for this

Kind of love
This kind of love

First you prance and then you preen
But light changes everything
It leans through the room at you
Outside rain pelts down
Inside I'm gonna drown
Unless I cling to you

Let me tell you this one last thing
Let me tell you tell you tell you this one last thing
You'll never convince me
There's no convincing me

I'm brave enough
Brave enough for this
Kind of love
This kind of love

"Again," Ernie says, when I've finished.

By the third measure, I hear him join me, and then the tentative clap of the drum, and Joe bobs, watching my fingers.

The next time through, Ernie leads in with a plaintive lick, and then a hiccup from the drum, and the song enlarges, rounds itself. Ernie plays a melody, and Joe has a ragged blues rhythm, and Trevor stutters and kicks and fires in a volley during the chorus.

"Again!" Trevor calls.

"Double the chorus," Joe shouts.

We play extra measures for a guitar solo, and a longer intro, and triple choruses, and finally, we're staggering lyric in the last minutes of the song, and ending with repeated cries of "I finally get it now."

Not mine anymore, the song belongs to us. They play it with as much concentration and awareness as they'd play anything real. The song isn't angry; it's too big and vibrant for anything so rudimentary as anger. Now it's ironic.

The drums stop abruptly. We all play another few measures, and then stall as well.

"Cole," Trevor says, "I want you to let go."

"What?"

"I want you to let go. We'll play it once through—no lyrics—and then I want you to come in and just feel it. OK?"

"Feel it?"

He smacks the high hat. "Yes." Trevor points his drumstick at Ernie, and nods his head.

Ernie's guitar licks a melody. The lyric in the notes—he could sing my voice with those strings. Joe double-strikes the notes: a heartbeat. He and Trevor counter me, run ahead and double back.

When I come in with the lyric, it teases from me. The furious rush of the guitar underlines the line breaks, but it doesn't jostle them any longer. I'm not hilarious or ironic, angry or clever. I'm all those things and none of them. I feel it. I finally get it now.

♫ ♫ ♫

Jeremy doesn't come to our joint birthday dinner. Kelly comes, and Meghan (doing her best "I love everybody here equally!") and Doggy Life, and Bangs, and Alicia, and a bunch of effusive kids from Nigel's chess club. Every time someone walks through the door, I think it must be him.

Ernie plays Happy Birthday on the piano—figures the guy can play piano—and everyone sings. Meghan sends me upstairs for my guitar, and we jam a little, trading the guitar between Joe and Bangs and me. Nigel keeps requesting U2 songs. Trevor tells us to buy a hand drum before the next party.

When Gabby stops by, around ten, to pick her brother up, she and Joe decide to cut my hair.

There are ancient peoples, right, that chop off all their hair

135

when they're in mourning. I've heard of these people. Greeks or Syrians or something. Anyway, that's what I'm thinking when Gabby chops my hair.

"This is going to be amazing," she promises.

Shorn. Their hair is shorn in their grief. It's like the ultimate physical gesture of loss, isn't it? Except for being temporary.

"You can just mousse it all out," Gabby says. "It'll be wild."

Amazing. Wild. Whatever. The three of us are in the bathroom; Joe reclines on the edge of the tub, Gabby shimmies around my chair, murmuring. She brought clippers and scissors with her, almost as if they'd planned it. Cross-legged on the carpet in my bedroom, Bangs strums my acoustic.

"This guitar is sonic." He watches the chop and buzz.

I figured she'd cut to my chin. She goes half again as short.

"Holy god," I say, when I look in the mirror.

"It suits you," Gabby says.

Joe puts his hand on my shoulder. "I want you to think about deep purple highlights."

"Holy god," I say.

Gabby grabs my hair dryer, and bends me forward. "All you have to do," she tells me over the roar, "is mousse, and blow-dry like this."

Bangs slouches in the doorframe. "What do you think?" I ask him once I'm upright.

"You're a little punk," he says.

♪ ♪ ♪

Friday morning, I wake, and try not to freak out. I won't need mousse and a blowdrier to get whacky hair. At the bus stop, Stacy grins at me. "Now do something unpredictable," she says. My face feels hot, despite the cold, and the considerable absence of hair. "It looks good."

"Thanks." Liar. Why couldn't I just tell them no? Why did I submit to this?

When we board the bus, Stacy squeezes into my seat. "I

136

thought Jeremy had chicken pox or something," she says as the bus lurches forward, "and then I saw him in the hall." Braiding the strings on her bag, she focuses on her fingers.

"Nothing like that," I say.

"Well, who wouldn't want to ride the bus, and get to school 45 minutes before it begins?"

When I first met Stacy Masteller, her hair was brown, and she wore these cute little striped sweaters, and played football with us, and got super-aggressive and would tackle the guys and sack the quarterback and everything. And then, halfway through eighth grade, she starts bleaching her hair, and worshipping cosmetics, and ignoring anyone who isn't dressed in a Metallica shirt.

We were never friends, really, but I liked her. Girls eager to tackle: fairly rare in my experience.

"Are you OK?" she asks now.

I shrug.

She hands me an orange square of gum. "I saw you guys play at Board."

"Did you? I didn't see you."

"There were a lot of people there. You guys are good. So many bands, they just pretend to be bands, you know what I mean? They're like in band costumes or whatever, but you guys—you are a band. And you sound good, which is a bonus."

"Thanks. You coming to the show this Saturday?"

"I'm thinking yes."

"You should say hey if you make it."

She nods.

"What about you?" I ask. "How are you?"

"If I shrug, will you believe I'm fine?"

"Sure," I say, "if you want."

She shrugs. "I'm totally over Jersey. I've never been so ready to go."

Over Jersey, the way Jeremy and Meghan are over me. Next year I'll be as far from this place as you can get and still be part of the U.S. Far from West Point, and Doggy Life, and this school, and this life. "Maybe we should switch places."

137

"No way." She laughs. "I could never pull off that haircut."

♫ ♫ ♫

So, Mr. Henderson, the lazy bastard, takes the entire week to grade our Geometry tests; at the end of class, he places them face down on our desks, and yes, wait for it: I got an 87.

Joe leans over my shoulder. I hold the test up for him to examine, and say, "I'm the queen of B."

"You're pretty righteous in E flat too." He shows me his 83. "Better than me."

Never mind that I studied for five hours, and still got a B. Whatever. I'm over it. Joe stuffs his test into his square green field bag. Bleached blond, and more than stubble, his hair has lost that sad chemo baldness.

"Walk you to class?" he asks.

I nod.

"That song you played, you wrote it?"

"Yeah."

"Do you have more?"

Hundreds probably. "I have more."

"I'd like to hear them," he says.

"Sure," I say. "If you want."

"Maybe next week you could come over for dinner, or whatever, and play them for me."

"Don't get your hopes up. They're all super simple, and don't really even have bridges."

He puts his hands on my shoulders and steers me toward the door to English. "You pick the night—any night—and let me know."

♫ ♫ ♫

Senor Fernandez gives us the entire period to write a story in Spanish. Tonight we have a gig at Ichabod's, and tomorrow at Board, and next week, we'll play at a new place in some kind of battle of the bands competition. I finished my mat routine in gym, and have been working on the balance beam. Lame doesn't come close to capturing how much I suck—even walking across the beam I barely keep from falling. Jeremy tried a handstand on the rings, and almost managed it. Diofelli cheered like a schoolgirl.

I want to kick something. Being civilized, wearing clothes, and walking upright, has officially become too much. Another two sentences, and I finish my story. Senor Fernandez will probably think I'm psycho—I've written about housecats banding together to take over the town. Los gatos aterrorizan a la ciudad. The humans, enslaved, beg for mercy, and grimness abounds until Pimienta el perro—Pepper the dog—frees them.

If I'd played basketball, I wouldn't have to take gym, and I'd never see Jeremy. Never have to walk the balance beam like a plank, or do jumping jacks, or pretend this is all no big deal. A haircut never made anyone new. At the bell, I turn in my story, and wander around the corner to Biology.

Once Bangs comes in, he digs through his bag and hands me a Charms Pop—sour apple, my favorite.

"Are you skating this afternoon?" I ask.

"Yeah, the guys want to go to Board."

"Shit, we have a quiz today, don't we?"

"Open book," he reminds me.

"When did I fall out of my life?"

He unwraps my lollipop, and grins at me. "You guys all play soccer, right—your brothers and Meghan and you?" When I nod, he goes on, "We're organizing an indoor game this Sunday afternoon. If you guys come, we'll have enough people for two teams. Interested?"

"Totally. I love indoor soccer." Just the idea of running up and down a gymnasium relieves me, not to mention the constructive, purposeful kicking. "I'll check with everybody else, and let you know tomorrow."

"Cool."

I have to take every book in my locker home for the weekend.

My bag weighs five million pounds, and I get to ride the bus home, and Jeremy passes us while Stacy and I wait in line, and he doesn't even look at me. I am invisible now.

I leave my bag on the landing outside the kitchen door, and follow the sawing sound. Uneven grey stone, a sheer staircase, all the exposed pipe work, I tend to avoid the basement. Mom's workspace, with interrogation lamps, myriad sharp implements, and a swivel chair like dentists use, actually amplifies the creep-out factor.

From the bottom step, I watch her—the giant ear protectors, the goggles and face mask—as she saws wood on a jigsaw or bandsaw or some whirring thing. The place smells of wood and machinery.

Mom turns, and pulls off her ear protection. "Cole? Is it so late?" She checks her watch, and then says my name once more, differently. "Nicole?" She crosses the room, and crouches down in front of me. We're almost level. She reaches around to rub small circles on my back.

"I hurt," I say. "I hurt all over." I'm telling my shoes. I want my shoes to know how hard it is. How much I want to stop feeling anything, to stop wanting. "He—I thought—I thought he—" I don't know what I thought. Something. I thought something once.

My mother isn't a murmurer. She doesn't say *Shh*, or *It's OK*, or *I know*, or any other lies. "Do you know what I thought about today?" she asks. "Your second day of kindergarten."

She moves around so that she's seated on the step beside me, still rubbing my back, a fine sawdust now on my knees and shoes. "The first day they took you all around—showed you the office, and the classroom, and the toilets. And the second day, you were just to start. Go right in and join the class."

I don't remember this. I remember kindergarten—the teachers speaking only German, the bins of toys, the great windows, and the bright yellow wooden furniture.

"Nigel was in a stroller," she continues, "and you walked beside him, holding his hand. And then, once we got to school, you stood there, looking at the doors. And finally you said, 'I don't want to go.' And then you let go of Nigel's hand, and you walked inside. You didn't hesitate or look back. 'I don't want to go'—and then you went. Nigel and I waited for you. Just in case. I don't know how long. I almost wished—" She coughs, and then says, "I almost wished you'd come back out, said you weren't ready, or needed a hug first, or more time. I needed more time. I think I cried every day that week."

I don't remember that either, her crying. "It's cold down here," I say.

She pats her knees, and stands. "Give me just a second, and I'll go up with you. I have to start dinner."

"What are we having?"

"Beef stroganoff."

I wait while she sweeps, and turns off the lights, and puts her tools away. I wait because I'm tired of struggling, and because she asked me to, and because for the first time since Jeremy left my room in his slippers, I've said that it hurts, and I've said it out loud, and I want to be with the person I told.

Parity. Equality, as in amount, status, or value. Noun. I think parity is a rarity.

Joe holds the tank top up to his own chest. "It's as blue as your eyes," he tells me. The ugly dog has its head back and bays into a microphone. Doggy Life in the same script as on the t-shirts— Trevor's wearing the new black one.

"You can change here," Trevor says, and winks.

"Aren't you supposed to be topless?" I ask.

"I will if you will," he says.

Seated on an amp with his guitar cradled in his lap, Ernie says, "Shut up."

Trevor looks at him. "Dude?"

"Cole," Ernie says, "you rock those sweatshirts. You don't need to wear some little tank top or spike your hair all out like Sid Vicious or any of that shit."

"Do you hear yourself?" Trevor asks Ernie.

"I thought we were serious about this," Ernie says. "I thought we meant it. This is us, all right, this—metal boy and Robert Smith's baby brother, and the sweet girl, and me. This is the wrong crew for safety pins and Mohawks. So leave her the fuck alone already." Ernie stands to take the tank top from Joe, and swaps it for his own button down. "I'll wear the tank top. I don't want to hear another fucking word about this."

"Dude," Trevor mutters, "menstrual much?"

We have the tightest set we've ever played. Ichabod's, smoky and dark, must be filled past capacity. The bouncers toss anyone with a drink off the dance floor. Whenever I note Ernie's blue tank top in my peripheral vision, I smile.

His knees bent, legs spread, he blitzes licks and power chords and solos. Joe's grind looks pornographic. Boys in the crowd thrash against one another, and up into the air like orcas. From the moment we took the stage, there's been steady screaming from the back of the bar.

Meghan, sporting an orange wristband to identify her as

underage, sits on a stool at the edge of the dance floor, and mouths lyrics. When we play my song, she jumps to her feet and dances with her arms over her head.

The sweet girl. Dig me, the sweet girl. Joe harmonizes for the chorus, and leans against me during Ernie's solo. Fuck, I'm alive. We will groove through you. We will sing you a rhythm. We are an electric current, the last thing you'll ever remember.

"You played one of Cole's songs," Meghan says when she comes backstage. She grabs my shoulders and hugs me. "You guys were absolutely unreal tonight." The three of them blush as she hugs them as well. With her arms still around Ernie, she says, "And I want one of these tank tops."

Meghan parks beneath the trees in front of our house. Just midnight, the car warm, the streets empty, both of us reek of cigarettes.

"Soccer on Sunday afternoon?" Meghan says.

"Nigel and Nate agreed already, and of course, Nate's bringing Kelly; and Bangs, and Gabby, and some of their friends."

"And Jeremy?" Meghan asks. "Will Jeremy come?"

"No."

"He wasn't at the birthday dinner."

"No."

"Why is that?"

"He wasn't interested."

"Wasn't he?" she asks.

"If he were interested, he'd have come, wouldn't he? So, I think I can say with certainty that he wasn't interested. That he isn't interested. I think I can guarantee you that."

"Cole, what happened?"

"There's something wrong with me." I tell her the story. The darkness helps. Could be any story I'm telling, just another grim fairytale. When I finally look at her, she has turned in her seat with her legs up so that she faces me, and her arm extends between us, her fingers sifting through my grief hair.

For Graphic Arts, we're supposed to shoot portraits. I've had trouble envisaging a portrait; I thought maybe I could get the

143

guys to pose for me with their instruments, or convince them this had publicity potential or something; but the truth is, I'm bored by the whole idea of portraits.

Yet, looking at Meghan—her blonde hair sitting at her shoulders, her knees pulled up against her chest, the night almost sifted down around her as if to illuminate her skin—she seems, in the car, to glow, and I wish I had my camera. I wish I could capture this.

"Say something," I say.

"I don't know what to say."

"Tell me I'm not a freak."

"You're not a freak."

"Then why?" I ask. "He left my room that night, and now it's like I don't exist. Like none of it ever happened, or mattered."

"Cole," she says softly.

"Whenever somebody asks me about him, I want to fucking punch them. I don't want to be this girl. This sad, dumped girl."

I bow my head and she runs her fingers along the back of my head, and down my neck to my shoulders. Soothing, and hypnotic, and something else—something I don't have a word for—maybe this is how it feels to have your head anointed with oil. To be blessed.

"That feels good," I murmur.

"Have you been dumped?" she asks.

"If I haven't, I have the shittiest boyfriend of all time."

"Maybe you should talk to him."

"Maybe I should just leave the whole thing alone. A week ago, I thought I couldn't possibly feel worse, and now I know I can, and I also know that I don't want to. This is plenty, thanks."

Her fingers tighten around my hair at the nape of my neck; she's gripping it in her fist, and she tugs and twists so that my face is turned toward her. And, all at once, in a single motion, she glides forward and kisses me. A launching, gliding, leaning kiss. And then she straddles me, and cocks my head back, and I see that glow again as she dips her face to mine. I cannot stop shaking. I cannot breathe.

Even with my eyes closed, I see that glow, that luminous dusting of night. I will put all my sorrow here, into her mouth. I will bury it, like a secret, and no one will ever know.

♫ ♫ ♫

Leroy has two chairs set up for us in the corner of the large room. "You don't look so good, kid," he says.

"Not sleeping."

He stares at me and strums his guitar. "You know this one?" He plays *Everybody Knows*, sings the lyric in his raspy blues voice.

"Concrete Blonde," I say when he finishes.

"Leonard Cohen," he corrects. "Concrete Blonde covered it."

"Will you teach me?" I ask. We go through the song, both of us singing now, the lyric intricate and painful. See, it can always be worse: Jeremy could have cheated, or left me for somebody. Bright side!

"How'd it go last night?" Leroy asks.

"Tight. Ernie is so good, he changes his lines a little, improvises, you know?"

Leroy nods. "Let's hear some scales."

Yes, scales, something monotonous and rote. Something mindless. I can still feel her hands in my hair. Her weight on me, her mouth, scales.

♫ ♫ ♫

Dad builds a fire. Nigel and I have taken over the living room— our books on the coffee table and both couches, our bags on the floor. Does Nate ever do homework? It's nearly two in the afternoon, and I don't even think he's out of bed yet.

From the kitchen, the teakettle whistles. "Hot chocolate?" Dad asks. "With marshmallows or whipped cream?"

"Whipped cream," we say.

He comes back with a tray and offers backrubs. In my family, you have to trade; no one gets a backrub for free, except right now apparently.

"What are you working on?" Dad asks.

I try not to be irritated. The backrub and everything; obviously he's trying. "My comparative essay on *The Lottery* and *A Good Man Is Hard to Find.*"

"*The Lottery*'s the one with the stoning?"

I nod. Dad knows a lot of shit. "Yeah, and they give the little kid pebbles to throw at his mom."

"Who wrote *A Good Man Is Hard to Find*?"

"Flannery O'Connor," I say. "You should read it. The story has a bunch of biblical allusions." I hand him the book—if you can distract Dad, he'll rub your back for half an hour.

"What's your essay topic?"

"Foreshadowing," I say, "to build suspense."

"Hmm." Dad reads.

Mom brings her novel, and sits in the rocking chair, with her tea, to read. Nigel flips back and forth in his Algebra book. The lackluster fire pops in the grate.

Aren't both stories about ordinary danger, the violence that rides behind us on a tandem bike? The kind of casual, horrible things that happen all the time? My atheist sent me an envelope with sand in it. No letter or anything, just sand. I poured it into the metal ashtray I made in seventh grade shop. I hope Meghan calls. I want to hear her voice. Does God hate me now?

"You're right," Dad tells me. "I do like this story. She's angry, isn't she? I'd like to read it again. Maybe tonight while you're at your show."

"Sure." My stomach hurts. Last night I lay in bed for hours, not sleeping, not tossing, just staring at the ceiling. Days of homework still to do, and I can't concentrate. I want to sit on the floor with my guitar and croon lamentations, like those heartbroken cowboys with their trashed guitars.

I abandon my essay for vertexes. Bangs calls, and we finish our Biology homework together over the phone. In spite of my wandering brain, I read the History chapters and answer all the study questions, then translate some ridiculous Spanish exercise about camping in Europe (where do they dream up this shit?).

By the time Dad returns with subs for our dinner, I've only got my English essay left to do.

If I had a cowboy hat, I'd wear it to the gig tonight. Distortion. I crave it like a drug.

🎵 🎵 🎵

The stage lights burn us. Ernie and Joe have sweat pouring off their faces, and I've shed my sweatshirt for the Doggy Life tank. Rather than slumping around languidly, they're sprinting all over the stage as though the cords and stands and amps were an obstacle course. Between vocals, I dance with them. Trevor uses a towel to wipe himself down, and keep from chucking his sticks at us. Tonight, for the first time, he asked for a mic to sing background vocals.

I can't see anybody in the crowd. Even the kids nearest the stage refract light, or they're moving so quickly that I can't make out any of their features. I hear the band—all three of them—chime in with me on choruses.

When you think of God, what do you imagine? That muscled old guy on the ceiling of the Sistine Chapel? I don't see a body at all—just two hands in the dark. When I was a kid, Dad would read stories at bedtime, and if I hadn't fallen asleep during the reading, he'd trace circles around my eyes and sing *Sandman's Coming*, and maybe that's where the hands came from: this comforting gesture in the night.

One afternoon, I walked to the parade ground, and climbed into the umbrella tree, and from my seat, I could see light fracture the clouds. I thought it was Heaven, that I'd witnessed a portal, or a vision or something. Later, this woman at church said she couldn't wait to get to Heaven where there'd be no sadness, only joy and adoration. No sadness? How would that work? If we were to be in a place with no sadness, we'd have to lose our memories too. Otherwise we'd bring sadness just by remembering, wouldn't we?

And adoration? I don't want to sing praises for the rest of

eternity. Heaven is basketball courts, and Elizabeth Bishop poems, and field hockey, and my guitars, and crisp bacon, and good music, and youth and vigor forever. Or Heaven is this: the four of us sweating under the lights. Now I get why native peoples used music to reach a religious ecstasy; it's a delirious madness—music—a sense of euphoria and adrenaline and community. I love these boys. I love this blank, yawping crowd. We give them some Violent Femmes, and our reverence, and Joe yanks his shirt off and flings it into the crowd. We give them Joe's shirt.

From atop the speaker, I sing to the spread of them, the kids pressed to the stage, seated near the ramps, all the way to the back wall. When we do my song, I hear Trevor harmonizing during the verses as well as the chorus. His voice, tender and higher than mine, adds another level still to the song.

We play for two hours. It's like a bloodletting, I'm pretty sure I'm anemic now. Bangs' band, Slim and None, opened for us. They hadn't played any gigs since the first time I saw them at Board. Bangs said his drummer kept hocking his kit to pay rent, and they couldn't find anyone to replace him.

"That's the best show," Bangs says backstage, "I've ever seen you guys play."

"Thanks, man," Ernie says. "It's good to see you playing again too."

Bangs shrugs the compliment off. "We just fuck around. Oh Cole, Meghan had to bail. She had a migraine. I said I'd make sure you got home safe."

"Dude," Trevor says, "your chaperone bailed. Now we can party."

"Another time," I tell him. "I'm exhausted. Trevor, you have a beautiful voice, and your harmonies . . . you've been holding out."

"I like to keep the ladies guessing," he says. And then I see the ladies he means: five of them, in outfits that make Daisy Duke seem modest, howl for him from the doorway. "Party bound." And he strides away from us.

Bangs and Joe and Ernie look at me. "Are you hungry?" Joe asks, handing me my sweatshirt.

"Why do you even ask?" Meghan left me. Left the show. I follow the boys to Joe's car, and we drive to the fluorescent diner for breakfast.

Surmount. To mount upon or prevail over. Verb. The obsolete usage meant to surpass in excellence. Kind of a hard fall for a word, don't you think?

Gabby meets up with us at the diner after she drops all her friends back at their houses. I eat the heart-attack special and finally quit, feeling faint.

"So," she says, on her fourth cup of coffee, "soccer tomorrow."

"Yeah, what about you guys?" Bangs asks Joe and Ernie. "Want to play some indoor with us?"

"Cool," Ernie says.

"Yeah, alright." Joe smiles. "I'm on Cole's team."

And the next afternoon, he is on my team, as well as Bangs and Ernie and Nigel, and Bangs' skater buds. Gabby and her friends join Nate and Kelly. Meghan phoned to say she couldn't make it.

We play in a middle-school gymnasium, the wooden bleachers drawn tight to the walls, the windows so high up as to be completely useless as a light source. We play seven on seven and have two substitutes. Though I stretched for twenty minutes, my groin feels tight, and my head light.

"Dude," Ernie asks Bangs, "how do you guys have access to this place?"

"Gabby knows everybody."

"Right." Ernie appears smaller in shorts. He's got on some crazy Bermudas and a white t-shirt and a pair of red Converse that he might have borrowed from Joe. I worry, the first time I pass him the ball.

He runs so quickly that no one comes close to taking the ball from him, or blocking his drive to the goal. He shoots, and without even bothering to watch the ball land, simply turns and runs back to our half of the gym, almost as though he can feel the goal.

"Ernie!" We shout. Bashful, and himself again, he lets us congratulate him.

Joe cannot stay on his feet. He tumbles and dives and drops

even in a clean run without defenders, but his aggression is unreal. Maybe because he knows he won't be upright for long, he attacks the other team with terrifying urgency. They start passing rather than engaging with him.

Bangs plays soccer like he skates: his movement balletic, his subtle shifts of the ball fluid, his height alarming in close quarters.

We beat them 7–0, and they're good sports but still ask if we can change up the teams for a fairer game. While we rehydrate between games, Kelly stretches beside Nate, her face turned up toward his with a look I never expected to see on her. Attentive. She's attentive to my brother.

When I was in second grade, Nate led us on an expedition to the orange clay pools. We hiked through the Missouri woods, past the creeks with turtles and tree-climbing frogs; we used our sticks as machetes, and wandered until the forest thinned, and the trees changed from evergreen to birch and finally gave way entirely to the orange clay pools. We stripped to our Underoos, and soaked in the warm water.

By the time we got back home, every parent on Gridley Loop had been mobilized. We'd taken some of the younger kids with us—maybe eight kids altogether—all of us damp, tired, and painted orange. Nate got in an unreal amount of trouble. Spankings, if I remember correctly, and he never told them it was my idea, that I'd begged him to take me.

Somehow, being punished for our innocuous adventure made it seem more remarkable, more daring than a walk through the woods. We treated Nate like a hero for years. Admired and aped him.

During our second game, we trade Ernie and one of the better skater boys for a timid girl, and a guy I swear is wearing dress shoes. I steal the ball from Ernie, pass to Bangs, and he arcs a beauty of a lob to Nigel, who heads it into the goal. Nate takes goal when we're up 4–2, and I score on him twice in quick succession—nobody telegraphs like Nate does.

He calls something shitty to me that I don't hear, but Bangs and Nigel do.

"Don't worry," Nigel tells our brother. "I'll score the next one on you."

Joe and I chase Ernie out of bounds, and Bangs flings the ball to Joe, who goes down almost at once, but the timid girl recovers the ball, and kicks it in Nigel's direction. Kelly gets to it first, and she and Nigel race back toward our goal, Ernie and Gabby flanking them.

Nigel's stride lengthens; he catches the ball, and guides Kelly into dress-shoes guy, then lifts the ball on top of his shoe for a flicking pass to one of the skater boys, and we all push back toward Nate. His team scrambles to defend goal, to slow us, to rally.

Bangs brings the ball under control with his chest, and spins once to angle a pass back at me, and then I lead Nigel, and he nails the ball right at Nate. For a moment they're both airborne—Nigel with his right leg extended, and Nate with both arms thrown wide to save the ball. I want to leave them like that.

♫ ♫ ♫

Afterward, in the parking lot, Bangs juggles a ball, almost lazily, between his feet, and asks, "Pizza?"

We look at Nate, our driver. "Sure," he agrees. "I just need to call home real quick."

Gabby tells everybody the pizza is her treat. In this half-tavern, half-arcade, the big-bellied staff model thick gold jewelry and sinister wisecracks. We order six large pies, and mean to finish every slice. Our group commandeers the jukebox, and the pool tables, while Bangs and I play air hockey.

"You kicked ass out there," I tell him.

"You sound surprised."

"Why don't you play on the varsity soccer team?"

"Jocks bore me."

"Is that right?" I point at Nate and Nigel and myself. "We all play varsity soccer."

"Hey, if I could play on the team with you, I'd be all over it."

"You're so weird," I tell him.

Two massive dudes with muttonchops throw darts in the corner by the Budweiser clock. I imagine I can hear the darts whistle. Bangs grabs us a couple of slices of pepperoni with black olives. "I haven't seen Jeremy around for a while," he says.

"Nope."

"I kinda miss the guy."

Nobody else has said this. "I miss him too." *Brilliant Disguise* on the jukebox, and the entire place sings the chorus—their voices lilting upward with Springsteen's. "What do you think God looks like?" I ask Bangs.

"Whose?"

"You know," I say, gesturing at him with my pizza, "yours."

"I think God's made of water." He flicks his hair, and chews on his thumb, thinking. The guy has left the crust from each slice piled on his plate. I eat them as he continues, "Ever notice how all the big stories involve water: Noah's ark, the *Epic of Gilgamesh*, *The Odyssey*, Osiris, Jonah and the whale, Oceanus, fishers of men, baptism, the Fountain of Youth, the parting of the Red Sea? And when the Israelites are punished, they're enslaved in Egypt, and then made to wander the desert—far from the ocean?" I think of my atheist, all these months in the desert, the awful waiting. "And Odysseus is marooned," Bangs says, "and trapped in caves and shit? Water figures in all of it, you know? So I think God is water."

He drains a mammoth glass of Coke, before adding, "Maybe that's why surfers are so insane; they have a chronic God rush. Have you ever thought about Eden maybe being submerged deep underwater?"

No, I haven't thought about that, but I'm still stuck on his initial assertion. "What the hell's the *Epic of Gilgamesh*?" I ask.

"It's this ancient story about this dude Gilgamesh, and his quests; there's a flood in it too."

"Oh sure," I say, "that dude Gilgamesh. It's all coming back to me." What if we got tossed out of some sunken paradise, and were forced to grow legs and breathe air? Somebody hits the

153

lamp above one of the pool tables, and it rocks back and forth, creaking.

Bangs' eyes skate across me, and away to the dartboard, and the pool tables, and our empty plates, and Nate and Kelly at the jukebox plugging quarters. Then he flicks his bangs a bunch of times, and finally admits, "My mom teaches Comparative Religion. Sometimes I read the books she leaves lying around. I've got this one about Confucius now. What a trip. Anyway," he says, "doesn't everything start with water?"

"I thought everything started with light," I say, "but I kinda dig your idea more." From the jukebox, *Livin' on a Prayer*, the second Bon Jovi song in a row—just a single would have been torture enough—and Nate and Kelly laugh like maniacs in the corner.

♫ ♫ ♫

My English essay, admittedly, blows. If something dynamic occurs to me in my sleep, at least I'll have 45 extra minutes in the morning to spice up my conclusion. (Bright side!)

I write to my atheist on ornate pink stationery my grandmother sent me last Christmas. Though I hadn't planned to tell him, I write the fight with Jeremy, and the kiss in Meghan's car, and whatever happened that night in her room, and Bangs' theory of an underwater Eden. The letter goes on for pages, my handwriting morphing from print to cursive. Will he be shocked? Will he disapprove? I'll send some Milky Way bars too, which should make the letter easier to swallow.

After midnight, I switch off my lamp, and lie in the dark. God as a giant squid, as a merman, as an old bearded guy with a trident; God as a wave, pulling, pulling.

♫ ♫ ♫

Monday evening, I have dinner with Joe and his mom. She cooks stir-fry with strips of pork and tons of vegetables, and the entire meal she tells us about the insane shit that happens at her work—she's a nurse in the trauma unit and has seen everything—like some guy with a thermos up his anus claiming to have fallen onto it while doing pull-ups naked in the woods.

After dessert, Joe and I head back out to the garage where we already had a two-hour practice this afternoon, and sit on stools facing each another.

"OK?" I say, nervous all the sudden.

He smiles at me. I've considered songs that would fit the band better, and chosen eight to play for him. I watch his foot as I play, the way it keeps time with my strum.

"Nice," he says, at the end of the first.

"Grab a guitar," I say, "and play the next with me."

We play together, with Joe occasionally plucking a bass line on his guitar, or harmonizing for the chorus. It's the last week before Christmas break, multiple tests pending, and the portrait project for Graphic Arts, two gigs with the band, in addition to the Battle of the Bands competition at some metal bar, and this feels like meditation. Kicking with Joe, our acoustics warm and bright, our voices intimate.

"Once more," Joe says a couple of times. And we weave back through.

Sometime later, his mom brings us another serving of apple pie and ice cream. When we finish eating, I tell Joe that I have to go.

On the drive back to the base, a pitiful snow swirls around, sticking to nothing.

"You guys going anywhere over break?" he asks.

"The boys are going skiing."

"Not you?"

"I hate skiing."

"Me too," he says. "We should hang out, if you want."

I don't mention Bangs' idea about a movie marathon: watching gangster films from the 40s, which showcase all the little guys waving guns around.

"I'm in," I say.

I had been worried, before dinner, when Ernie and Trevor left, and I stayed, that things might get tense with Joe, but it was easy, tensionless. And when he drops me off, I'm grateful to have had the respite, a leisurely evening away from my life.

Two days later, we take the stage at the metal club—Metallic— how's that for originality? Imagine a penguin habitat without the water or the penguins, but complete with penetrating smell, and you've got Metallic. Longhaired, scrawny dudes, entwined with thick-lashed hippy chicks, stand around smoking cigarettes and drinking beer from plastic cups.

We play fourth, and open with The Ramones. On the second chorus, the first beer missile clips my mic stand, and splashes up into my face. Ernie and Joe are hit simultaneously—Ernie in the shoulder, and Joe, kicking up to defend himself, in the knee. More beer comes; I've crouched, and ducked behind a speaker, but some asshole lobs a pitcher, and a spray hits me before the pitcher crashes into the wall.

"Fucking punks!" comes the cry from the crowd.

I yank my guitar free from the cord, and cradle it protectively. The crowd's roar and another launch of beer chase us from the stage. Trevor, at the last, picks up a speaker and hurls it into the crowd. Backstage, the manager tries to chide us about hurling equipment at his patrons.

"Fuck you, douche bag," Trevor says. "Get your fucking monkeys out there to break our gear down right now, before I call the police." The guy tries to argue, and Trevor steps up so close that the manager flinches. "Get your fucking monkeys out there to break our gear down now. I won't tell you again."

The guy vanishes. Even backstage we hear the crowd roaring. Musicians from other bands stand around, glancing at us, then at each other.

Ernie rubs his guitar down, and packs it inside his case before toweling the beer from his hair. Nobody but Trevor has spoken. "How much must that beer suck?" Ernie says now. "They were throwing entire pitchers."

Dismal. Our party, reeking of cheap beer, sits on the bench

seats in Trevor's van, staring at our cigarettes. Trevor drinks two Budweisers, crushing the emptied can and hurling it to the floor each time.

"Fuck," he says again to no one in particular.

The first gig I've ever played without my chaperone, and we're attacked by beer-catapulting metalheads. Of course, my parents have no inkling that I'm unchaperoned and it's not like I could explain it, anyway. I start laughing.

"You're hysterical," Trevor observes disgustedly.

"That was really scary," I say.

"I wish I'd thought to throw speakers," Ernie says.

"That should be the plan," Joe says, "for next time."

"Next time?" Trevor asks. He shakes his head.

"Those are your people, man," Ernie tells Trevor. "Your own people attacked us."

"Those fuckers," Trevor says, jabbing his cigarette at the night for emphasis, "are not my people. We should burn that fucking place down. Cole, dude, you're gonna be sick if you keep laughing like that."

"I'm sorry," I gasp.

"We smell," Joe says, "like we've been to a really bad party."

The worst, we agree. The worst party imaginable.

♫ ♫ ♫

Soaking in the bath, I call Bangs and wonder, briefly, if I'll be electrocuted.

"They what?" he asks.

I tell him again.

"That's horrible," he says.

"Yes. The look on Trevor's face when he said *fucking monkeys*—unreal—he was actually the scariest thing in the whole place."

"I should come over there," he says.

"What?"

"I feel like I should come over. Make sure you're OK."

"I'm OK."

157

"Cole," he says.

"Don't worry," I tell him. How to explain that this is the least of it? Tonight in the bar pales compared to Jeremy walking out, or Meghan vanishing. Nothing, anywhere, is certain. "Everything gets corrupted, doesn't it?"

"Fifteen minutes," Bangs says, and rings off.

For a while, I stare at the phone. I bought it with babysitting money when I was twelve, and allowed, for the first time, to have a phone in my bedroom. I pull my flannel pajama pants on when I hear the scratch at the door.

"I'm sorry," he whispers as he slides past me into the room. He doesn't ask where my shirt is, why I'm damp, why the light's out; in fact, he doesn't say anything as he tips my face back and kisses me.

We kiss for so long that I stop crying, and brush my palm against his jawline. "Christian," I say, and cry again.

He lifts me onto the bed, and holds me. He's singing *Prove My Love*, by the Violent Femmes, maybe the most hilarious lullaby I've ever heard. And I laugh and he kisses me again. My laugh in both our mouths.

Ascension 1991

Tragedy.

That's the header, the only word I've written on my sheet of lined paper. We're supposed to write 500 words about tragedy before the bell rings. Everyone else—head bent and pen scrabbling—has engaged with this assignment. I've written: Tragedy.

What exactly am I supposed to write? I haven't seen Meghan in 26 days—since the night she left Board with a migraine. That's my tragedy. One of them. But shouldn't tragedy have more scope than my particular life? Shouldn't tragedy affect some other people too? What about my atheist? Deployed, running drills in the desert, anticipating the inevitable invasion, the chemical warfare, the horrible death. That's tragic.

He wrote me again:

> I wish I could take you out for coffee, or a soda, or something. Maybe just a drive. I used to drive all the time in high school. Your letters make me nostalgic. I'm going to tell you something, but you're never allowed to repeat it—to anyone—in fact, you must burn this letter directly after reading it. Do you promise?
>
> The first time I had sex, my knees kept slipping on the bed sheets, and I had no leverage and really sucked. It was bad. Not bad, it was embarrassing. I thought sex would be systematic or intuitive or something, but it wasn't. In the end, I was ashamed of myself, and made her feel bad.
>
> It's lonely at first, being young. I remember it that way too, I remember the loneliness. It's like being here at night. Like you're nothing.
>
> I've considered making up some advice for you. Something sage like, You'll fall in and out of love for the rest of your life. But I can see how you

might not find that reassuring. Listen to a lot of music. There's great heartbreak music out there. Or revenge music. I used to listen to "Babe, I'm Gonna Leave You"—you know that Led Zeppelin song?—whenever I was bummed out. It's a heartbreak/revenge classic.

I've started smoking again. I figure, what the fuck?

But I don't want to share my atheist, or his tragedy, especially with Overhead. Then I think about the Space Shuttle Challenger. We were sitting in Ms. Moos' class, learning how to divide fractions, when someone came to the door. The women murmured to one another, and Ms. Moos turned back to us, and announced the news in a trembling voice.

They pulled a television in from the A/V room and we watched the shuttle explode again and again that afternoon. The teachers consoled one another, while we sat at our desks, and were awestruck. Alive and then not. Momentum and then pieces. I'd just turned eleven and was startled to discover it could all be over so quickly—blinked out—that's what could happen.

I can hear the clock on the wall tick, and the sweeping hand of my Swatch sweep; Alicia's furious erasing, and the dash of her hand as she wipes away the pink skin.

The last year we lived in Missouri, I was a fourth grader, and my father had taken over the division chapel where the basic trainees came every Sunday by the hundreds. (If they attended a church service, they could skip drills.) What I remember most from that year is a family down the street from us, who discovered, in a heavy trunk in their garage, the body of their four-year-old son, who'd climbed into the trunk with three newborn kittens and suffocated. My father performed the funeral. He cried when he told us.

Fuck you, Overhead. Fuck you and your tragedy. Fuck Jeremy and his precious soul. Fuck Meghan and her stupid career.

Fuck Iraq and Kuwait and sand and shuttles and heavy trunks.

My atheist's advice about heartbreak/revenge songs is sage. During Christmas break, Bangs played *Babe, I'm Gonna Leave You* on his record player all afternoon, and I lay with my head on his thigh and felt righteous.

Our fourth day back in classes, and I can't fake caring anymore. I'm out of the habit, I guess. Tonight we have a gig at one of the new places. Trevor has us playing all over the place. He said we'd become old news at Board if we played there every week, so now we play eight different places in some kind of random order that I can't figure at all. Every Thursday, Friday, and Saturday we have gigs, Monday we have practice, and the rest of the time I'm free to do a bunch of homework, or babysit. I worried my parents might freak about my schedule, but they said as long as I maintain a 3.8 GPA, I'm golden.

And Christmas break? Christmas break began with several bags on our doorstep, tagged to each of us from Meghan, along with a hasty note explaining how sorry she was to miss us but she had to leave immediately for the trip down to see her folks, and would see us again in January. Merry Christmas and Happy New Year!

Yeah. Whatever. My parents haven't said anything about my being unchaperoned. They have mentioned several times that they think Joe is a surprisingly responsible teenager. Last year I wasn't allowed to date, and now my parents are trying to pick out my boyfriends. Over break, Nate and Nigel took two ski trips. I shot a portrait of my mother in her tool belt—something black smudged across her cheek, and a wicked drill held to her chest like she's going to pledge allegiance—which Mr. Pang claims he'll enter in some state competition.

Tragedy. I miss the weekly vocabulary lists. I miss the sheet of words in Meghan's handwriting. I miss the band—the way it used to feel less like business and more like invention. I miss watching Hitchcock movies with Jeremy. I miss Nate. And sometimes, especially in the morning, on the walk from homeroom to Graphic Arts, I miss Kelly.

Finally, just before the bell rings, I write: *I don't even know where to begin.*

♫ ♫ ♫

I've got cramps, and am breaking out around my mouth, and engaged in full glower-mode with all the other kids waiting in line to board the bus.

"What's with you?" Stacy Masteller asks.

I glower at her.

"Oh," she says. "You want some gum? I think I've got watermelon."

"OK," I say.

It's snowing, and Stacy's dressed in her denim jacket without a proper coat. Her bangs, recently Aqua-netted, stand at frizzy attention; she reeks of fresh cigarette, and practically crawls into her giant acid-washed purse to get me a piece of watermelon gum.

"Hey!" a voice shouts. Every kid in line looks up. On the far side of the scraggly parking strip, Doug leans out the window of Nate's hatchback and waves at Stacy and me. "Hey, you two, get your scrawny asses over here."

We stall a moment, and then she links her arm through mine, and pulls me to Nate's car. Doug doesn't bother to get out, but grabs the handle of his bucket seat and leans forward. When I climb in, I give the seat a vicious push and crush into him.

"God," he grunts. "I take it back. Your asses aren't at all scrawny."

"Thanks," Stacy tells Nate.

She turns her head rapidly to the left twice, and I hear Nigel say, "I'm growing my hair out."

"Is that what you're doing?" she asks. "Gum?"

We blow bubbles—the car pungent with artificial watermelon—and Doug demonstrates the bubble within a bubble technique that made him famous around the neighborhood a couple of years ago.

"What's your deal?" Doug asks me. "You catch chicken pox, or something?"

"You're such a dick," I say.

"Maybe we should've left you in the snow with the other losers."

"Losers?" I say. "When was the last time you had a date with a girl that didn't have scabs?"

He twists around in his seat and punches me hard, right in the middle of my thigh. I grab his hair and pull so hard that he cries out.

"You fucking bitch," he yells, and then we're all thrown forward.

"Doug," Nate says. His tone is exactly our father's—stern and cold and final—and I'm ashamed.

But Doug's totally gone—screaming the kind of apocalyptic raving you hear at tent revivals—spittle in the air around him like gnats in the summer. Horns honk behind us.

"Doug," Nate says again. Nate looks at me. "Are you OK?"

"I'm sorry," I say, and start to cry.

"Doug," Nate says. "Dude, enough. Calm down, or I'll throw you out of the car."

A driver behind us pins his horn, and yells out the window, "Get your ass out the way!"

Doug turns in his seat to stare out the window, his arms folded around his torso. No one says anything for the rest of the ride home.

I'm leaking, I can feel it, and the cramps make breathing difficult. In the kitchen, pausing just long enough to get a pudding and an apple, I hear my mother call my name.

"Yes?" I ask.

"You've got a letter," she says. "On the kitchen table."

My atheist. No one else writes me. But the letter on the table shows a single word in the return address space: Meghan. I forget, for a moment, even my cramps.

Snacks stuffed in my bag, I open the letter as I climb to my room, and find a single sheet of paper.

Cole,
I've enclosed your next vocabulary list—
just 15 words this time—consider it an

165

*other Christmas present. Please don't be
angry. I couldn't bear that.*

DEPREDATION
ANTEDILUVIAN
ENCOMIUM
CADGE
DESICCATE
NOISOME
IMPECUNIOUS
SATURNINE
INCHOATE
PANEGYRIC
HAPLESS
PREVARICATE
EXCULPATE
SEDULOUS
OCCIDENTAL

*Yours,
Meghan*

The truth, I'll tell you the truth. I make it to the bathroom, but not to the tub, not even to the mat. I collapse on the freezing tile and cry and tremble until nothing else will come, and then I lie there sniveling with my eyes burning. For a while, nothing, not a single thought, forms itself. I'm anonymous.

Cadge. To beg. Or obtain by begging. Verb. Boy, I'm surprised we don't see this on signs all over the place: ABSOLUTELY NO CADGING ON THESE PREMISES. VIOLATORS WILL BE OBJURGATED!

Bangs and I are watching *The Big Sleep* on the television in his bedroom. It's part of the Sunday afternoon gangster film festival, and we're at the climax (Humphrey Bogart and Lauren Bacall taking time between gun battles to shorthand their feelings) in a bizarrely incestuous story about porn, blackmail, gambling, and murder.

"He's kind of a little guy, isn't he?" I say.

"Who?"

"Humphrey Bogart."

"You think so?" he asks.

"Why else would she be slumped down in the car like that—she can't be comfortable—but it makes her look small and vulnerable compared to him." We watch Bogart kiss her. Her slumped posture renders her strategically kissable. I whisper, "He has a scrawny little chest, and a giant head like a Chihuahua."

"He's a good actor, though," Bangs whispers back, "interesting to watch."

This is true. He's compelling. The lisping loser tough guy fascinates me. You want to see him beat these smooth, evil bastards and get the dangerous blonde.

Bangs' room gets toasty warm. Pitched on the couch in our socks, with a couple of cotton blankets, Burger King wrappers on the chest/ottoman thing, Hawaiian Punch in Coca Cola glasses—packed with ice so they'll keep bracingly cold because we still have half a box of Ding Dongs to get through. I've been over here every Sunday for weeks, in Bangs' room with the door locked, unsupervised. His parents may be a myth.

"There's a lot going on in this movie," I say.

"It's pretty close to the book—the basic plot, I mean; they've toned down the porn angle in the movie—and the sex—and devised a love story."

"You've read the book?"

"I've read all the Chandler novels. They're pretty much like this."

Bangs surprises me. That night he slept over, I woke early in the morning to find him raised up on his elbow watching me.

"Can't you sleep?" I asked.

"Can't you?"

"How did you get here last night?"

"Gabby dropped me off."

"What'd you tell her?"

"That it was an emergency and I'd explain later." He touched my ear with his finger. "You're pretty when you sleep."

"Just when I sleep?"

"You're harder to see when you're awake."

"What?" I said. "What do you mean?"

"I should go." He climbed from the bed, and knelt to scour for his shoes.

"How are you going to get home?"

"Skate," he said.

"Skate? It must be miles."

He shrugged. "It's all flat."

"Should I walk you out or something?"

"No," he said, and pressed me backward into the warm bed. "You should sleep."

"It's freezing, and dark. You can't skate home like this."

He kissed me and I stopped protesting.

"Less traffic," he said. And then he slipped through the door, and I didn't hear so much as a creak of the stairs.

In Bangs' room, the artwork makes me feel like I'm inside a comic book. I'd kind of like to put on gloves and box with Alice; the Cheshire Cat, in his snappy little black bowtie, separating us, his arms stretched wide in warning.

A third spray of bullets through a door, and another guy drops without visible injury. "They're all a bunch of racketeers," I say.

Bangs nods, his face beaming.

"OK," he says, after he ejects *The Big Sleep*. "Another Bogart, or another Chandler?"

"Which do you want?"

"I've seen both these films."

"Which is better?"

"Well." He bites his thumb, considering. "*To Have and Have Not* is romanticized, and *Double Indemnity* is heartless betrayal, so they're pretty different. I wouldn't call them gangster films, they're really noirs."

"Oh, noirs." I smile at him. "By romanticized, do you mean cheesy, or romantic?"

"Both."

"All right, the romantic, cheesy one, then."

He puts *To Have and Have Not* on, and offers to give me a backrub. Bogart is a genius antihero; it probably helps that he's unlikely and compromised—an ex-believer—and that the girls are always more fucked up than he is.

Bangs unlatches my bra, and massages down from my tight shoulders to the knot in my hip. "Jesus," he says. "Stress much?"

"*You just put your lips together and blow!*" I repeat. "My god, I can't believe they let her say that. Censorship was really shoddy in the forties."

"She's talking about whistling."

"Sure she is."

He laughs. "You're tight everywhere," he says.

I hope he means my back. You see it coming, this movie, and you still don't mind.

♫ ♫ ♫

When I get home later that evening, the lights are off through the house. "Hello?" I call.

"Hello."

I follow the voice and find Nate standing in the kitchen in the dark.

"What are you doing?" I ask.

"Nothing," he says.

"Why are the lights off?"

"I just got back."

"Where is everybody?"

"I just got back," he says again.

"Are you OK?" He doesn't say anything. There's something wrong. Besides the lights, and his voice—the vacancy of it—even his posture feels wrong. "Nate?" I ask. "What happened?"

"I don't know. I don't know what happened. She just started crying. She wouldn't stop, and it was that deep sobbing like with little kids, you know? I was afraid she'd choke. Maybe I hurt her." He turns to me. "Do you think I hurt her? She wouldn't say. She just kept sobbing."

"I don't know," I say. Even though my coat's still on, I shiver.

"Cole," he says. "I think maybe I hurt her."

How? I want to ask. How did you hurt her? And then, I say the only thing I can think to say, "Do you want a burger? We could go to Wendy's or whatever."

"We should leave a note," he says. When he flips the light switch, both of us flinch. His bloodshot eyes give him a deranged look. Neither of his shoes is tied.

We order from the drive-through, and eat in the parking lot, our fries spread between us as though we're sharing.

"If you tell any of this," Nate says, "to anybody—"

"I won't," I promise. When did he get so harried and suspicious?

His profile is as much of him as I see. In his Toyota hatchback, the grey roof cover sags in three sad bubbles. The heat blasts our feet, and one of the tapes I made him for Christmas plays Jane's Addiction.

"We've come really close a bunch of times," he says. "I mean really close." He eats two fistfuls of fries.

Behind us, a dude unlocks the dumpster, tosses four large black bags in, and slams the lid before locking it again. Now the dude moves around sweeping the parking lot. He doesn't even have a coat on.

"Tonight," Nate says, "her mom went to the city, and we had the house to ourselves."

I want to touch the tear in Nate's letterman jacket. I want to

170

console him. How do you console somebody? Meghan does it just by listening, with the intensity of her attention. Bangs does it with gestures: with a touch of his hand on your face, or a Charms Pop.

Nate looks at me. He stares into my face like we're strangers. "We did it." I won't look away from him—I can't look away. I have to see and hear whatever he tells me. "We did it, and I laughed. Not at her or anything. I laughed because it was all so big. This huge amazing thing. I kissed her, and said something—I don't even remember what—something stupid. And then she rolled away from me and burst out crying." His voice shatters. He swallows several times, and clears his throat. "She wouldn't even look at me."

Nate. If anyone else were here, that person would know what to say. If it were Meghan or Bangs or my father, any of them would know.

"Do you think," Nate says, "do you think I hurt her?"

"I don't know." I whisper this to him.

"What should I do?" he asks. "Maybe I shouldn't have left. I wrapped her in the comforter, and patted her back for a while, but she just kept crying."

My favorite Nate story? The summer before fifth grade, in Washington, I rode my dirt bike down a hill without using my hands. I'd done it a million times. This time the front tire caught in the road and pitched me down the hill. I skidded on both elbows, and the bike landed on top of me.

Nigel had been riding beside me, and he jumped off and started screaming about how I'd been killed. A neighbor ran over and straightened the handlebars on my bike. She asked if she should call my mom.

I shook my head and began to push my bike home. Nigel circled around me, freaking out. I told him to ride and get Nate.

"Nate?" he asked.

"Yes," I said. "Go get Nate."

"Where is he?" Nigel asked.

"At the field," I said. "They're playing football."

Nigel sped away. My elbows had gravel lodged deep in the skin, my cheek burned, and both knees bled. I'd ripped my bike seat, and the grip on the handlebars.

I'd limped three blocks, to a house with a rock garden, and one of those cool sundials, when Nate came racing back on Nigel's bike, with Nigel mounted on the handlebars. They skidded to a stop, and Nigel launched forward.

"You crashed?" Nate said, laying my bike down and examining me. I nodded, tears down my face. "These burn, don't they?" he asked. "Come on. You sit, and I'll pedal."

He biked me home, Nigel racing ahead. Our parents weren't home. Nate had me sit on the toilet seat, and cleaned the cuts with peroxide. The whole time, he kept telling me how spectacular the crash must have been. How Nigel thought I'd broken my neck. How Evil Knievel had nothing on me.

In the entryway upstairs, we heard the door, and then Nigel yelling at my folks. "She could have died," he told them. "And you weren't even home."

They came into the bathroom, and checked my injuries. Nate vanished before I could thank him. He'd left in the middle of the football game, and had promised the other kids he'd be right back.

Winter in Jersey, the fries gone cold, this brother asking about unfathomable injuries.

"Maybe I should call Kelly," I say. "Check if she's alright."

"Would you?" he asks.

"Sure," I say. "I'll call the second we get home."

He crushes the trash and leaps from the car to throw it away. On the drive home, I try to imagine how this phone call will go. Hey, Kelly, just calling to see how you're handling the whole post-coital thing. Hi Kelly, any chance you've quit crying?

♫ ♫ ♫

On the third ring, someone picks up, but doesn't speak.

"Kelly?" I ask.

Nothing.

"Kelly? It's Cole."

"Hey," she says.

"Hey." This is as far as I've thought this through. I'll say hey, and see how it goes.

"Hey," she says again.

"So I'm calling," I say, for a damage report, "to say that I've missed talking to you. All this mad stuff has happened, and, you know, I used to talk to you about it. And now I don't." Oh my god.

She doesn't say anything. I am stupid. Why am I always so stupid?

"Well," I say.

"You're with Bangs now?" she asks.

"Yes. Not this minute, but yes, in general. I'm with him."

"How is that?"

"Oh," I say. I have no idea. I don't understand Bangs any more than I understand the others. Less maybe. "He's surprising."

"Yeah?"

"I thought he'd be an anarchist."

"Right," she says. "His backpack."

"But he's really sweet."

"Did Nate tell you?" she asks.

"He said you were upset."

"Upset." She says this wonderingly. "I cried like an orphan."

My room feels arctic after Bangs' room, and the heat-blasted hatchback. Nate didn't try to wheedle his way up here. He just asked me to find him after I'd spoken to Kelly.

I want to ask if it hurt. Did she cry because it hurt?

"Was he worried?" Kelly asks.

"Yes. He thought maybe he'd hurt you."

"No," Kelly says. "He didn't."

"Should I tell him?"

"Yes."

"Should I tell him anything else?"

"I'm sorry," she says. "I've missed you too. Tell him to call me. Will you do that?"

"Yes," I say.

"I'll see you in homeroom." She hangs up.

♫ ♫ ♫

After I tell Nate, I stand in front of the open refrigerator, trying to decide. Why now? Why should I want Jeremy now? I have this urge to run over to his room, to scratch at the door like a cat begging to be let back in.

Somebody ate all the chocolate pudding, and the swirled, and left only the vanilla. The people in this house upset me.

"Hello, Cole," Dad says.

"Hello," I say.

"I haven't seen much of you lately. How's everything?"

"We don't have any chocolate pudding."

He peers over my shoulder. "There's vanilla."

"Yeah." I close the door. Then open it again, and grab a yogurt.

"Do you feel like a walk?" he asks.

Pepper barks once, and runs to the door. She stares at it, knowing the walk is on the other side, that it's close.

We don't see anyone outdoors. Not a car on the road. Eleven, on a Sunday night, and I can't bring myself to look at Jeremy's window. Does he wonder? Does he wonder if he hurt me? Does he worry about me at all?

"How's the band?" Dad asks.

"Busy," I say. "We play all the time." The cold swirls around us: we're wrapped in it. The evergreens loom.

"And that's good?"

"Usually." I've been wondering about soccer. Will I be able to play soccer in the spring? Could I be on the varsity team, and still play with the band? There was a time, I'm pretty sure, when things seemed simpler. Maybe all that really means is that I used to have fewer options. "Are you unhappy—in Jersey—are you unhappy here?"

We stand together a moment while Pepper pees, and Dad stares at something I can't see. "I'm ready to do something different," he says. "I'd like to have a church again."

174

"Next assignment, right?"

"Yes," he says. "Next assignment."

"A church in Alaska—an igloo with a steeple."

"They might have a couple of buildings on the base. What about you? Will you miss this place: traffic and honking horns, the tolls and sarcasm, the tireless East Coast ambition?"

God, yes. I grew up here. These, these are my formative years. "Some of it."

"The band?"

"Sure," I say. Dad grew up in Spokane, Washington. His whole life, he went to school with most of the same kids, had the same neighbors. In college he joined a fraternity. He didn't find Jesus until he was in his twenties. Before that, he was a regular guy.

I wonder about that: Dad's conversion. I never got to be converted. I had Jesus from the start.

"It's good to see you and Nate talking again," Dad says.

He can't let anything go. Pepper tries for a squirrel. Dad leans back, steers her away. If I could have anything I wanted, what would I choose? To stay here in Jersey? Another chance with Jeremy? Sundays with Meghan? What do I want?

The only constellation I've ever been able to recognize is the Big Dipper. Or maybe the little one, what's the difference, after all? Tonight the stars seem farther away than usual, but I can see one of the dippers overhead. If I were better at Geometry, I could reckon my position with the stars, or maybe that's Trig.

"Will we go to war?" I ask.

"Yes."

"Any day now?"

"Yes."

"I hope my soldier lives."

Dad pats Pepper's head. I think he's praying. Will it be like World War II, or like Vietnam? What kind of war will this be? Which side will be virtuous?

"Will we bomb schools?" I ask.

"Not on purpose."

"But kids will die."

175

"Yes."

"Don't you ever worry," I say, "that it's wrong?"

"The wrong decision?" Dad asks.

"No. That it's wrong—war."

"Of course."

"Would you go—even if it were wrong?"

"Yes."

"Would you fight?"

"I'd probably be assigned to a unit. Be with them. Minister to them."

Jesus saves. Jesus saves unless you happen to be in the way of a two-ton bomb, or a sniper, or a hand grenade. I imagine, sometimes, that I answer the door, and it's my atheist dressed in a leather jacket and blue jeans, with sunglasses pushed up into his buzz cut, and a motorcycle helmet tucked under his arm. On leave States side, and he's come to visit me. To take the drive he wrote about. If Dad were assigned to the atheist's unit, would I worry more, or less?

Dad loves Walt Whitman. He reads me poems sometimes. He loves that vigil for a dead soldier poem best. He says that poem expresses what it's like to be a chaplain, the constant vigil over the dead and the dying. And the living, I always think. They need your vigilance too. They need your watchfulness and your attention. If I were in a field somewhere, my soul escaping, could I tell him? Could I confess to my father at last?

I have doubts. I have so many doubts. A plague of them. The old stories don't make a lot of sense, if you think about them. What was the snake doing in Eden? Didn't God know the snake was there? What the hell did anyone need a tree of everlasting life for—isn't God immortal? Does he need to eat fruit to be immortal? If God so loved us, then why does he punish without mercy? Why did John the Baptist end up with his head on a platter? Service to God is not incentive enough, really. Service to God rarely ends well. If you read Revelation—I mean, you know, study it—well, it's fucking terrifying. Eternal torment, not so much, but the alternative doesn't appeal to me either. I mean, who lets his own kid get crucified? God runs kind of hot and cold for my taste, you know, if I'm being honest.

"It's a beautiful night," Dad says. "Even if we're in Jersey."

"Beats the desert," I say.

Dad nods. I hope he's praying. I hope he's praying for all of us.

Exculpate. Free from blame; vindicate. Verb. This reminds me of amnesty. I have a funny story about amnesty. If I ever see you again, I'll be sure to tell you.

During freshman year, the guidance counselors met with each of us twice, and gave presentations at orientation and school assemblies, and beat it into us that we should letter in at least two sports, join multiple clubs, and run for student council, in addition to volunteering for community organizations. And because we have nothing but time, study for our SATs between coursework for our eight classes.

Of course, we believed them. Freshman year, I joined the Spanish Club, SADD, the Ski Club, and Amnesty International. I don't know what I thought Amnesty International did, but I remember being really surprised by that first meeting. I'd just joined because I liked their stickers. Clubs used to meet after school at 3:30, but, in an effort to be more athletics friendly, this year most clubs began meeting at lunchtime.

Alicia and I joined Amnesty together, but she isn't in the classroom when I arrive. We're supposed to write letters, or something, today. I think everybody in this club expects to be a lawyer, and bring reforms on the scale of Martin Luther.

"Cole," the head girl says—I can't remember her name—Sharon?—she has crazy bushy hair and the beginnings of a mustache. "Do you want to stuff envelopes?"

"Sure," I say. "I love stuffing envelopes." All the earnest kids stare at me. From the row of desks by the windows, Monica Prader waves at me. "Load me up."

The head girl reads to us from the Amnesty International Newsletter. It's all horrible—most of the reports so vague as to be especially terrifying. How is this happening while we're sitting here stuffing envelopes?

Monica seems to be doing homework.

"What is that?" I ask, indicating her notebook.

"Chemistry."

It never occurred to me to refuse to stuff envelopes. "What is this letter?" I ask, without bothering to open and read it.

"A vital political cause." She reaches across and pats my shoulder. "We're in the business of freedom here at Amnesty International."

"You don't know either, do you?"

Her laugh is sudden, and, judging from the reaction of the other kids in the room, highly inappropriate. "You're a trip," Monica Prader tells me.

While the head girl carries on reading, I skim the letter. "It's pro-war," I say.

"An increasingly inevitable position," says the reputed genius.

"Do you believe that?"

"Read the paper. Watch the news. The whole thing'll start any minute." She shrugs. "That's how it is."

The reality, she means. The inevitable reality. I still think of wars as trenches and tanks and those Poles racing across the field on their horses. And jungles. I think of jungles too.

I can't imagine a war in the desert: the soldiers in their light fatigues, the humvees, the air campaign. I keep thinking of David with his slingshot, and guys riding on camels. Will my atheist have to shoot someone? Will he think, as he pulls the trigger, of his friend's eye? Will he hesitate? Will he live?

As we leave the classroom, I slam into Jeremy. My books crash to the floor, and I stumble backward into the door.

"Sorry," he says, bending to pick up my texts. "I didn't see you."

I stand there, watching him collect my stuff. The kids behind me step around us. Monica Prader winks at me.

"Sorry," he says again, and hands my books to me. He starts to dash away, but turns and says, "You alright?"

I can't think of anything—not a single thing—to say.

♫ ♫ ♫

My mother hands me a stack of plates. "Set for six," she says.

I set the table, noticing the new unlit candles in the holders, the bouquet of yellow flowers, and figure Kelly for our sixth. She and Nate are inseparable again. This morning, on the walk from homeroom to Graphic Arts, Kelly updated me about the new clothes her mother brought back from New York, and even spun so I could admire her pink silk shirt. Meanwhile, Stacy and I no longer ride the bus. Doug at his worst cannot diminish the bright side of carpooling with Nate: 45 extra minutes in the morning, and strolling into school just as the bell rings.

"What are we having?" I ask Mom.

"It's a surprise," she says.

I look around the kitchen—nothing in or on the stove. I check the fridge, pretty barren. "No, for real," I say. "What are we having?"

"Pizza?" Nigel asks from the living room.

"Nope," Mom says.

"Subs?" I ask.

"It's a surprise," she repeats.

"How soon do we get this surprise?"

"That's a surprise too," she says.

"Man," Nigel says, "the endless adventure!"

"I have to babysit at seven," I say.

"We'll eat before seven," Mom assures me.

"What will we eat?"

"Go away," she says.

Dad brings home takeout from Little Szechuan. If God eats, I swear to you, he devours nothing but Little Szechuan. The sweet and sour pork, the noodles, the crisp vegetables, the tang and bite! We're all so happy and surprised, that we don't register Meghan at first.

"You're back," Nigel yells, scrambling up from his chair to throw his arms around her.

Blushing, dressed in cords and a sea-foam wool sweater, she looks thinner, older somehow. For the first few minutes, as we gather at the table, pray, and then load our plates, I'm unaccountably furious. I'm so mad that I can't speak; I haven't even welcomed her home. In fact, as I think the word *home*, I get madder still.

I can't explain it. I don't know why I'm angry, or how to stop being angry, but I understand if I don't say something posthaste, my parents will make remarks, and ask questions, and demand answers. Before I can think of anything, Nate asks about her vacation.

She tells us about Christmas with the folks in Georgia; sounds like a lot of sleeping in and eating out to me. "I'm sorry I didn't get a chance to wish anyone Merry Christmas," she says. "If it helps at all, I've brought back tins of my mother's almond roca and gingerbread cookies."

"You're forgiven," Nate says.

The food tastes different, soggy, or something.

"How have you been, Cole?" Meghan asks.

"Good," I say, nodding. The nodding sells it. Beneath the table, Pepper whines. Nate has been slipping her all of his broccoli.

"How's Doggy Life?" Meghan asks.

"We're super-busy. Gigs every place."

"I can't wait to hear you," Meghan says.

I wish aliens would extract me right from the table. A tractor beam, isn't that what it's called? I need a tractor beam to slice through the ceiling, and spotlight the candles and the yellow flowers and the sad remnants of my favorite food, and lift me the fuck out of here.

"Cole's in love with Christian now," Nigel tells everyone.

I stare at him. I feel the whole room shift.

"Christian Sorrentino?" my mother asks.

If I broke my plate over Nigel's head, what would happen? Grounding? Two weeks without phone privileges? How high would the fine be? "Why are you wearing pajamas?" I ask him. "It's like 6 o'clock."

"No," Nigel tells my mother. "The other Christian."

"The boy with the haircut?" Mom asks.

"Yeah," Nigel says. "That one."

"Dude," Nate tells him, "share your own news."

"I think I'm done," I say, standing with my plate. "I have a ton of homework." I glance at Meghan and add, "I already finished the vocab list you sent." The statement comes out rougher than I intended—a challenge almost.

♫ ♫ ♫

Annie and I build approximate cars with Play-Doh. Happily, Karen crushes them with her little fists almost the moment the cars are formed.

"Make a cat," Annie says. And then, a bit later, "Not a cow. Make a cat."

"This is a cat."

"No. It isn't."

"What's wrong with it?" I ask.

"It's a cow."

I turn the blue creature around in my hands. "It isn't."

"The ears," she tells me.

Karen smashes the green and blue and red together, and hands the lump to me. "House," she says.

"No," Annie says. "A cat."

I try again. Annie stands on her chair to observe the sculpting process. "Good," she says when I hand the cat to her. "Now a house."

I sit on the floor next to Annie's bed while I read stories. Karen plays with my earrings.

"The peach one," Annie tells me.

I read *Each Peach Pear Plum* three times. They sleep with the hall light on, and the door thrown open. I get extra kisses before I leave them.

On the Thorns' couch, both cats tucked against me, I flip through my Biology text, and try to remember which questions we're supposed to answer. Odds? I could call Bangs. *Cole's in love with Christian now.* I object to practically every word in Nigel's construction. I'm not in love. I'm not in love with Christian. And *now? Now* is the worst. Now makes me sound slutty.

Meghan comes back and we get Little Szechuan for dinner. That should be ideal, right? Hours later and I still don't know if I'm angry with her for leaving, or for coming back. She sat there asking about the band as though she were interested, as though it were important to her. I don't believe her. I don't believe her anymore.

I answer all the Biology questions, and then read about congruent and symmetrical shapes in Geometry. This all sounds familiar. Sometimes I think I'm having math flashbacks. Being a military kid is like doing a slow Houdini: an escape over two or three years. Why can't I be unaffected? Why can't I slam into Jeremy and collect his shit and walk off again? No big. Why can't I screw someone, and then vanish, and then come back and chat about whatever? Why does any of this get to me?

Overhead wants us to discuss the difference between hero and protagonist. Specifically, we're supposed to discuss the difference as evidenced by the short story, *The Most Dangerous Game*.

"Deep thoughts," Alicia whispered to me while Overhead wrote our assignment on the board.

Halfway through the essay, I call Bangs. "What are you doing?" I ask.

"Changing guitar strings. What about you, are you home already?"

"Not yet."

"Did you finish Bio?"

"Yeah, you want the answers?" After he takes them down, I ask, "Are you the protagonist or the hero?"

"In this story? I'm the sidekick."

"Whose?"

"Yours," he says.

"You're my sidekick?" Should I be insulted? Isn't he the romantic interest? "How do you figure you're my sidekick?"

"Hey, you're the narrator. What are you asking me for?"

"I'm the narrator?"

"Yes," he says, "and you're unreliable."

I think about this, and then ask, "Are you mad at me?"

"No."

"Do you mean the story of this conversation, or the ongoing story of us—our acquaintance or whatever?"

"I mean all of it. The whole thing."

The ginger cat's tail flicks against my leg. The cats hide until the kids go to bed, and then they emerge to lay claim to me. I'd expected Bangs to say he was the antihero. "If I'm the narrator," I say, "who's the writer?"

"An old lady sitting at a desk in the garret. She writes with a fountain pen."

I see her. Hunched over a stack of parchment, her fingers black where she has had to blot the ink. She looks feeble. "She lives on apples," I say.

"And a tiny bit of bread and cheese."

"Meager."

"Yes, a meager bit of bread and cheese."

But I don't want to play anymore. Some impoverished old woman writing any of this horrifies me. "I should go," I say. "I still have to finish my essay."

I employ the five-paragraph essay and write three pages, including an apposite point about antagonist and villain, a sort of cherry on the sundae of my argument, and one sure to irritate my teacher. Overhead hates to be given a bigger answer than she asked for.

On my walk home, the recorded bugle plays Taps. Eleven o'-clock. I'm surprised to find the kitchen light on when I arrive home. Dad, in his whitey tighties and t-shirt, stands beside the fridge, talking on the phone. His hand covers his mouth, and his shoulders draw up as he shakes his head at me. "No, sir," he tells the phone. And a moment later, "I understand. Absolutely. Yes, sir. We'll write a memo first thing in the morning, and inform all the students. Yes, General. Good night, sir."

Before he replaces the phone in the cradle, he covers his mouth again. You can see the little boy Dad was: the naughty doorbell-ditch kid who terrorized the neighbors up and down 17th Avenue in Spokane. He snickers on and on.

"What happened?" I say, laughing along with him.

"You know General Trent's wife?" Dad asks.

"The big one with the hats?"

184

Dad nods, his eyes rimmed with tears. "She drove through the gate today, and didn't present her ID card to the sentry."

General Trent's wife has been trouble before. When they first arrived, she made a stink about other cars parking in the General's spot at the commissary. When Dad told Mom, she said, "A little walk wouldn't kill her."

"She just drove right through?" I ask.

"Yes."

"What did the guards do?"

"They dropped the gate," Dad says. "And pulled their weapons."

"They dropped the gate?" I see the gate landing squarely on the hood of the General's Cadillac.

Dad, gasping now, nods again. "She crashed right into it. The sentries approached with their pistols drawn, and ordered her out of the car."

"Did they shoot her?" I ask in a small voice.

"No," Dad says, "but they cuffed her, and called their supervisor."

These poor guys are so going to be shipped to Saudi Arabia. "Then what?" I ask.

"Well, an alert went out, and a dozen MPs swarmed the gate, and they had her in the back of one of the cars when Colonel Reid drove up to the gate and asked what had happened. He cleared the whole thing up in minutes, but the General's wife is not a forgiving woman."

"No," I say, and feel a great deal of pity for the military police.

"The sentries are on high alert—under the Provost's orders— but even if they weren't, she should have stopped and presented her ID."

"I'll bet she will next time. Was that the General on the phone?"

"I'm to draft a memo to all military personnel and their families: anyone entering this base will stop at the gate and present an ID card. No exceptions will be made. Not even for wives."

"He didn't say the thing about wives."

"He did," Dad says.

"Gosh," I say. "Now I kinda feel sorry for the General's wife."

♫ ♫ ♫

Several knocks on my door wake me.

"What?" I mutter.

"Let me in."

I peer at the clock, and then climb from the bed. "It's 6:15," I tell Nigel. He wears the hat with earflaps Meghan gave him for Christmas.

"Come for a run."

"Are you insane?"

From the hook in the bathroom, he grabs my sweats, and tosses them to me. "We'll just do four miles."

Not until I'm brushing my teeth do I remember how much I hate Nigel.

As we're stretching in the front yard, I ask, "What was all that about last night?"

"All what?"

"At dinner."

"Oh," he says. "I'm sorry about that. I didn't know it was a secret—you and Christian."

"It's not a secret."

"Then what are you mad about?"

"I'm mad that you told a table full of people that I'm in love with Christian. When I'm not."

"Fine, dating him, whatever."

"No," I say. "We're not dating. We're not anything. We're just—" sidekicks, my mind interjects. "We hang out." Nigel bends to touch the top of his socks. "Since when do you editorialize?" I ask him.

"I said I was sorry," he murmurs.

We lap the parade ground, neither of us speaking. I love morning runs. Occasionally, a car passes with its lights glancing off us. We're breathing sharp air, each inhalation a prick to the lungs. By the end, I know he's holding back.

"Oh god," I say, pinching the stitch in my side.

Nigel bounces beside me. "I'll make oatmeal," he says. As we walk back to the house, he asks, "So you're really not dating Christian?"

"No."

"I thought you two were dating."

"We're not."

"Well, I thought you were."

He looks upset—his posture and tone defensive. "You told Jeremy," I say.

"Yes."

"Did he ask about me?"

"Yes."

"What did he ask?"

"He asked if you were seeing anyone, and I said you were dating Christian."

"What did he say?"

"He said he figured."

"That's all he said? He figured?"

Nigel hesitates.

"Tell me," I say.

"He said he figured, a girl like you."

A girl like me. I am so over Jersey.

Viscous. Seriously? This is a word people use in public?

Diofelli gives us a handout explaining the positions and rules for indoor soccer. "Today," she says, "we'll work on dribbling and passing."

We stand in lines to dribble, one by one, through orange cones. Our passing drills, also choreographed to orange cones, involve all the other kids passing the ball to me, after which I lead a pass back to them, and they shoot on an empty goal. Still (bright side!), we could be doing gymnastics routines.

Diofelli blows her whistle, and hollers, "Fifteen minutes to scrimmage."

It's a relief to run. Sonja, a tall black girl with a weave and glorious red fingernails, tells me to play sweeper. She and I take the ball up and score in three passes. On the opposite team, Jeremy plays halfback. I take the ball from him, and Sonja passes to Tom Richardson, who shoots wide.

I feel a wild thrill. I push myself, play as though this means something. Pass to the girl in the giant glasses, and watch, astonished, as she kicks the ball across the gym to Tom Richardson, who's open and scores. We're magic—all of us—enchanted during this scrimmage with focus and delight and killer passes.

We have an early set tonight—early for us. We're playing at a teen club called Stoked that wants us from 8 to 10. "They're afraid they'll have crowd control problems if we play the second set," Trevor told us.

"What's this club like?" I asked.

"You've never been *Stroked?*" Trevor asked.

"Don't you ever get tired?" I said.

"A little—after the first couple of hours."

I laughed and punched him.

"We'll hang out after our set," Trevor said, "and party."

Nigel and Nate and Kelly have all agreed to come. I'm excited about the show. For the first time in weeks, I can't wait to play. A couple of nights ago, Dad and I were talking about improvisation in music, and he took out one of his old jazz albums—*Time Out*—and played it for me. The Dave Brubeck Quartet has changed everything, especially the way I think about tempo. Tempo might be fluid. Melody might be experimental. They might vary to reflect urgency or seriousness or comedy. Just because Doggy Life has found a great way to play music, doesn't mean we can't seek an even better way, or at least a newer one.

I've been playing my songs differently every time I sit down with my guitar. Adding strums, or breaking a song on the bridge to let the words air a little, or pumping a stop into the crescendo; and when I talked to Ernie about it, he said rather than practice the variations, we should watch me for changes, and let the music happen.

I can't wait to let the music happen. And the school day, rather than tormenting me, has sped by. Mrs. Brooks gives us a pop quiz in History, and then lectures some more on Peter the Great, and none of us can get our minds around such a Russia. *Czar* really is the coolest title ever.

Do you ever have a day when you marvel at your health, at the way your arms feel when you pull books from your locker, at the glow on a boy's face when you walk past him and glance back, and for a moment, he loves you? Do you ever feel as though your clothes fit you differently, and better, that your body has changed somehow without your even noticing? A day when everything reminds you: I'm alive!

In Biology, Bangs hands me a pencil drawing of a girl in knee-high boots, with flaring finned gloves, and hips, and huge soulful eyes. She appears to be riding an electric guitar like an airborne skateboard. Her hair tufts.

"Cool," I say, imagining her superpower is high soprano notes that incinerate buildings.

"Now you see why I don't mind being her sidekick," he tells me.

"This is supposed to be me?"

"That's you."

I look harder at his drawing. She doesn't look a thing like me. I could never pull off those boots.

"What's her power?" I ask.

"She has several."

I wait, but he doesn't say more. What am I supposed to do with this?

Later, on stage, I tell the crowd of teens in their Benetton shirts to sing along, and then we roar into *London Calling*, and I realize who Bangs drew: Gig Girl. My guitar on my hip, my outfit completely outside my comfort zone, but accurate—spot on for this delivery. I feast on the songs; the ragged stroke of my guitar feeds an airy wildness into Ernie's solos as Joe bounds around, and finally climbs a speaker, tears away his shirt, and thunders at the crowd. I hear Trevor scream, "Yeah" into the mic, and I am airborne.

At the end, I sing our crowd a lullaby; the band shining with sweat and vibrancy, hardly moving on the stage, the music hushing around us like new snow as my voice rasps: *I've fallen out of love. I've fallen out of time. I miss the days. I miss the days. I've fallen out of love. I've fallen out of time. I miss the days when you were mine.*

"Where the fuck," Trevor asks me backstage, "did that come from?"

As my alter ego, I've slipped my sweatshirt back on, and put my guitar in its case after wiping the strings, and am mild again. "What?" I ask.

"You. Out there. Where did that come from?"

"I've been listening to jazz."

He stares at me a second, and then laughs. For the first time in living memory, Trevor wears a button-down shirt. One of those weird snapping cowboy shirts—I don't know if he means to be ironic.

"You," he tells me, "are one far-out chick." We finish loading the van with our gear; the boys smoke out, and then we return to the club. Tucked around the bar: stools, and high tables with more stools, and on the far side, a bouncer guards a flight of stairs, which leads to a small, roped section for the consumption of alcoholic beverages. Anyone with alcohol can watch the stage from the balcony. The interior of the club is painted a burnt orange, and has sweeping arches on the ceiling that remind me of flying buttresses.

Kelly, Nigel, Nate, and Bangs have the table nearest the bar, and a partially obstructed view of the dance floor.

"What are you drinking?" I ask Kelly.

"Coke," she says. She stands, "Let me buy you a drink."

"Shirley Temple."

"We should dance," Trevor tells us.

"Dude," Bangs says, "we're resting. You wore us out."

Trevor turns to me. "How 'bout it?"

"I can't dance."

He takes my hand, and leads me between groups of hopping kids at the outskirts of the dance floor, then deep into the heated center. This isn't dancing. We're thrashing and pushing and trying not to be crushed. House music blares *Gonna Make You Sweat (Everybody Dance Now)* as Trevor, with one hand on my waist, guides me through the chaos. The dude towers above most of the kids here, and seems incongruous with his lanky hair, his snapping shirt, and his huge laugh.

As I decide the house music sucks, they play *Just Like Heaven.* Suddenly, Joe and Ernie appear, and we're all four bobbing with drunken grins. The first time I listened to The Cure's *Kiss Me Kiss Me Kiss Me* was basketball camp in seventh grade. Between sessions, I lay alone in my dorm room, playing the tape over and over. It felt like consciousness, as though I'd discovered myself in the music, as though the album were written for me in particular, alone in all the world.

The next band plays a bunch of radio songs, but they aren't terrible, and occasionally we dance. (Even to Bon Jovi's *Wanted Dead or Alive,* which is a song I secretly love.) I realize, swigging my third Shirley Temple, this has been the perfect evening to cap a perfect day.

And then, good Jersey boys, the band on stage plays Bruce

Springsteen's *Dancing in the Dark*. And we do. We dance in the dark until we cannot breathe.

♫ ♫ ♫

"Do I know anything about jazz?" Leroy repeats. Behind him, the radiator clatters and kicks itself awake. This morning, we're the only two people in this long, decrepit room. "You kidding me?"

"Well," I say, flushing, "I didn't want to assume."

"'Course not," he laughs. When Leroy laughs, he pulls his legs up, and shakes his shoulders, and kind of hunches over his right arm as though he's trying to catch the sound in his hand. "Kid, I know all kinds of things about jazz."

"I've been listening to Dave Brubeck, and I think I understand something new—about tempo and how it relates to tone."

"How tempo relates to tone," he says, cocking his head inquisitively.

"Performance—being on stage—the way I deliver the songs is up to my interpretation, right? I can make them new each time. You know what I mean? Like maybe the line just occurred to me. I can make the songs feel spontaneous just by the way I manipulate the lyrics, and the stutter of the rhythm, and whether or not I slow the whole thing down, or rush along to the chorus."

"Show me."

I play him the first verse of a tragic ballad, and then, for the second verse, pluck the strings playfully and clip the lines, and suddenly the song's comic, the lyric subversive.

"Dave Brubeck taught you that?" he asks.

"Yes."

"Next week, I'll bring you a couple tapes. Change everything you know every time you listen to 'em." He gestures toward my guitar. "You write that one?"

I nod.

"Play it again—all the way through with the plucking. Jazz never was an excuse for sloppy downbeats."

192

We do scales, and he plays me some Hendrix and talks to me about melody.

"The thing about tempo," I say. "Have I got it wrong?"

"Not even a little. If the song sounds the same each time you play it, you're not trying."

"You won't forget about the tapes? Next week?"

"I won't forget." He stands, and puts his suit coat back on, smoothes his hand over his tie, slides on his cap. "Who gave you this Brubeck?"

"My dad has tons of old jazz albums."

"Check for Ella Fitzgerald. That woman singing *Summertime* will kill you."

♫ ♫ ♫

After church on Sunday, I head upstairs for a bath, and another go at *Tess of the D'Urbervilles*. I don't know how to break it to you, but Thomas Hardy hates all of us.

Maybe, after all these Sundays, I'm out of practice. Maybe Thomas Hardy does something devastating and irreversible to my brain. When the knocking starts, and persists—though I holler that I'm in the bath—and I'm forced to climb from the tub, dripping across the tiny tile, and the brown carpet, right up to the metal door, even then, I don't expect Meghan.

She looks at me in my towel. "We have our vocab list," she says, and holds up her notebook.

"Right," I say. I leave the door open, and stalk back into the bathroom. Scalded pink, but marginally dry, I scramble into pajamas, and hurl my towel at the draining tub. She's standing at the foot of the bed, looking around. Nothing has changed, except the piles of albums on the chairs, and the record player on the desk.

"You're listening to jazz," she observes.

"Not right this minute," I say, before I can stop myself. If I were Kelly, I'd have snide skills. I'd nail disdain into every word, and the meanness wouldn't ricochet; I'd never be wounded.

Meghan hasn't moved, but agrees, softly, "No, not this minute."

I sit cross-legged on the floor, and open my notebook. Pen uncapped, and dutifully perched above my completed list, my expression wiped away, I look up at her, waiting. Her face is chapped. Her sweater, a cabled blue grey, as intricate as a web, falls at her hip.

"Don't you want to do the list anymore?" she asks.

"I never wanted to do these lists. This was your idea, remember?"

"I'm sorry I hurt you."

"You didn't."

"Cole." She crouches down, and puts her hand out, the way you would in a petting zoo to a goat.

"Don't. Don't you dare."

"Cole, I panicked. I started thinking about everything—about what your family would say, and what the Army would do—you're sixteen, you're just a kid. It's wrong to do this to you—to ask this." She drops to her knees, and grabs my arms. Her hair has come loose from her ponytail, and a strand snags in her mouth. "And every time I'm near you I don't care, and I can't think, and you're so angry. I've never seen you so angry."

"You're babbling," I tell her. "You're totally incoherent. And thanks for telling me I'm just a kid. It makes me feel loads better about everything. Thanks for keeping all of this to yourself—I mean, why talk to me? Thanks for leaving. Thanks for vanishing before Christmas and leaving a stupid note. Thanks for coming back a month later and acting like nothing had happened. Thanks for protecting me. What a champ you've been. What a hero."

"Cole."

I hate her for saying my name. I hate her for that most of all. "No, it's too late to be noble and heartfelt. You're the villain. How could you start this and then leave me with all of it?"

"I'm sorry," she says.

"I don't want your apology."

"What do you want?"

A little of everything. I want a little of everything. "Nothing.

I don't want a fucking thing." I smooth my hand over my note-book. The first vocab word is *viscous*. I misread it as *vicious*.

"Look at me," Meghan says. "Cole, please, look at me. I'm sorry. I'm sorry I hurt you. I won't anymore. I swear. I won't hurt you again."

Lies. The villain telling intoxicating lies. But I'm just a kid, and I want to believe.

Fulminate. Verb. To utter or send out with denunciation. To send forth censures or invectives. Hey buddy, go fulminate yourself!

When I get home from school, the war is on television. On a couch in the sunroom, with her basket of receipts, her ledger and checkbook, Mom listens to CNN while she pays the household bills.

"An air campaign?" I say, trying to decipher the image of a trembling hotel.

"The reporters keep changing the name," Mom says. "First it was Operation Desert Shield and then Sword and now Storm. Operation Desert Storm sounds like camping gear."

Vietnam was on television: the war right in your living room. Anyway, that's what my History teachers always tell us. This isn't that at all. We can't really see anything. Terrific booms and shaking structures—scary, of course; but unclear. "Are they using chemical bombs?" I ask.

"Who?"

"The Iraqis."

"Not yet."

In an air campaign, my atheist will be safe a while yet. Ground forces won't be deployed until we have air superiority. (I've been an Army brat for sixteen years. I know some things.) Besides, Saddam would have to be insane to attack Saudi Arabia. "How insane is Saddam, do you think?"

"Off the charts."

"Oh."

Taking off her half-moon librarian glasses in order to see me, Mom asks, "Are you hungry?"

"No."

"You sure? I just bought some apples—they're in the basket."

"I'm sure." Will we have to ration butter and sugar and meat? Have victory gardens in the courtyard? "What will he do, do you think?"

"Saddam? Your father thinks he'll attack Israel."

"What do you think?"

Mom peers at me overtop her glasses. Sometimes I can imagine her as a schoolteacher. Dad says the first time he visited her classroom, he found Mom in the hallway spanking some poor little kid. "I think your father's right."

"And then what? What'll happen after he attacks Israel?"

Mom opens and closes her ledger. "I don't know, honey."

I watch the news for clues, to decipher this. I need a signal. I need them to interview my atheist, and he can pull at his ear, or scratch his nose, give me some sign that it'll be all right.

It's like watching one of the videos of my basketball games that Nigel filmed last year. You just want the camera to be still, so you can get your balance; orientate yourself to your surroundings. You can't really figure out what you're looking at. It's all so amateur: messy and unfocused.

♫ ♫ ♫

I have to write my eulogy for English. I doubt Overhead realized the war would start today when she assigned this, but it wouldn't surprise me. I'd rather write my epitaph. Wouldn't the assignment be more interesting if we had to be brief? I mean, who can't go on and on about herself?

She said we could write it as though we'd died today, or invent a future for ourselves. Pick already: reality or fiction.

Born into a military family, Nicole Alyssa Peters lived a life of variety and adventure. She played guitar in a rock band, and excelled at soccer, field hockey, and basketball. Nicole is survived by her brothers, and her parents, and her beloved dog, Pepper. She has been known to mess around with girls—one anyway— but it doesn't mean anything. Don't worry. Also, she died with an intact hymen, but not for lack of trying.

Today we mourn the loss of Nicole Alyssa Peters, Nobel Laureate, Pulitzer Prize winner, and fabulous philanthropist. A woman devoted to the poor, and to sensible shoes.

Nicole wrote a eulogy, but unfortunately we've misplaced it. We, the bereaved, can assure you that Nicole worded her eulogy eloquently. You would have been quite touched. As it is, we probably won't remember half of her accomplishments, and we certainly must be vague about her feelings, and her character. But we do know she enjoyed her life. We will vouch for that. In her later years, Nicole cheated at cards, and played doubles every morning on a grass court. She took a lot of photographs of tree branches.

On the record player: Ella Fitzgerald sings *Summertime* with Louis Armstrong—turns out Dad had a recording in his collection. At night, I play it over and over, and have come to love the verse Armstrong sings as well. It's a mourning song, isn't it? A sorrowful song. Her voice a string on a balloon, a staircase, a trade wind: *So hush little baby. Don't you cry.* They could play this song at my funeral.

Nicole Alyssa Peters died today. She had so much still to do.

On Friday, I have to debate for women in combat. Timely, huh? Monica Prader promised to meet me in the library during lunch to prep our argument. Maybe in two years I'll get drafted, and meet my atheist on a desert sortie.

For Biology, Bangs is typing up our lab notes—he types faster and more accurately than I do—and this afternoon during commercial breaks, I finished Spanish and Geometry. Now I've only my eulogy to write.

Cole Peters believed in God a good deal of the time. She envied kids playing stickball, or jumping naked into swimming holes. She wished she'd lived in a less formal time—one without electricity. She should never have let Jeremy leave angry.

♫ ♫ ♫

Nate is alone in the kitchen when I go down for a pudding cup.

"What happened to the pudding?" I say, staring into the fridge.

"Have some yogurt."

"There was pudding this afternoon."

"Have yogurt and hot chocolate. That's practically pudding."

"Jeez," I say. I grab a yogurt, and sit down across from him. "I've been writing my eulogy all night."

"What are you doing that for?"

"English."

"That sounds kinda sick to me."

"What would you say," I ask him, "if you had to write one?"

"Billionaire Nathan Parker Peters died today in a fiery explosion. He leaves his fortune to the charitable organizations he founded, and also, relief in Africa. Nathan Parker Peters will be remembered as a man of singular vision and vast accomplishment. His wife, the former supermodel Christy Turlington, is in mourning, and asks the press to respect her privacy. Also, she encourages mourners to make donations to one of her husband's many philanthropic interests. *We must find some way to carry on his vital work without him,* Turlington wrote. Flags around the world will be flown at half-mast."

"A fiery explosion?" I ask.

"It could happen."

"It's a little more likely than you marrying Christy Turlington."

"You always underestimate my charm." He stands and stretches. In the last month, Nate has finally grown taller than Dad. He made a big ceremony of penciling their heights on the back of the kitchen door. "You want me to make hot chocolate?" he asks.

"Sure. How about you? What are you doing up this late?"

"Chemistry." He stretches again. "I gotta start running with Nigel. Soccer trials start in March. Kelly keeps asking me if you're gonna play."

"I don't know yet."

"You're totally gonna play. I call it."

"I'm going to quit the band and play soccer?"

"No, genius. You're gonna do both. And babysit for the Thorns, and get straight A's. You're that girl."

"Am I?"

"This is news? You're accelerated. You do everything faster than everybody else. I'll bet you score more goals this year than you did last year. I'll put money on it."

"Where's my brother, Nate—tall guy, charming?"

"He died today in a fiery explosion."

The kettle whistles, and Nate makes two mugs of hot chocolate, adding whipped cream and a bunch of rainbow sprinkles.

♫ ♫ ♫

In Geometry, we have a substitute who gives us a free period to do homework so long as we're quiet and let her read her newspaper.

"I love this lady," Joe whispers. "She subbed in my physics class last month, and let us watch television all period."

"Nice."

"We're playing at Stoked again on Friday. Did Ernie tell you?"

"No."

"Well, we are."

"OK."

"I had a good time last week—the dancing."

"Yeah."

"Cool." Joe flicks his pencil against his notebook. "The new Kelly kind of freaks me out. When did she go all Fabulous Humanitarian on us?"

"Nate explained it to me last night. I've been underestimating his charm."

"Of course." Joe laughs. "He charmed the bitchy cunt right out of her."

"Joe!"

"All right over there," the sub calls, rattling her paper at us. "No talking."

We duck our heads, and snicker.

"You are such a bad guy," I tell him.

"Hey, I mean it as a compliment."

"She'd be so pleased."

"Don't tell her," he pleads. "I think she could take me in a fight."

200

"Joe, I really want to play soccer."

"I know you do."

"Don't you think—don't you think maybe I could manage both? Play in the band, and play soccer?"

"No gigs on Thursday, no practices Monday night?"

"You never know. I'd get study hall again instead of gym, and last year, Jennifer Cairn starred in the senior play, and played varsity soccer."

"She was a lousy Sandy."

"Stay on topic."

"You're right," he says. "She managed to do both. She looked like a junkie there at the end, but she managed. And it would be tragic to miss you in those little shorts with the socks pulled all the way up to your knees."

♫ ♫ ♫

Joe walks me to English, and we pick Alicia up along the way.

"My obituary is so embarrassing," Alicia says, "I don't even want it read when I'm dead."

"I wrote like thirty drafts," I tell her.

"She should have had you write each other's obituaries," Joe says. "At least that would have been interesting."

"She can't be interesting," Alicia says. "It requires character. If she makes us read these aloud," she adds, glaring at us, "I'm going to leave. I'm serious. I'll walk right out."

Once we're seated, Alicia breaks her last stick of lead, and borrows some from me.

"There's a war on, you know," I tell her. "You should be better prepared."

"You're going to get tired of saying that," Alicia says. "Not soon enough, but eventually."

"Well." Overhead surveys us with her mole eyes. "Since Cole and Alicia have so much to say, they can read their obituaries first. Cole, come on up and read for us."

I stall a moment, just in case Alicia walks out. Nope. Up front, by the blackboard, I unfold my paper and look at the class. "You're sorry to have died," I begin. Ruth, the first girl I ever saw wearing white braces, laughs. I cough once, then start over. "You're sorry to have died. Not because death was painful, it wasn't, but because you're beyond feeling anymore. The first kiss, and the last kiss, don't matter, or the suck of the wet playing field on your cleats. Your brothers' lumbering gait like giraffe on the savannah, your mother's lullaby in the feverish dark, your father's story voice, they're forgotten now. Gone are fireflies and cicada shells, the sound of a minor key. Here in this box, neither comfort nor chill. The sun cannot burn your neck, or freckle your skin. Outside, the soldiers crouch with their guns, and the engines drone, and the children open their books to begin again. Valor and fear have no weight here. You can't hear girls laughing, or the bugle's call. The bracelet taken from your wrist, misplaced at some distance, in some time you no longer recall. Without surname, fingerprints, first person. Beyond indifference and corruption, you don't even sleep now."

I cough again, and glance at Overhead. Her eyes are closed. I hesitate, waiting. Did I bore her into a coma? Her eyes blink open, and she says, "Cole, read that once more, if you would."

I swallow and start again.

"Thank you," she says when I've finished. She reaches out her hand for my paper. "An inventive approach to the assignment."

"Maybe she had a stroke," I tell Alicia in the hallway afterward. "She can't actually have meant to compliment me."

"I can't believe she made us read our eulogies aloud. The woman is just wrong wrong wrong. And don't you even think about complaining. Yours was good, and you got a gold star in front of everybody. No, don't you say another word to me about it. I want to forget the whole dead thing." She flings her arms up like a hallelujah, and shoots down the stairs.

♫ ♫ ♫

At lunch, Bangs and Joe have a table, and a box of pepperoni pizza.

Bangs winks at me. "I couldn't bear to watch you eat another peanut butter and jelly sandwich."

"I'm tired of school," I say.

"We should ditch and go to the shore," Joe says.

"I've never ditched," I say.

"Never?" they ask.

"Well, just first period." The pizza isn't hot, but tastes spicy and fattening and perfect.

Someone hung a bunch of yellow bows up around the cafeteria. At the table next to us, three boys aim and flick bottle caps at the drama girls.

"Stop!" the girls squeal between bouts of giggles. They attempt to launch caps back, and hit Joe instead.

"Sorry!" they cry in the same chorus.

"What are you guys up to?" Stacy Masteller asks, as she slides into the chair beside me.

"Pizza?" Bangs offers.

"Thanks. I'm fucking famished. What a shitty day. I just got detention for chewing gum. Since when does anyone give detention for gum chewing? Fascism. Mr. Crucifelli thinks he's in the Gestapo or something. And why is watermelon so offensive, you know what I mean? He said the outcome might have been different if I hadn't chosen watermelon. What does that even mean? This pizza is seriously good." Bangs hands her another slice, and a napkin. "Is it true you guys are playing Stoked this weekend?"

"Yup," Joe says.

"What's the cover?"

"Five bucks."

"I am so there," she says. Another bottle cap slaps our table and wings over Stacy's shoulder. "Once more with the bottle cap and I put my fist through your asshole." For the first time, the drama girls hush. "I'm fucking serious," Stacy tells the three boys beside us.

"Whatever," one mutters as he turns back to his tray.

Bangs' grin stretches around his entire head.

"Anyhoo," Stacy says, turning to me. "I have a letter for you."

"Yeah?"

She digs in her denim purse. "Shit. Hold this." She hands me her comb, her styling gel, her mascara, and three lipsticks. "Oh, I have more watermelon. The day keeps looking up. You guys want?" She passes watermelon to each of us. "Maybe it's in my coat." She roots through the pockets of her jeans jacket. "Weird. I just had it."

As the bell rings, and we climb, slowly, from our plastic chairs, Stacy pulls the envelope from her purse. "There. He said to tell you he meant to send a proper letter, but he didn't have any stamps."

♫ ♫ ♫

The bell rang like ten minutes ago, but Tabitha Goddard is just standing at the podium not speaking. She is entirely red—a full-body blush—and appears to be waiting for Jesus. When she gets up in front of the class, trembling and vermilion, you actually give odds to fainting versus a seizure. Her speech topic today: The Right to Die.

I open my letter, and read.

> Dear Nicole,
> You know The Cure's lyric from "Disintegration": "A woman now standing where once there was only a girl"? They meant you.
> Desire should be straightforward, right? You see what you want, and you go after it. Never mind rejection, and mixed messages, and fear, and the possibility of failure. See. Claim.
> I told him to wait. I told him to take his time and savor and enjoy the buildup. Not to scare him. Not to freak him out. But I did. I freaked him out. Maybe that doesn't matter to you. Maybe it's too late, and nothing will help. But I had something to do with this, and I want to say how wrong I've been. How sorry.

We learn early, move after move, base after base, in different economies, sometimes in different languages, that no one stays. We learn early not to be sentimental. Boxes get lost, furniture broken, orders change. We learn to disengage. He loves you. He's an idiot, but he loves you. He's afraid. He's unkind. And he loves you. That hasn't changed. He's a mopey little shit if you want the truth. I actually feel sorry for the guy.

Mike

I have to write my own eulogy, but Jeremy gets his brother to write his love letter.

Tabitha Goddard bangs her fist on the podium and scares the shit out of us. She's fiery—her speech as well as her skin. Outside, the day blues, and a wet snow falls indiscriminately.

Tyro. Noun. Beginner; novice; person lacking experience in a specific endeavor. The vampires craved the blood of twenty teenaged tyros.

It's midnight. Joe and I finally persuaded the sentry to let him drive onto the base. I had my I.D. card, but the guard kept saying I'd broken curfew, and couldn't be admitted onto the base until 6 a.m.

"Curfew is 2 a.m.," I told the guard.

"Not when we're at war. When we're at war, curfew is midnight."

"For Chrissake, it's three minutes till midnight."

"Not by my watch."

"You can't be serious. We play in a band. I'm rarely home by midnight."

"Then," he said, "you'll rarely be admitted back onto the base."

"You must have a list of exceptions," I said. The sentry blanched. "You do, don't you? Nicole Peters." I reminded him.

He returned to the guard shack, and checked his clipboard. In a moment, the gate raised and he waved us through.

"Don't say anything," I warned Joe.

"Is he going to let me back through?" Joe asked.

"If he doesn't, come around back. I'll leave the door open for you."

"Maybe I should just stay."

"You're cute. Thanks for the ride."

"Tomorrow."

Midnight. I stand on the pavement looking up at Jeremy's attic room. The glow may be from the fish tank, or the desk lamp. I've had two beers. We played for sixty raucous fans, and made $175.

I smell of cigarettes and pot and beer. The backdoor of Jeremy's building is unlocked. I climb two steps at a time, stepping near the railing.

At his door, I wait for my heart to slow, for my breath to quiet, and then I try the doorknob. It opens. In flannel pajama bottoms and a white t-shirt, he's sprawled on the carpet on his belly. When he looks up, his eyes widen.

"What are you doing here?" he asks.

"I got your brother's letter."

"What letter?"

"Your brother wrote a love letter for you."

"Why?"

"Didn't he tell you?"

Jeremy stands, and smoothes his black hair down. His pajama pants are blue plaid and ridiculously large. Three of him could fit inside them. I take the letter from my coat pocket and hand it to him.

As he reads, Jeremy colors a Tabitha Goddard shade of red.

"You really didn't know?"

He shakes his head.

Well, that's awkward. I come marching into his room with my two-beer logic, and my bar perfume, and the guy doesn't know anything about the letter. "I'm sorry I barged in here. I thought you knew Mike had written that letter. I thought you expected me." Oh, worse and worse. "I'm sorry," I say again.

"Don't go."

I stop. Faced away from him with my hand on the doorknob. A turn and two steps from an exit—a graceless, desperately desired exit.

"It's all true," he says. "Mike's letter. Every word. Except none of it was his fault."

Warm and close, the boy and his room. He pulls my coat off my shoulders, and spins me toward him. Oh, I'd give my right hand for a piece of watermelon bubble gum.

His face scratches mine. Sweet and sour, his breath gasps between us as he yanks my skirt up and tells me the bathroom floor will be easiest to clean.

I hold my breath until I think I have to tell him to stop, and then the tension is gone, and it's not horrible at all, and then he's finished.

"I'll get a towel," he says.

I prop up on my elbows and see a small shallow puddle of blood. So this is it. This puddle of blood. I don't feel like I've

207

compromised my soul. More than anything, I'm sleepy. Jeremy mops the floor with a towel, and hands a second one to me.

"We probably shouldn't shower," he says.

I wrap the towel around my shoulders before I realize why he handed it to me. Even the cold of the tile is comforting.

"High five," I say. "We totally did it."

He doesn't move or meet my hand. Poor sportsmanship.

"OK, then," I say, bundling my clothes together. "I'll call you tomorrow."

Marching Papers

Quiescence. Noun. Inactivity; stillness. Sunday should be a day of quiescence, but instead we're dragged to church every week. (Just kidding, God.)

Kelly has her right leg propped on one of the metal kitchen chairs, and a huge ice pack draped across her ankle. We're both in our black Umbro soccer shorts and Monmouth Regional sweatshirts. We smell sweaty and look windblown, and should have showered after practice.

Today is Mom's birthday; Nate took her on some totally fabricated errands in order for Kelly and Nigel and Dad and Meghan and me to prepare a lavish dinner. Except Kelly torqued her ankle at practice and can't stand, and Meghan has yet to show, and Nigel keeps yelling at me about improvising with ingredients, and Dad disappeared twenty minutes ago without putting the steaks on the grill.

"You're slicing those too thinly," Nigel scolds.

"Dude, they're carrots."

"And you're slicing them too thinly."

"You know what, feel free." I hand him the knife. "Slice away."

"How much longer for the casserole?" Kelly asks.

I check the timer. "Twenty minutes."

"This is insane. We should put the steaks on. I've seen people grill things. How hard can it be? Put the steaks on the grill, stand around holding the spatula."

"Where's Meghan?" I say again.

A moment later the kitchen door opens, and Jeremy brings in two sacks with French bread, and sparkling apple cider, and the ice-cream pie he picked up from Carvels.

He kisses me, and lays his purchases on the kitchen table. "Cooking injury?" he asks Kelly.

"Becky Shrader slide tackled me at practice." Kelly grins. "I landed on her with my elbow. Hard."

"Well done." He folds the paper sacks, adds them to Mom's

211

stockpile, and belts his arms around me. "What do you need me to do?"

"Can you grill?" Kelly asks.

He takes the marinated steaks and ventures back outdoors, only to return empty-handed a minute later. "Your dad's back."

"You bought orange and yellow peppers," Nigel tells Jeremy. "I did."

"I love orange and yellow peppers."

"I know."

"Mom only ever buys green."

"I picked up some Greek olives and feta cheese too. Spice up the salad a little."

"You should buy all our food," Nigel says.

I set the table; Kelly fills the glasses; Meghan finally arrives with a box of decadent chocolates and a beautifully wrapped gift.

"I have the best excuse ever," Meghan says. We wait. "I'm going to West Point!"

"Shut up!" We yell. Even Kelly hops up to stagger across the room and hug Meghan.

"I got the letter this afternoon." She takes it from her pocket and shows us. "I've read it five thousand times in the last half hour."

"Congratulations," I say, thinking of the package I received this morning. My atheist is stateside again. He arrived home with two weeks' leave before he has to report to Kaneohe Bay Marine Corps Base in Hawaii. **From the desert to the tropics . . . at least my tan won't suffer.** He sent me a mixed tape of Heartbreak Songs for Teenagers, and a photograph of himself in civilian clothes. I totally knew he'd be a fox.

So the war was anticlimactic. Isn't that a good thing? Who the hell wants a climactic war? Despite oil fires, and scud missiles; precision-guided bombs, and months of anxiety about chemical and biological weapons, my atheist has come home with both eyes, and all his limbs, and the same irreverent sense of humor. That's the best news ever—right up there with Meghan attending West Point, and Mom turning 45.

212

"Cole," Kelly says, peeking inside the oven, "this casserole is perfect. Get it out of here, quick."

Even as Dad brings the platter of steaks into the dining room, Mom and Nate walk in the front door. Mom actually tears up when she sees the table.

"What have you done?" she asks.

A fairly decent job actually—no matter what Nigel says. Mom even compliments the casserole. We keep making toasts. Somehow I feel drunk and sparkling.

After dinner, while the coffee brews, Meghan and I load the dishwasher. Who knew I'd envy Kelly her swollen ankle?

"What are we going to do to celebrate West Point?" I ask Meghan.

"Skip our vocabulary list for a week?"

"A whole week? You reckless deviant."

Once the coffee has finished brewing, we rejoin the table with the box of chocolates.

"More?" Mom asks. "Are you trying to kill me on my birthday?"

"You'll need the sugar just to open all these presents," Nate says.

Woodworking tools, a sweater knitted by Meghan's mother, a couple of tapes, a Doggy Life t-shirt, and a final slender package in a tie box: pearls and a folded sheet of paper.

"They're gorgeous," she tells my father. "And this?" She unfolds the paper, stares at it for a long minute, then looks up at Dad. "Do they know?"

He shakes his head.

"Know what?" Nigel asks.

"We're going to Hawaii," Mom says, handing the Army's orders to Nate.

"We aren't," Nigel says. "It's supposed to be Alaska."

"In Hawaii," Dad tells Nigel, "you can drive at 15."

"When do we go?" Nigel asks.

"Dad reports August 1st," Nate says. "I can't wait to visit you guys."

"Me either," Kelly and Jeremy chorus.

213

"Which base?" Meghan asks. "Schofield Barracks?"

"Aliamanu Military Reservation," Dad says. "I'm assigned to the brand-new chapel there. I'll give the inaugural sermon."

The first sermon in a brand-new chapel in Hawaii on your last assignment for the Army, assigned to a church again, exactly as you wanted. Seated on Dad's right, I haven't said anything. My atheist will be in Hawaii. That should soften the blow, right? But softened or not, it feels like a blow—sudden and unavoidable—and sets me reeling.

"What do you think?" Dad looks at me.

"I have to get ready," I say, standing. "I need to be at the club in an hour."

♫ ♫ ♫

We take the van; Dad lets Meghan drive all of us kids. The band hasn't played at Board since January. Nate piggybacks Kelly indoors, her ankle wrapped in one of Nigel's many ankle braces.

I'm leaving. For real, with an expiration date and everything, I'm leaving Jersey this summer. Had I expected a reprieve? The Army to send my father an official letter: Colonel Peters, we'd like to extend your assignment at Fort Monmouth for another two years; enough time for your only daughter to graduate from high school. No doubt you are aware of how much the United States Army values stability and continuity and the lives of teenaged girls.

When I join the guys backstage, Trevor says, "Peters, I think we should open with the new song. What do you think?"

"I agree," I say.

Ernie shakes his head. "It's such a naked song. We should build to it."

"What do you think, Joe?" I ask.

"Tell her your idea, Trevor," Joe says.

"OK," Trevor puts his hand on my shoulder and goes all man-of-vision on me. "You sing the first verse with just the bass. The guitars come in on *Leave your arguments*, and I lead in for the chorus. Yeah?"

214

Open the show with a bass line. Me and a bass line. "We should try it," I say.

They nod.

Mr. Hand introduces the band. On stage, a single light trains on me. From the crowd at my feet, the screaming has not let up. Everywhere I feel the shift of bodies, the movement amplified. I hold on to the mic.

And then, Joe's box-step rhythm:

Pack your letters, and pack your suitcase
Haul your furniture out of our place
Take your books, take all your photographs
Drag them anywhere and don't look back

Ernie climbs eight notes, and I drive beneath him. My voice a clear, warm growl, not at war, for once, with the thunderous drums. This could be my attic room, or Joe's garage.

Leave your arguments, leave all your pity
As starter to burn our city

When Trevor crashes into the chorus, I hear Ernie lick a counter-melody line.

I won't ask you to touch my skin.
I won't ask you to plunge back in.
All we were, all we have ever been
I'll remember as golden.

They all sing golden. I could weep they are so beautiful—these boys beside me. We back Ernie's solo; he pulls the measures apart only to circle back to build better, more heartbreaking lines.

It's just a story—a fiction now
A girl so loved, she glowed somehow

I will wander these emptied rooms
Dreaming of the life I knew
If I could tell you what I have lost
Would I feel less robbed?

We repeat the chorus until the crowd joins us. The whole fucking place chants I'll remember as golden. I'll remember as golden. I'll remember as golden.

♫ ♫ ♫

In the van, without stage lights or my guitar, I feel smaller: a reduction of Gig Girl, the boring aftermath. The rest of them go on laughing, and maybe they haven't stopped since dinner. I wanted to stay with the band. We broke and loaded the gear in silence, and stood around while Joe and Trevor smoked. Comrades. The brothers I can't tell about Hawaii.

Kelly steps down from the van gingerly, then leans against Nate, up the walk to her doorstep. How many more nights do they have? Or any of us?

Nigel scans radio stations. "This?" he asks, and no one argues.

Beside me, on the backseat, Jeremy whispers, "In an hour?"

"Not tonight."

"No?"

"I'm exhausted," I say.

He peers at me in the dark, but doesn't speak. Minutes later, in the street behind my house, he kisses me a light, final goodnight, and I am nearly across the backyard, the screen door closing behind Nate and Nigel, when I realize that Meghan is still with us.

"Why didn't we drop you at the dorm?" I ask.

"I need to walk. I'm so awake."

"Can I come?"

"I thought you were exhausted." She laughs.

"Did you hear us?"

"I heard." She holds out her hand, and I take it, and fall in

216

beside her. "The long way?" she asks. "Through the parade field?"

"Sure."

The field is sodden, and the night chilled, though next week it'll be April.

"Will you visit?" I ask her.

"I hope so."

"Will you miss me?"

"Yes," she says. She squeezes my hand. "Jersey for Hawaii isn't a bad trade."

"Do you promise?"

"Yes."

She stops beside me, and points at the tree by the memorial. "Bats."

I see an indistinct, flitting shape. "Are there bats here?"

"Right there," she says.

"I can't tell." My knees ache with cold. Anxious to keep walking, I pull her forward, my body strangely keen. "My atheist wrote me. He's back home."

"On leave?"

"Yeah. His next assignment is Hawaii—Kaneohe Bay."

"You're kidding? See, you'll already know people."

"Right. I can hang out with my pen pal, who happens to be in his twenties, and in the Marines."

"What is it you'll miss?" Meghan asks.

"The band, my friends, school—I might even miss Overhead—soccer, field hockey, our crummy house and the bugles and my attic and you and Jeremy and Bangs. My whole life. I'll miss my whole life."

"Tropical beaches, a driver's license, surfers, new friends, new teams, a new school."

"New doesn't mean better."

"It doesn't mean worse, either."

"I'm cold," I say, and she presses her shoulder to mine, hurrying us through the empty field. I wish I'd brought Pepper, to have company on the walk home. "Brooks told us countless lives were saved because we nuked Japan. How can that possibly be true?"

Meghan's laugh is so huge and sudden that I actually shy.

"Jesus," I say, and punch her. "You scared me." Practically bent in half, Meghan clutches her belly, and carries on laughing. "What's so funny?" I ask. "She really said nuking Japan was a better option than going on with the war. I know it doesn't sound true, but what if she's right?" More laughter. She seems to be collapsing under the weight of it. "Seriously, where's the comedy?"

After some length of time, she gasps, "Where did that come from? We were talking about tropical beaches."

"I was thinking about beaches, and then Pearl Harbor, and kamikaze pilots, and POW camps, and how crazy the war in the Pacific was; and when Brooks told us the thing about the nuking, I wanted to ask Dad, but I forgot, and when I remembered just now, I asked you instead." Flustered, still not getting it, I look at her—as much as I can see in the near dark: her red wool jacket, a glint from her necklace and her eyes. "They're all connected," I say, almost defiantly.

"Doesn't your brain ever get tired?"

It's tired now, I'm tempted to say, but her tone surprises me.

She takes my hand again. "Come on, crazy." And eventually adds, "My father agrees with your teacher. Your father probably does too. For my part, I have no idea. Was it racism? Would we have nuked German cities? Was the war in the Pacific so different that you can't even compare? Would the Japanese have gone on fighting until every one of them was dead? I don't know. In a war filled with horrible atrocities, I'm not sure I understand any of it."

"Don't worry. West Point will teach you all the right answers."

"I hope not. I'd rather learn to ask the sort of questions you do."

"Do you think I'm disloyal to you?" I ask.

"When?"

"With Jeremy?"

"I don't understand how any of this works, Cole. How can it be wrong when it feels like this?"

We don't reach her dorm until 2 in the morning. It feels as though we've walked for years, around the planet maybe. I don't want to let go of her hand, or the night. I don't want to be afraid anymore.

"Come on," she whispers. "I'll drive you home."

"You'll only have to drive back."

"Don't argue. You're always arguing."

"I am not."

"Hush," she says. "Just this once, shut up and do as you're told."

Turgid. Swollen; distended; tumid. Adj. Oh my god, tumid?

Only midway through warm-ups, and our team is completely demoralized. Somehow, since we climbed from the bus, the following information has found its way to us: Point Pleasant Boro has nine returning seniors, an undefeated record, plans to play their second string and still annihilate us, and is led by a superstar—recruited to play for some exclusive club when she was eight—of such skill that she currently has her pick of full-ride scholarships to prestigious universities. If we doubt the truth of any of these statements, you'd never know from our sloppy shots on goal, our errant passes, or our crushed expressions.

The whole ride up here, Kelly was all Spanish Inquisition. She kept asking if Nate had talked to any of us about the two of them coming for a visit next Christmas, or if he'd said anything about which colleges he'd applied to. Would they at least be on the East Coast together? And if the two of them did come to visit next Christmas, would they be allowed to sleep in the same room if they stayed with my parents, and did I think Nate was sorry to leave? The bus drove on and on as though nobody suffered.

When we finally ran out onto the field, I wanted voltage and elegance. Instead, every one of us sucks, and mostly now I just want to sneak back to the bus for a quick nap. So, of course, I step into Amy Kent's path, and catch a soccer ball with my face. Sometime later, years possibly, when I open my eyes, I see sky and three worried faces.

"I didn't see you," Amy Kent says as Renee and Kelly bend down to examine me. "Your face. I'm so sorry."

"Am I bleeding?" I ask, afraid to touch my nose.

"No," Renee says.

Kelly brushes her fingers along my right eye, down the bridge of my nose, and along my cheekbone. "That's gonna be some bruise."

"I'm so sorry," Amy Kent says again. "Seriously."

I touch my face. Check my hands afterward for blood. Renee and Kelly pull me up, and pat my back. Aside from the stinging, I feel fine. "I'm OK," I tell Amy.

We take wild shots on goal with the rest of the team, until we see a tall black girl waving to us from the sideline. "What's up, kids!"

"Jayna!" Renee and I run over. Seven of the basketball girls have come to cheer us on. Dressed in MRHS letterman jackets, they're huge and imposing; their presence alone kicks something into us.

"Ya'll look like shit out there," Jayna says. "We drove forty minutes to watch ya'll look like shit?" She leans closer to me. "What the hell happened to your face?"

"Soccer ball," I say.

The girls laugh. And Denise Jordan, the one who replaced me as point guard, says, "I don't like to say you deserve it, but you mighta had a black eye coming."

"What'd you say?" Renee asks.

Denise Jordan slaps my arm. "She knows I'm playing."

"You all through playing," Renee says.

Nobody says anything. In the silence, we watch the other team drill. Three girls weave and pass toward the goal; after they score, the next three weave and pass. They're like paramilitary units.

"Scrawny little things," Jayna says. "Don't look like much to me."

"They are scrawny," Renee says, her voice low and almost wondering.

The refs whistle captains to the center of the field, and we join our team for the last few minutes of warm-up.

"What the hell happened to you?" Becky Shrader says. "Jesus. Your face."

I touch my eye. My face has the same weird feeling you get after shots at the dentist.

Renee squeezes my arm at the elbow and tells Becky, "One of those scrawny girls over there did it." She points at the other team. "Kicked a soccer ball right into Cole's face. On purpose."

"What?" Becky glares at us, and then at the other team. "You fucking hear this?" She tells the girls around us Renee's story.

"Those scrawny little things are dead," Renee tells me as we hustle over to Coach Robins. "I'm even a little sorry for them."

As sweeper, I should be attacking with the forwards, but for most of the game, I hang back with Kelly and defend our goal. Renee scores three times in the first half. She seems to glide across the field, dance past the defenders, and guide the ball into the net as though the whole thing were choreographed. My right eye has swollen shut. At halftime, me and my legendary injury get benched with an ice pack.

Mom and Meghan squeeze in behind me on the bleachers.

"What happened?" Meghan asks.

"I took a ball to the face."

"When?" Mom asks. She has her hand under my chin, and swivels my face around to examine the bruising.

"During warm-ups," I say.

"Does it hurt?" Mom asks.

"It's kind of numb actually."

Nigel leans between them and says, "It'd be so cool if you got a black eye."

"Yeah," I say, "super cool."

After halftime, Point Pleasant Boro scores almost nonstop and beats us 8–3: our first loss all season.

I ride home in our van, everyone else rehashing the game, the almost possessed way their team moved the ball, and the nightmarish twist of the second half. Lackluster—this loss, and my attitude, and I think I've never been so tired.

♫ ♫ ♫

When Jeremy sneaks over, I still have seven Geometry problems to solve.

"I can barely see it," he tells me.

"You're sweet," I say.

"Tell everybody you got into a fight at a gig."

"Anything sounds better than getting friendly-fired with a soccer ball."

"I had kind of a weird night too," he says.

"Weird how?"

"My dad's been reassigned. Effective July 1st, they'll be in Fort Benning."

"Won't you go as well?"

"I thought we'd have more time. Half the summer anyway."

"Mom says we're leaving the Saturday after school ends," I say. "She just told me." This isn't true. I've known for several days, but I haven't told him. I thought we'd have more time too. "Will you go to Georgia?"

"I don't know." Jeremy wears red sweatpants and a long-sleeved white t-shirt with a giant rooster logo on it. Whenever he wears some goofy t-shirt, it's always a hand-me-down from Mike. Stretched beside me on the bed, with his head tucked in his palm, he plays with my hair. "What happens afterward—you leave and I leave—and then what?"

I can't imagine any of it. Not the leaving, or the separation. I can't imagine living on an island in the Pacific. Of all the lousy ways to finish high school, that's the lousiest. Why not send me to Alcatraz?

"We could write letters," I say.

"Great. Pen pals."

"Maybe we should talk about something else."

"Yeah." He stands. "Maybe I should go."

I grab his hand. "Why are you mad?"

"When does it end? When do we get to be normal? I thought, once high school was over, I'd be free. Now you're leaving the country, and I have no idea where I'm going to be, and you don't even care. You're talking about being pen pals. Have you already picked out my nickname? The Lutheran? The preacher's son? The first?"

"Don't," I say.

"We never get to keep anything. Never. Temporary quarters, and temporary friends, and temporary schools, and we lost so much time this winter. Now it won't be months we're losing, it'll

223

be years. I'll go years without you. Years. Don't you see? Don't you get it? You won't even be on this continent."

He throws himself on the bed again, and covers his head with a pillow. I would touch him, but I'm afraid. I wonder if his skin will burn me.

When he sits up, his face is wet. "I won't even know what your room looks like."

"Just as crappy as this one," I say, "unless the movers break something."

"I love everything in this room," he says.

I should comfort him, but I keep thinking about how much I hate this furniture, these paintings of mossy rocks and scrawny streams, every one of these ornate lamps. And I still have my math to finish.

♪ ♪ ♪

At lunch the next afternoon, Kelly and I are alone at the table when Stacy Masteller joins us.

"Where is everybody?" Stacy asks.

"Since you mean Bangs," Kelly tells her, "he and Joe are in line for burgers and fries."

Stacy blushes.

"Bangs?" I say.

"Is that uncool?" Stacy asks me. "I thought you were back with Jeremy."

"It's totally cool," I say. "I had no idea."

Kelly groans. "You see nothing."

"He secretly worships Satan or something, right?" Stacy asks. "I've never liked anybody who wasn't completely fucked, you know, underneath."

"He's one of the best guys I know," I tell her.

"Will he be at your show on Saturday?"

"Yeah. You should come."

"Maybe I'll do that," she says, standing. "But now you have to come with me. Ms. Ruhl wants to see you."

"What for?"

"Beats the shit out of me. I'm just incarcerated here."

We walk down the hall together, and Stacy offers me a piece of strawberry gum before asking, "Did you have sex with him?"

"Bangs? No."

"Did he want to?"

"He never asked."

"No shit?"

"Nope."

"Why?"

"Why what?" I ask.

"Why didn't he want to have sex with you?"

"I don't know. Maybe he wasn't into me."

"See, that sounds weird. I think he must be weird."

"We're all weird, aren't we? Bangs isn't creepy, or a bastard, or anything. I promise you."

Stacy whispers, "Mom let me go on birth control after—after the last time—and Dad doesn't know. And I promised I'd tell her if I, you know, if I need it, or whatever, which seems totally insane since I'm already taking it, so what's the diff if she knows or not, but I promised, and I don't want to tell her and then it turns out I've got another asshole on my hands, you know? I'm at my, like, quota with assholes already."

"Do you want me to tell him?"

She stops and backs me into a bank of lockers. "I will scalp you if you tell him. I will sneak into your room and cut your tits off."

"Hey!"

"Don't you fucking say a word to him. Promise me." She jabs me in the chest. "Promise me."

"I promise, Jesus." For a small chick, she's terrifying.

Ms. Ruhl is in her office, eating a salad. Her black sweater drapes over her shoulders, and something about the pale skin set against the black wool reminds me of vampires.

"Here she is," Stacy says. She stands in the doorway with her arms crossed, posing as an enforcer, while I take the seat across from Ms. Ruhl.

"Cole, I have a proposition for you." She registers my black eye, but doesn't ask. I'm starting to love the people who don't ask. "I've been given twenty minutes in the spring assembly, and I'd like to have the chorus sing with your band."

"What?" Her salad looks disgusting: twigs and bark and ranch dressing. No wonder she weighs twelve and a half pounds.

"Your band, Doggy Life. I'd like you to play, say, three of your songs, for the assembly, and the chorus will harmonize. What do you think?"

"We're a punk band," I say, stating the first of my many reservations.

"You're brilliant," Ms. Ruhl says. "I heard you at Stoked. We could collaborate, and create something utterly unexpected. The assembly is scheduled for the last Thursday in May—we'd have plenty of time to prepare."

I frown at Stacy, hoping to appeal to her for some sane perspective here. Doggy Life playing with the chorus during a school assembly—how could anyone support such a notion?

"I think it's freaking genius," Stacy says. She and Ruhl look maniacal, their eyes practically glowing.

"Well," I say, rubbing my hands together. "I'll have to talk it over with the band. Trevor has a full-time job and his boss is pretty strict." I edge from my chair and press past Stacy. "But I'll talk it over with the guys and see what they think about a collaboration."

"And you'll let us know," Ms. Ruhl says, "right away?"

"Right away," I call back to them.

♫ ♫ ♫

We have an exam in Spanish. Senor Fernandez always turns the lights off during an exam, which makes it difficult to stay awake, let alone conjugate irregular verbs.

When the bell rings, I still have three questions to answer, and am the last to turn my test in.

"Que le paso a su ojo?" Senor Fernandez asks me, nodding at my eye.

226

I mime boxing since I don't know the word for it. He pulls his glasses down his nose and arches a quizzical eyebrow.

"Futbol," I say.

"Ah," he says, "si, futbol." He squeezes my shoulder. "Tenga cuidado, por favor."

"Como desee." Life sounds cooler in Spanish. If I'd known the word for mascot, I'd have said I got my black eye auditioning to be the team mascot. Rally around me everybody. Let my stupidity be your inspiration, but just for the first half. It's like I've made a mockery of my own life. I'm one of those effigies. And not only in soccer—now the band'll be ridiculous too, playing for a school assembly with a bunch of chorus girls dressed as waitresses.

In the hallway, Monica Prader shouts my name, and throws some kind of heavy metal salute.

"Where are you going?" Kelly asks me.

I stare around me, and realize I have no idea. "Biology?" I say.

"We drop Biology today," she says.

"Oh right."

"What's wrong with you?" she asks. I shrug. She hooks her arm through mine, and pulls. "We have to get to practice."

Practice. Jesus, as much practicing as I do, shouldn't I be better at everything? "How did you know," I ask Kelly, "about Stacy liking Bangs?"

"Well it was obvious, wasn't it?"

"Was it?"

"Sure," she says. We're nearly at my hall locker.

"You used to think I dug him."

"You did."

I don't remember anymore. For months I've thought of Bangs as my sidekick, the guy who draws a comic universe where we get to be heroic.

"Anyway," she says, as I swap my books around, "it was always you and Jeremy. Joe knew that from the beginning, and so did Bangs. It was only me—I misunderstood."

"What do you mean?"

"You were both so sad. All winter. This one day over break, we were throwing snowballs outside, do you remember? Nigel kept putting rocks in his. Anyway, I saw Jeremy at the window, and his face—" She touches her own face, remembering. "I was wrong about him. I had it all backward."

Lugubrious. This word is gross. Just reading it makes me think of snot. It probably means something like pompous, right? Adjective.

The chaplain preaching this morning is new: young, with light black skin, and a vague mustache. Alicia has been so still, I've had to check to make sure she's breathing. I think maybe she's lovesick. Meanwhile I've been guessing at my vocabulary list. It's not going at all well. Have you ever heard of the word *accretion?*

I flip through the bulletin and read his name again, Chaplain Harris, and his sermon title: Lot's lot. What do you make of a guy who opens with a biblical story of drunken incest? Unabashed. At the very least, he's unabashed.

We stand for the final hymn, and he raises his arms to us. "May the Lord bless you and keep you. May the Lord make His face to shine upon you, and be gracious to you. May the Lord lift up His countenance upon you, and give you peace."

I like this guy. He's dramatic.

"Cookies?" I ask Alicia.

"Hmm?"

"The service is over. If we don't hurry, there'll only be wafers left."

"His voice is like a cello."

I almost say *how romantic* but catch it just in time. "Very musical," I agree.

"We should go shake hands."

"What?" I try to pull away, but she's bigger than I am. In line with all the comely grown-ups, I don't have the nerve to struggle.

Then Alicia's shaking hands with him. "I enjoyed your sermon very much," she says.

He smiles at us. "I appreciate your seriousness," he tells Alicia. He looks at me.

"Very nice," I say.

"Nice?" He grins, and looks like a child, suddenly, in someone else's robes.

"The first time I read that passage I thought I'd be sick, but I get what you're saying. We're not all good stories, are we?"

"No." His grin is, if anything, wider. "Every lineage has its shameful secrets."

I consider punching Alicia as we snake through the hallway, and into the fellowship hall. She's bigger, yes, but I'm probably quicker, even in my Sunday clothes. When we finally make it to the refreshment table, we find a single, broken chocolate chip cookie.

"Very nice," I say, and chug the nearest cup of punch in as recriminatory a way as possible.

"You need new modifiers," she tells me.

"And new friends apparently. I guess I'll head home. I have fifteen words left to define."

"Why are you still doing those stupid lists?"

Because Meghan keeps giving them to me, because I'm afraid to alter any of my habits, because at some point we'll run out of words, and then what? "I have no idea."

♫ ♫ ♫

Nigel and Nate and I cut across the parade ground. A group of virile, muscular men plays lacrosse. If it weren't for my list, I'd watch for a while. Despite the muddy field, the day is sunny and tolerably warm. We squirm out of our jackets before we reach the road.

"We won't need to wear coats in Hawaii," Nigel says. His new thing involves listing the endless bright sides of living in Hawaii.

"Or make snowballs, or go skiing," I say.

"The Big Island has a ski resort," he says.

"It's artificial snow," I say. I've flipped through all of his library books too.

"It's going to happen," Nigel says, "no matter how you feel about it."

"Yes. That's exactly the problem."

He stops in the field, and says, "Cole, this is how it is. We

230

move. And this time, we're moving to Hawaii. Just accept it already."

"It might be easier if all I had to leave behind was the Chess Club."

"Cole." Nate says my name as an order: cease and desist.

But Nigel laughs. "Go on, then," he says. "Go on. Say whatever will make you feel better. I've been all the same places you've been. I've left all the same places you've left. You can't make me different. So go on, say whatever you want."

"I want to be like everybody else."

"What would that look like?"

"I'd have shiny hair and no pimples," I say.

Nate and Nigel laugh, and we're on the same side again.

After we've resumed our walk, Nate kicking halfheartedly at our shoes, Nigel says, "The Pacific is bluer than the Atlantic."

"Bluer, huh?"

"And the water's warm most of the year. And they have sea turtles, like right there in the coves. It's supposed to be beautiful."

We come through the trees across from the house and see Nate's car with the hatch open, and Mom and Dad—already in their play clothes—loading bags into the back.

"Hey," Nate says. "What're you doing?"

"Oh, Nate," Dad says. "We'd like to borrow your car."

"Yeah?"

"I'll make sure it's returned with a full tank of gas."

All the resistance drops out of Nate, and he grins. "Cool."

"Where are you going?" Nigel asks.

"Cape May," Mom says. "Just for a few days. Don't worry, Cole, we'll be back in time for your game Wednesday afternoon."

"Who's worried?" I say. Three days with no parents is a miracle right up there with the loaves and fishes.

"Now wait, you two," Dad says, and tucks Nate and me into casual headlocks. "I know I can trust you two not to have overnight guests, or throw a party, or anything of the kind. Can't I?"

"Yes," we concur.

231

"I know I don't need to have Meghan stay with you, or appeal to your characters."

We model innocence: two trustworthy, virginal teenagers, looking respectfully up at their father.

"Nevertheless," Dad continues, "Meghan is going to stay with you, and I am appealing to your characters." His hazel eyes bore into us. "No overnight guests. Agreed?"

"I'm eighteen," Nate says, "and you got us a babysitter?"

"Yes," Mom says. "Your father asked you a question."

"This is crap," Nate says.

"Don't say crap," Mom says.

"But Dad—" Nate protests.

"Meghan's inside," Dad says, "with subs. And I don't expect her to have to argue with you about anything. I expect exemplary behavior. Nathan, I want your word."

"This is such cr—" He glares at my mother, "Crud! What are you gonna do next year, send me to college with a chaperone?"

"I agree," I say. "No overnight guests. No orgies or animal mutilation. We won't even swap needles."

Mom folds her arms, and pinches her face up in that Keep Joking and Die expression.

"I'm kidding," I say. "You can trust us." I smile at them.

"Nathan?" Dad says.

"Fine. I agree." Nate stamps up the walk to the house, and calls back, "Enjoy my car."

"This," Dad says, slamming the hatchback closed, "is why we need a vacation."

♫ ♫ ♫

Meghan lets us watch *Bonnie and Clyde* and *Dr. Strangelove*. We eat our subs, make brownies, and popcorn, and then order take-out for dinner. At ten, the boys promise not to play more than an hour of Sega, and Meghan and I take Pepper for a walk.

"It's sprinkling," she says.

Spitting, more like, but we raise our collars anyway.

"What will Nate do?" she asks.

"Sneak out probably."

"And what? Walk to her house?"

"I forgot he doesn't have his car. He might take the van, I guess, even though he's ashamed to drive it. Or maybe Kelly's mom would pick him up."

"And drop him back off before dawn?"

"It does sound kind of unlikely." Pepper stiffens, and raises her hackles, but it's just a couple of black garbage bags.

Meghan's hair seems to catch the soft glow of the porch lights. As the rain falls more heavily, the sound in the leaves is sleepy and warm.

"What about you?" Meghan asks. "Will you have an overnight guest?"

"I've given my word."

"Ah," she says.

"Don't say it like that."

"Like what?"

"Like you don't believe me." The rope slaps against the flagpole. From the promenade, we can see the guard shack, and the entry gates, and the naked dogwoods. "God, Pepper, what did you eat!"

It doesn't occur to me until we're home again, on the back steps. "Where will you sleep?" I ask her.

She's looking up at the house; the light in the McIntyres' kitchen window blinks out. I got my ears pierced in that kitchen—three holes—when I was twelve. Mrs. McIntyre used a needle from her medical bag, and an ice cube.

"On one of the couches," Meghan says. It's almost a question, the inflection on that final word.

"They're best for napping really, not too comfortable for sleeping."

"I should check on the boys."

I wipe Pepper's feet, and give her a treat, and wait for a while in the dark kitchen. In the end, I climb the stairs to the attic alone, worried that I've upset her.

Before I turn off the lights, I finish my vocabulary list. Lugubrious means mournful or gloomy, as in: *Wuthering Heights* is a way lugubrious novel. I know it doesn't sound right, but it's true.

♫ ♫ ♫

Mr. Pang has on his pink fake-Izod shirt today. "I've got some exciting news," he says, once the bell's rung. "Cole and Christian both took prizes in the statewide art competition." He starts clapping, and everyone else joins in. "Cole won honorable mention for her photograph, *Wood Work,* and Christian won third place for his *Photo in a Field.*"

Wood Work. I didn't think Mr. Pang was serious when he said he'd enter the photo of my mom in the competition.

"Cash prizes?" Kelly asks.

"Yes," Mr. Pang says. He hands both Bangs and me a sealed envelope.

"For real?" Bangs asks. "There's money in here?"

"For real," Mr. Pang says. "Every prize winner is on display at a special exhibit at the Newark Museum through the end of April."

"How much?" Kelly whispers to me.

"$25." So, first my parents leave on a surprise vacation for three days, and then, this morning, Meghan has a bag of warm bagels waiting for us in the kitchen—poppy seed and plain with spreads of lox and cream cheese. And now the state is awarding me money for a photograph of my mother. "How much did you get?" I ask Bangs. He holds up his check for $30. "Nice. I don't remember *Photo in a Field.*"

"It's of you," he says. "From that day at the baseball diamond."

"So, really, you should split the prize money with me."

"Probably."

"Why don't we take both your winnings," Kelly says, "and spend the rest of the day at the shore."

"Yeah?" I say. "Who'd drive us?"

"Joe?"

Bangs grins, shaking his head. "We have a test today in Bio, remember?"

"We have a test today?" I ask. "You're joking."

"'Fraid not."

"Fuck," I say, "so much for my charmed life. Dude, a Bio test today makes me feel totally lugubrious."

"Makes you feel what?" Kelly asks.

"Lugubrious," I say.

"What language is that?" she asks.

"This one," I say.

"Points for usage," Bangs says.

"Thank you. Yesterday, I thought it had something to do with snot."

"No, that's loogies."

Kelly glances between us. "Geeks of the world," she says, "unite!"

"Do either of you have your Biology book?" I ask.

We quiz each other using Bangs' study sheets. The margins of his papers have pencil drawings of superheroes and skateboards and lightning-shaped words.

I think one chick in this class might actually be doing something appropriate to the study of photography, but everybody else is doing homework for some other class. Mr. Pang is talking movies with a couple of guys up front. The droopy-eyed senior fell asleep before the bell rang; in fact, it's possible that he slept in here all weekend.

"Your friend called me," Bangs says.

Kelly looks up.

"Which friend?" I say.

"Stacy," he says. On his sketchpad he has drawn a werewolf in surf trunks.

"Oh yeah?" I say. We're studying him, like Biology notes. "How'd that go?"

"She's funny."

Kelly makes an encouraging grunt of affirmation.

"I told her," Bangs says, "that we should hang out."

"You should," I say.

"All of us," Bangs says. "At your show. We should all hang out."

"Oh," I say. "Oh, totally. That'd be fun."

"Cool," he says.

"You're going to be a virgin until you're like thirty, aren't you?" Kelly says.

Bangs and I both stare at her. I can actually feel the red burn from my ears down my face to my neck. "Dude," I whisper.

"What?" Bangs asks her. His expression is curious more than offended or embarrassed.

"She likes you," Kelly says. "What do you need all the padding for?"

"I don't know her," he says.

"So?"

"So, I'd like to get to know her, and that'll be easier if she's comfortable. And she'll be more comfortable around her friends, right? And you guys are her friends."

Kelly taps her fingernails on the desk. "And then what?" she says, finally.

"Then what *what*?"

"What happens after you get to know her?"

"I have no idea. That's the whole point."

"Not to have any idea is the point?"

"No," he says. "Not to have any expectations. We have the rest of our lives, you know? We don't have to experience everything right now, right this minute."

Oh god, I have totally heard this speech already. This is the savor speech. It's like they've all been going to the same meetings or something.

"I get it," Kelly says. "Get to know her. Take your time. And in the end, when Stacy goes back to her old boyfriend too, you won't actually have risked anything, and it'll be just fine."

"I'm not in a hurry," Bangs tells her. "That doesn't mean I'm a coward." His voice is as soft and even as always.

"I haven't called you a coward."

Bangs chews his thumb, then asks me, "What do you think?"

236

"About which part?"

"Any of it."

I think of the glow of Meghan's hair, and the walk up those stairs to the attic alone. Of Jeremy loving my room, and Bangs skating through the winter night, and Joe perched on a stool, listening. "Isn't all of it risk?" I say. Nate crying in the kitchen, afraid he'd hurt her. Stacy with her birth control.

Obloquy. Censure, blame, or abusive language intended to discredit. Ill repute. Noun. How does this word work? Sir, I would like an opportunity to respond to your obloquies.

After soccer practice, Jeremy picks me up to drive me to band practice. Paused at a stoplight, he kisses me again, and says, "Why do I feel like I haven't seen you in ages?"

"Because you're a sap."

"Nigel says your parents are out of town."

Nigel. "I promised them," I say. "No overnight guests."

"How about just half the night?"

"I don't think so."

"Why?"

"I don't want Meghan to get in trouble."

"Why would she?"

"She's watching us."

"You're not serious."

"Totally. They left Meghan in charge. It's crazy."

"Your parents have no faith."

"None at all."

We're the last to arrive, and the boys are dinking around with some Jane's Addiction. They've left the garage door up, and have four opened bags of chips on the table with their sodas.

I've plugged in and turned on my amp before I notice Trevor. "What the hell happened to you?" I say. Trevor's hair is shorn—above his ears—and his sideburns and chin have been tidied as well.

"He's got a girlfriend." Ernie smirks.

"Are you wearing a rugby shirt?" I ask Trevor.

He nails the high hat a couple of times. "All right, get it all out."

"Are you dating a hypnotist or a witch or something? How'd she get you to cut your hair and lay off the leather vests?"

"Peters," Trevor says, "when you see her, you'll understand."

"Oh, she has super-huge tits?" I ask.

"Peters." He shakes his head. "That's no way to talk about

women. And, yes," he holds his hands out for emphasis, "she's gifted."

"Well, she has some kind of gift. Prep school looks good on you."

Trevor blushes. "Yeah, yeah," he says.

I tell them about Ms. Ruhl's proposal for the school assembly.

"Just the chorus?" Joe asks.

"Yeah, just us and the chorus."

"Full kit?" Trevor asks.

"I guess so."

Joe asks Ernie. "What do you think?"

"I think we should play *Love Song.*"

Trevor groans. "Dude, no sentimental crap. If we're gonna play The Cure, let's play something rugged."

"Not The Cure's *Love Song*; I'm talking about Cole's. Just imagine it, with all those sopranos."

We do. We imagine.

♫ ♫ ♫

In Jeremy's car after practice, he and I eat hot wings. With our windows down, the street noise of honks and shouts plays along with his Phish tape. The night smells of rain and garbage.

"I thought you didn't want to play with the chorus," he says.

"It seemed cooler, somehow, once the boys started talking about it. It'd be a completely different kind of sound for us, you know?"

"I've been reading about giraffes," he says.

This comes from absolutely nowhere. "Why?" I ask.

"You're into them, right? You told me you're a giraffe person." He has barbeque sauce on his mouth. I can feel it between us, the thing I've pushed him away with. What I know, in this car, watching this black-haired boy gesture with grubby fingers, is how tender my ache is.

"You've been reading about giraffes?" I say.

"Yeah, I thought I could find an origin myth or something. I wanted to be able to tell you a story about them. But, mostly I've just found kids' books with random facts."

"Like what?"

"Like baby giraffes join nurseries called crèches, and are left pretty much unsupervised. And giraffes sleep standing up—never for more than a few minutes at a time. They get half an hour of sleep a day. And they're the only mammals born with horns, the males and the females."

"I didn't know any of that."

"And nobody really understands how they evolved. The animal they're descended from had a short neck."

"What else?" I say.

"The males eat a different part of the tree from the females, so they don't have to compete with females for food. And the herds can be spread over a large distance, because they're tall and easily spotted by one another."

It is a story, after all. His hands are sticky, and his mouth. And there is no impediment between us. None at all.

♬ ♬ ♬

Meghan opens the front door before I get my key in the lock. Dressed in pajamas, with her hair frazzled and her face flushed, she looks kind of wild. "Where have you been?" she demands.

"At practice," I say.

"It's midnight," she says. "You don't really expect me to believe you've been practicing with the band until midnight on a school night."

"Well." I take a step back, bewildered by her intensity. I'm still on the front porch as she's blocked my way inside. "We were at practice, and then we stopped on the way back to get some dinner."

"Dinner. I see."

"If I'd known you were going to freak out, I would have called."

"That's what I love about you, Cole, you're so considerate."

"Why are you mad?" I say.

240

"Because it's midnight, and I had no idea where you were—in pieces in somebody's trunk for all I knew. You've taken advantage of my being here. You'd never have pulled this shit with your parents."

"I'm sorry," I say.

"Fuck you."

"Meghan." I stretch my arm out to touch her, but she slaps it away.

"Fuck you." She turns, and without another word, or a backward look, disappears into the house.

Have you ever wanted to throw a piano? Lift it right up over your head and hurl it through the living-room wall, right into the dining table in the next room, or, better yet, through the living-room wall, and the dining table, and on through the next wall, and the exterior brick, to crush the grill and the clothesline in the backyard? Spectacular destruction. A burst water main, a gouged-out building.

Honestly, I'm too tired for a tantrum. Too tired, at midnight, to turn around and stomp back into the dark. Anyway, where would I go?

We should open *Love Song* with the piano, guitar, and bass. The sopranos will kill. The song's kind of high for me, and I can't wait to hear the sopranos hit those notes. I haven't done any homework. I'm not even certain what's due. I could sleep on my feet. Like a giraffe.

♫ ♫ ♫

The next morning, I wake at 6. Though I only have twelve Geometry problems to solve, they take a whole freaking hour. I finish one of my two assigned History chapters. During homeroom, I inadvertently stab myself in the palm with my mechanical pencil, and immediately worry about lead poisoning. Overhead gives us a pop quiz on some William Blake poem. She has written it on the board with her instructions: YOU HAVE THE ENTIRE PERIOD TO EXPLICATE ME. Blake is such a clown. For

241

Speech, I get to deliver an impromptu speech on trade. Two minutes. On trade.

At soccer practice, Coach Robins thinks we're fucking about and has us run sprints.

"This a game to you?" he hollers at us. "This a big joke? You like losing so much you just want to keep at it? Murphy, pick up the pace, or I'll bench you for the rest of the season."

Afterward, in the locker room, nobody speaks. Locker doors slam. Somebody keeps sniffling. Sprawled on the floor, Kelly has her eyes closed, and her arm thrown across her face.

"God," she whispers, "even my hair hurts."

She and I wait for the boys in the hallway outside the gym. Today they're lifting weights. We've finished our lab summary for Biology, and I'm midway through Spanish translations when Nigel peeks his head into the hallway and grins at us. "We'll be out in ten minutes."

"I think," I tell Kelly, "that's the highlight of my entire day. We only have to be here another ten minutes."

"Yeah, and then you get to spend the rest of the day with the prison matron. How is it possible Meghan is more of a rag than your parents?"

"What do you mean?" I ask.

"Nate said she yelled at him a bunch of times last night. He didn't tell you?"

"No."

"She freaked because he was playing Sega too much, and on the phone too long, and up too late. He said she even yelled at Nigel. Can you imagine anyone yelling at Nigel? Like, for what, being too quiet and diligent?"

"Why'd she yell at Nigel?"

"Apparently he was reading too late."

"Well, this is the last night she'll have to put up with us."

"And vice versa."

Instead of going home, we hit Salsa, and order three nacho platters with the works, and chicken quesadillas. Long after the toppings are decimated, and only soggy chips left, the four of us stall. Nate was so reluctant to go home that he offered to treat us to dinner.

"We better go," Nigel says at last. "She's probably mad we aren't home already."

We drop Kelly first, and make it home by seven. The house dark, Pepper a launching maniac. While I feed the dog, Nigel does recon.

"She isn't here," he calls from the sunroom.

Nate checks around. "She hasn't left a note." He punches Nigel. "Quick, let's play Sega."

I leash Pepper, and am dragged down the back steps and straight into Stacy Masteller.

"Hey," she says, holding her lit cigarette over her head like Pepper might try to sneak a drag, "What are you doing?"

"Hey." I gesture at Pepper. We fall into step without further comment, and then Stacy holds out her pack of cigarettes. I take one, and we let Pepper pull us toward the parade ground.

"Today was the weirdest day," Stacy says, "ever."

"Way weird," I agree.

"Mr. Green told me I'd forfeited the privilege of bathroom breaks for the rest of the school year. I mean, what? Has he ever been to the girls' room? The place is radioactive. And my mother is wigging out about Metal again. How can I prove I'm not worshipping Satan? Listen to Country? Take a urine sample and leave me the fuck alone already, Jesus."

At the memorial, we sit on the slabs of cement everyone says mark the crypts of dead Civil War soldiers. We smoke another cigarette while Pepper investigates the bushes.

Stacy digs through her purse. "I'm out of gum, but I know I've got some orange Tic Tacs."

As my Tic Tac dissolves, I hop discreetly, chilled now by the cryptic cement and the night air.

"Christian called." Stacy cocks her head back like a Pez mid-extraction. "He told me all about the comic book he's writing. Like I actually got excited just hearing about it. A comic book. Weirdest day ever."

Stacy and I stall outside for ages, talking about how Tic Tacs are disappointing. Like for a second you're hopeful, but it comes to nothing.

Later, I let Pepper into the kitchen, give her a treat, then climb to my bedroom. By ten, I've finished my homework, abandoned *As I Lay Dying,* and put on a Cure tape—*Kiss Me, Kiss Me, Kiss Me*—to strum along.

The knock at the door is loud enough to rule out Jeremy. I fling it open, and return to bed without a word.

Meghan has let herself in, and closed the door, before she observes, "Aren't you speaking to me either?"

"What do you want me to say?" I keep my arms around the guitar.

"Nothing. I'm the one to apologize." She sits at the foot of my bed. "I'm sorry, Cole, about last night. I was awful. Awful to you, and Nate and Nigel, and I have no excuse, none at all, but I hope you'll forgive me."

"Why?"

"Why what?"

"Why do you want me to forgive you?"

She stares at me; her expressions flutter across her face. Flattened by the cap she wore earlier, her hair appears listless. Robert Smith sings, *How beautiful. How beautiful you are.* "Because I'm sorry."

"This time, yes. And last time you were sorry, and next time you'll be sorry, but Jesus, how about if you just stop? How about if you stop being an ass, and needing forgiveness?"

She stands, walks toward my desk, the angle of the ceiling cutting down upon her, as though she'd suddenly grown. Boxing Alice. She puts her hands in her hair. "Because this is easy?"

"What's that got to do with it? You chose this, didn't you? You make all the rules. You draw every line. I'm just a kid, right? And so you can kiss me, but that's as far as it'll go. Until you fuck me, but just the once. OK, twice, but then you can vanish and treat me like shit and atone for all of it, right? As long as you're sorry, that's all that matters. Never mind how many times it happens, or how much you want it. And more than that: never mind what

I want. Never mind asking me, or taking it into account. What I want has never mattered. You want forgiveness? I forgive you. I forgive you for all of it. Now get the fuck out of my room."

"Cole?" Her voice punctures the wail of Robert Smith, and the raging bass, and the raging child.

In stop motion, I set my guitar in its stand, and step toward her. "Get the fuck out of my room. I mean it. Get out."

She stares at me. And the worst part is how much I want to comfort her. I want to apologize. To hold her. To take her hands from her hair, and put them around my waist, and lean against her, hold on. I want to hold on despite everything.

"Come closer," she says.

"No."

"Do as you're told."

I cross to her. Her hand comes up so slowly I think it stuns me, like hypnosis or something. "I want you more than West Point."

"Liar." Fuck. God.

"I want you." She draws her hands in a "v" up my belly and drags her thumb across my nipple. I help her lift my shirt over my head. "I smell you on my clothes. On my fingers. I think of you in my bed, soft as a mouth, begging me. Lie down."

I fall against the bed and she straddles me, pins my arms. "Say you want me to break you open."

"Please. Break me. Please."

"Say you want me."

"I want you, you selfish fuck. Stop teasing."

Laconic. Using few words; terse. Adjective. I speak laconic Spanish.

The turf of the stadium field looks different, the green more green, denser and softer. Our first game in the stadium—the overhead lights; the huge, cheering crowd; the flare of cameras—and we're intoxicated. Drunk on the idea that we might be athletes. This is where the boys play, but they're out now, booted in regular season, so we don't have to play on the upper field, by the teachers' parking lot, in the afternoon. The stadium lights and the huge, cheering crowd make us feel like gods.

I can see Mrs. Brooks (in a cap and jeans!) and Jay with most of the baseball team, and Bangs and Gabby, and Doggy Life, and, actually, I think half the school is here. This morning, the *Asbury Park Press* announced Point Pleasant Boro, the favorite to win state playoffs, would annihilate us. My mother already has her hands clasped in prayer. I hope it works.

Robins pulls us into a huddle. "Annihilate," he growls. "They wrote you're going to be annihilated tonight. They put that in the goddam paper and sold thousands of copies to everyone you know. What are you gonna do about it? What's your answer? Tonight, it's up to you. Now get your asses out there!"

Kelly throws an arm over my shoulder as we take the field. "Here's our strategy," she tells me. "Slide tackles. Let's bring every one of those bitches down."

Slide tackles are no longer legal, if they're from behind. As long as you slide from the side, or from the front, and are clearly after the ball, dropping girls is fair play. So we drop them. Kelly and I take down three just in the first few minutes of play. If they cross onto our side of the field, they are tackled, and we take possession, scanning for the forwards, for the breakaway, the chip, the quick score.

Kelly passes to me, and I see Jamie, our sweeper, dash up and

246

left. At midfield, two defenders come at me, and I skirt to the right, take three strides, and punt the ball high and long. Jamie's head comes back, her arms wide, and she chests the ball straight into their goal.

Robins screams at us from the sideline, "Don't get complacent! Re-form your lines!"

Now they come at us four at a time, passing quickly between girls to make it impossible to target any single one for a tackle. Our forwards rush back to midfield, and the midfielders hunker with the fullbacks, and when Sue saves the ball, and kicks it across the entire field, we break their lines and Renee assists to Jamie, who heads another goal.

It's a dream. A dream beneath the stadium lights. This time we're the military unit—disciplined and sharp. Their coach calls timeout. Diofelli, in an official-looking collared shirt, has positioned herself at our right corner arc, and bellows murderous instructions to—well, I'm not sure who she's bellowing at—possibly the refs, the opposing team, their fans, or everyone in attendance. Point Pleasant Boro brings in two subs, and then another several minutes later. Still we drop them. Drop, dart, dance. We come at them wave after wave. Someone in the crowd blows an air horn every time we recover possession.

I chip the corner kick to Renee, and she scores. And then Jamie takes the ball back from them in a scuffle, and one of their fullbacks steals it, and in the ensuing scuffle the ball lobs high into the lights, an arc that bisects the night. I step right, bend my knees, and, as the crowd murmurs a collective "Yes!" head the ball back down the field.

If any of us remembers that Point Pleasant Boro is slow to warm, rests their best players early in the game, and tends to bring wrath to the second half, you wouldn't know it from our halftime huddle.

"You've got them," Robins tells us. "You've got them, and you're going all the way."

Nigel screams something encouraging, waving his arms like a

pinwheel. And the dream unravels, almost as we walk back onto the field.

♫ ♫ ♫

Jeremy removes the screen from his bedroom window, and winds the window open. He stretches his arm back to me.

"You seriously think I'm going to climb out your bedroom window," I say, "and sit on the roof of your house."

"Don't worry, I've got a blanket we can sit on. An old comforter."

"A blanket?"

"You won't believe the stars—"

But I've already heard his pitch about the stars. "No fucking way."

"Cole, I promise you, it's perfectly safe."

"No. Fucking. Way." I throw myself onto his bed, and stare up at his ceiling. My mother had the nerve to say, "At least you weren't annihilated." 5–4. No, the score doesn't reflect annihilation, nor does it reflect the fact that we never managed to cross their penalty line the entire second half. We were effectively shut out. Helpless, as we watched them score five goals, and eliminate us from playoffs, under the big lights, before our home crowd.

Before I could walk off the field, Diofelli came over and hugged me. "I hear we're losing you."

"Hawaii."

"It's heartbreaking, Peters. You military kids, you're like gunpowder for our teams, and then, just as suddenly, you're gone. I haven't watched anybody fly down the field like you in years."

"Thanks, Coach," I said.

"Years!" she called after me. "Well played tonight, Peters. That was one hell of a header."

Framed in his bedroom window, Jeremy asks, "Will you sit on the windowsill?"

"Will you let it go already? I don't want to see any goddam stars."

He sits on the edge of the bed, and lays his hand across my

248

belly. I want to slap it off, but the truth is, he's comforting, and gradually I feel the poison drain away. I'm only tired now.

"As far as the sill," I relent.

He sits between my legs, on the roof proper, and he's right, the stars are glorious. Brighter than camera flashes and stadium lights. Bright and merciful.

"We're out," I say. "I can't believe it." The last of my Monmouth teams, and the checklist becomes another tick shorter: Finish soccer season.

"How are practices going? With the chorus?"

I know what he's doing. I know, and I'm grateful. "Ernie says they give us another texture. At first, I had no idea what he was talking about, but I think I get it now. Ms. Ruhl on the piano gives a different rhythm to the songs—and the harmonizing stretches the lyric—and we sound better. We sound better than we've ever been. The songs are a building now, when they used to be a room."

"I thought they were cities."

"You're biased," I tell him.

"My parents are coming—to the assembly. I guess your dad's been telling everyone. Dad says there's a buzz around the chaplain school."

"Are you joking?" With my hands in his hair, I'm tempted to give him a tweak.

"No."

"Why would he do that?"

"Why are you upset?" Jeremy asks, twisting around to look at me.

"Why am I upset? Are you kidding me?"

Jeremy shrugs. "He's proud of you. He's excited, and he wants everyone to know he's excited. I don't blame him. I've been having dreams about it. In my dream, you guys are all wearing cloaks like friars."

I laugh, and the anxiety vanishes. Jeremy's a tonic tonight, an antidote to every snakebite. What difference does it make if Dad brings everyone he knows? I'll never see any of these people again. In five weeks we'll be gone for good. A flash of gunpowder.

"You're sure you don't want to go to prom?" he asks. He has one knee propped up, and the other stretched out. He's in shorts and a sweatshirt, and must be cold. I wish I'd showered after the game. I'll taste of salt.

"Yes," I say. "Aren't you?"

"I thought the girl always wanted to go."

"Not this girl."

"You want a beer?"

"Where are your parents?"

"With your parents, at the Officers' Club for their Hail and Farewell."

"God, that's tonight?"

"Yes."

"No wonder Mom wore her pearls to my game."

He winks at me. "You don't miss anything. Can you reach the cooler—on the floor behind you—and grab us both a beer?"

"Yeah, the view is sweet and all, but I'm not drinking out here." We climb back inside, starved, suddenly, for chips and salsa and bottled beer.

"I've picked William & Mary," Jeremy tells me once I've sat, cross-legged, on his comforter.

"Last week it was Georgetown."

"William & Mary. I've decided."

"So it's settled."

"Yup."

"William & Mary."

"Yup. In stone. Irrevocable."

"Will you send me a long-sleeved t-shirt in the fall?"

"Of course."

"Hawaii's no place for hooded sweatshirts."

"I'll see if the campus bookstore sells bikinis. Oh, and Mike's promised to come down for the movers, and graduation."

"In order of significance?"

"Yes. He's worried about his baseball cards."

250

We finish the six-pack, and watch the fish in their tank, and later when he kisses me, his mouth is filled with sleep. Heavy, and deep, I drink my fill.

♫ ♫ ♫

Dad says the prayer. We hold hands and bow our heads, though Nate keeps his eyes open. "Lord, thank you for this meal, for the opportunity to be together as a family, for your grace and your son. Amen."

Spaghetti with meatballs, garlic bread, green beans, and a fresh salad; I can't remember the last time I ate family dinner.

"Well, Cole," Dad says, "we're excited about your school assembly. Miss Jensen is coming, and Colonel Masteller, and all of my staff."

"Great," I say.

"Nicole," my mother says. "Modify your tone."

"Great," I say again, and sneer at her. Dad's puzzled. He stares back and forth between me and my mother. Alright, so I'm a jerk. Jesus. "I wish you'd asked me."

"Asked you what?" he says.

"Asked me if you could bring everyone you know to my school assembly."

"I didn't think—I'm sorry."

"It's OK. Forget it."

Mom shoves the breadbasket at me. "Pass some bread to your father."

"Sorry," I say again.

"It starts at two, right?" Dad asks.

"Yes," Nigel says. "You should all wear your Doggy Life t-shirts."

"Dork," Nate coughs.

"I'm wearing mine," Nigel says.

"Don't forget to iron it," Nate says.

"Nathan!" Mom warns.

Nate rolls his eyes, and eats an impossible softball-sized forkful of spaghetti.

"Nate," Dad says congenially, "what'd they teach you at school today?"

"Einstein worked in a patent office." Nate stuffs the rest of his bread into his mouth. "When he was young."

"Is that right?" Dad looks hopeful.

"Yes."

"Interesting."

"If you say so."

Dad plods on. "What about you, Nigel? What'd you learn?"

"Shakespeare plagiarized from other writers."

Dad scowls. "Which writers?"

"German ones."

Dad scowls around the table at us; you can almost see him decide to let it go. "Cole?" He raises his eyebrows at me.

"Mr. Pang wants us to alter a photograph. He says it'll be our final project."

"Alter it how?" Mom asks.

"Any way we like. We can alter it with flash, or light, or whatever, while we're taking the photo; or we can alter it while we're processing the negative; or we can alter the photo itself after it's fixed. We're supposed to experiment with all three, but we'll only be graded on two photographs." I don't mention Bangs' plan to take shots of the band performing at the school assembly. After all, they'll know soon enough. An experiment within an experiment as witnessed by every student at Monmouth, and the entire chaplain school.

"Well, I've had some exciting news," Dad tells us. "For the first two weeks we're in Hawaii, we'll be staying at a hotel right in downtown Waikiki. Practically on the beach."

"Why?" Nate asks.

"And, we'll be housed—eventually—in a volcanic crater called Aliamanu Military Reservation."

"Eventually?" I ask.

"A volcanic crater?" Nigel says.

"What do you mean eventually?"

"Well," Dad says, " there's a bit of a wait."

"How long a wait?" I ask.

Dad glances at Mom. "It might be three months. Six at the most."

"So," I say, "where do we go after the hotel in Waikiki?"

"Temporary housing," Mom says.

"So we get to move a bunch of times. That's awesome. I can't wait."

"Nicole—" my mother begins, but I'm on my feet, and nearly through the door.

"I'm not hungry," I say, and send myself to my room.

Nascent. Beginning to exist or develop. Adjective. Insert breast joke here.

All four heavy doors of the activities hall are propped open. I've been shunted through these rooms all my life, usually for youth activities, like Sunday school—always the same linoleum, the same fluorescent lights, the same gimpy foosball table—never the ball, just the table—as well as a chalkboard with a single stub of yellow chalk. Not yet ten on Saturday morning, the lights in the long, rectangular room still off, and two men at the back, a chessboard between them, have paused to listen. From the doorway, I watch Leroy, his cap turned backward, his head bowed, play *Motherless Child.* His guitar a furious rush of bass and lick, the musical equivalent of call and response, and then, his ragged voice: "If I mistreat you girl, I sure don't mean no harm. I'm a motherless child, I don't know right from wrong."

I stand at the door for the entire song, hold my breath through the long, tearing solo, and if I had any skill at all, I'd rush in and give him a rhythm to play against. When the guitar comes to an abrupt halt, he bows a little lower, and then the chessmen applaud, and I do too, with my own guitar case tucked between my knees, and Leroy seems to wake all at once. He smoothes his tie, and waves me over.

"You're early, kid," he observes. It's true. But this is the last time, and I don't want to waste any of it. "Tell me," he says. "How'd your assembly go?"

"We played that little satirical love song, you know?"

He nods toward my case. "Play it for me."

I take my guitar out, and run my fingers over the neck. I can't even do the song justice anymore, not on my own; not after the chorus, and the band, and the undercurrent of piano.

"E flat," I tell him. He gives me four measures, and then he joins in.

I'm gonna sing you a love song
And I'm gonna get all the words wrong.
In the end, I'll make you cry
In the end, yeah, we'll both die.
Love is tragedy and hopelessness and misery.
And I'm gonna sing you,
I'm gonna sing you a love song.

I sing it for him, and then we both keep playing, going round and round, the notes tiny now, in the dim room.

"The sopranos were so big," I say. "They just hit the thing through the auditorium, and the harmonies made it seem like a real song, you know? And with the piano and everything—I can't even tell you. It's one thing in bars, with the amps, and pedals—but on the school stage, it all seemed—" and I can't believe the last word, even as I say it, "legitimate."

"Second verse," he orders.

I'm gonna sing you a love song.
Soon enough you'll be gone
And while you're retreating
Holding my heart, still beating,
In the dust-bowl swirl, I'm a fractured girl
Between the earth and the sky,
Between the earth and the sky.

"You found another sound," he tells me.

"Another sound?"

"You play with other people, mix it up, try different instruments, different voices, and you discover another sound. It might just be a layer at first, but it might be more than that, too. It might be a whole different sound. Like what you got at the school assembly."

Something inside my chest tightens. "You play until you hear it?"

"Until you create it. You'll know. You'll know it when you hear it."

Another sound. You can find another sound. It's the most encouraging thing anyone has ever said to me.

Leroy takes his glasses off, and wipes them with his pocket handkerchief. "The music isn't done with you yet," he says. "Today, I'm gonna teach you an old blues song. Put some growl in your voice, now. Dig deep."

At the end of the lesson, I crouch to wipe my guitar down, and put it back in the case. I take longer to do this than anyone ever has. Stall stall stalling.

"You don't seem like a t-shirt guy," I tell Leroy, handing him the shirt wrapped in a brown paper bag. "But you can wear this on laundry day, or whatever."

He unfurls the shirt, and grins. "Doggy Life! Well, all right! A mutt playing the bass."

♫ ♫ ♫

In the parking lot, Meghan idles in her convertible.

"Why is it you?" I ask.

She grins. "Your mom had to rush off somewhere to get Nate. How was your lesson?"

"Traumatic."

"How about Little Szechuan for lunch? My treat?"

"Yes, please." I launch my seat back, rest my hand on her thigh.

"It's too beautiful to be indoors," she says. So we order carry-out, bring the lot to the park.

The day beyond lovely: bright, with low humidity, and a lazy breeze meandering through the grass.

"Bring your guitar," she says. I follow along behind her. She has a blanket and citrus soda. Was her smile always this wide? She wears a striped tank top, and short denim shorts. Her body fluid, muscled, already browning in the first days of June.

"Play something."

I glance around: some children by the play structure, a few adults on the periphery, but no one nearby. I tune my guitar, watching her, waiting for my next instruction.

"Something slow," she says.

I play something slow, and then something fast, and the afternoon falls down around us. The blanket soft, the grass dense, the strings holding their pitch admirably, and I keep playing. My strum seems to be changing. Even the old songs sound different.

A small child shrieks down the metal slide, his arms raised straight up to God. Boys play Nerf football in the field by the bus shed. The bugle blows.

She has cleared away the empty cartons, and soda cans, and lies now, staring at the sky, her head in her clasped hands. "More," is all she says. And I obey.

Seminal. Meghan? Are you kidding me? Seminal? Alright, *highly original,* and *influencing the development of future events* sound pretty groovy, but you know people just think *semen* whenever they hear this word, right? Adjective. And I get the theme of this list, by the way. Subtlety, not what you're best at.

Bangs and I watch *Charade.* Cary Grant, Audrey Hepburn, Walter Matthau, it's a classic. For most of the second act, Bangs has been sketching in one of his notebooks. We had this idea for altering the photographs—well, Bangs did—he hand-painted the guitars in a shot from the assembly, and in another he painted the microphones and the stage lights. The shots are freaking eerie. You look at them, and aren't quite sure, at first, what's wrong with the photos. You just know they're wrong somehow—sharper and blurrier all at once.

I came over to see his work, and to eat snacks and watch movies.

"What are you working on," I ask. "Your comic book?"

He winks, then passes his notebook across to me. A girl appears to be playing the clarinet in an orchestra.

"A mild-mannered musician?" I ask.

"Aren't we all?" he says. "Natasha plays the clarinet. And when she plays certain songs, the listeners forget. She makes them forget. She concentrates on whomever she chooses while she's playing, and her notes bore into their memories and wipe them out."

"That's horrible."

"Yes."

"So she's a villain."

"Well." Bangs takes his notebook back. "Doesn't that always depend?"

"No," I say. "You're the writer. You choose the hero and the villain."

"I think the characters just happen. I mean, they choose themselves. I draw them, but it's their story, you know? Is Natasha evil? Is she villainous? Partly. She's other things too. She's a really good cook—risotto is her specialty."

Even his penmanship is interesting, each letter precisely etched. Natasha looks a little like Meghan. "What if there's nobody to talk to," I say. "In Hawaii. What if I don't meet anyone these next two years—anyone real?"

"Planes go back and forth between here and there. And the postal service, and telephone lines."

"I'll be so lonely."

"Me too," he says. Someone in the movie screams, probably Audrey Hepburn.

"I'll miss all these afternoons when nothing happened."

Bangs chews his thumb, nods.

♫ ♫ ♫

Germans love parades. When we lived in Mainz, we went to parades or on Volksmarches all the freaking time. During kindergarten, we made paper lanterns for some festival, and returned at dusk with our families, to march around the town in the gathering night. Ancient magic, the shadowed streets lit with our own delicate contraptions, the excitement of the late hour, and the cold. For some reason, standing on my porch, watching our parents prepare the tables for the garden party brings our lantern walk to mind. My parentss and Jeremy's parents have combined forces. They've unfolded tables between the houses, and piled summer food for the party. Dad has grilled burgers and hotdogs, and we have salads, deviled eggs, watermelon, cantaloupe, ears of corn, potato chips, sodas and juice, baked beans, fried chicken, cobbler, pies, and homemade ice cream.

Nate and Nigel have Frisbees, hacky sacks, soccer and foot-balls in a bin behind the garage so we'll have our options readily at hand. Mom has asked twice if I'm sure I don't want to wear a summer dress. Ancient magic. The final party. A kind of wake. Goodbye to this life we have known. And though it's barely noon, I wish for paper lanterns, for something to glow.

Gabby and Bangs stock the coolers with ice and drinks, and fetch and carry with Meghan. The requisite checkered tablecloth, the children's table, benches, blankets, folding chairs; we might be at the beach, or a church picnic. Trevor, his girlfriend—her bangs teased high enough to qualify as antennae—Joe, and Ernie arrive together in Trevor's van. They've all promised to watch their language, and remain sober. Trevor carries a hand drum.

When Monica Prader arrives, we're midway through a game of Ultimate Frisbee, and the girls are decimating the boys— Alicia is a Frisbee god, her passes arc out like a boomerang and wing back to our waiting fingertips—and Monica joins, despite the fact that she's attired in a billowing summer dress decorated with little cherries.

"A dress?" I say by way of greeting.

She kicks a glossy, black-booted leg up. "I've got shorts on underneath."

"Of course," I say. "Frisbee?"

"Totally," she says.

Every kid in the neighborhood has cruised by on a bike or skateboard, and ended up joining our party. The Thorns bring Annie and Karen, and Karen wants me to run with her as we dash up and down the lawns tossing the Frisbee. She squeals with delight, grabbing at anyone near us, laughing harder when we tumble. The day's fiercely bright, humid, and riddled with bugs.

Jeremy and Mike intercept impossible passes—their arms tip tip tipping the Frisbee up, and then snagging it. Trevor and Joe collide so often we've stopped checking to ensure no one's broken anything.

We take frequent breaks to eat. We're like locusts, alighting to devour before collectively moving elsewhere.

Chaplains come from the school—some bring their families— and stand around in bunches telling classic stories. "Oh, he was a wild one. Wasn't he one of the Three Amigos?" "What do you mean you've never heard about the Three Amigos? Brother, you haven't lived!"

Miss Jensen arrives with an ice-cream cake, and—what

could I have been thinking?—the woman's old enough to wear garters, sasses everybody, and could never have had an affair with my father. "Well, now, you must be KNEEcole. It's a pleasure to meet you, KNEEcole. The stories your daddy tells about you would light you up. What's the one about the bomb in the girls' locker room? I know I've got it right, now, just by the look on your face."

Jeremy, Meghan, and Ernie crash into a bush, and have to be helped upright. I have Meghan's hands in mine, and pull her up, and into my arms, her laugh like cannon fire. I pick evergreen needles from her hair. I've had it so wrong.

♫ ♫ ♫

We break for dinner, and the adults have replenished the coolers and the platters. The dads want to play football with us.

"Touch," one of them says, in case we might have mistaken them for athletes.

We play heavy-handed touch. Trevor tackles me into Stacy Masteller, and she drops a knee into him on the next play. Even Nate hasn't lost his temper. The bugle calls, and the sun drops, and the dads light a fire in a pit, and the littlest kids sleep on blankets, or against their mothers.

"Grab your ax," Trevor tells me.

Meghan comes upstairs with me. The room emptied except for a suitcase, a duffel, a sleeping bag, and my acoustic guitar. Even the carpet's gone.

She stands beside me, the edges of our hands touching. From the opened window, I hear shouts and laughter. School is over. We leave in two days for the West Coast, for a family reunion in Seattle; and then, Hawaii. My atheist will meet us at the Honolulu Airport. He's promised to give me a tour of the island. I'm going to live on an island you can drive around in a single day.

We kiss until I'm not afraid. I slide two fingers inside her. Oh! That's the sum of my technique, but she grabs onto me and kind of thrashes, and I can feel her entire body. Her throat tips back,

and her feet press against mine like I'm a ladder. Her face. I can see inside her.

With a hand on my wrist, she whispers, "I'm done."

"Already? Do you want to go again?"

"Yes."

God loves me more than I ever imagined.

I have my guitar in my hands, but I already hear it. Without strumming, I hear a new sound.

"What is it?" she says.

"Do you know what giraffe nurseries are called?"

"No."

"Crèches."

"I love that word. Crèches," she whispers into my hair.

"Say it again."

She does. I imagine I can hear Trevor's hand drum. Ernie and Joe and Bangs will have their guitars out as well. We'll play late into the night, but at some point the party will disband. Disband.

Meghan takes my hand, and leads me down the stairs. Mom and Dad make s'mores—they are marshmallow-toasting experts—and the boys are seated in a row with their instruments. Jeremy eases my guitar from my hands, and takes the open seat beside Ernie.

"We've arranged one for you," Ernie says.

He strums the opening measures of *This Flight Tonight,* and five teenaged boys sing Joni Mitchell in falsetto, and for the final chorus, which they play ten or fifteen times, they call for us to join them, and we do, the chaplains and their families, the neighborhood kids, and Nigel's chess club buds, and Kelly with her head rested on Nate's shoulder, and the Thorns, and Gabby and Stacy Masteller, and Monica Prader in her cherry dress, Trevor's antennaed girlfriend, and Alicia and me as well.

When I look for Meghan, she's beside the fire, and if I wanted a lantern, I had only to ask.

Aver. State confidently, declare as true. Verb.

Bangs altered his photograph for our final project by hand painting masks onto each of us. Afterward, I scratched the negatives, and ended up with some really cool effects. My photographs looked like they'd been recovered from a bombed house or something, like reels from old movies with a stray hair flitting through them. Mr. Pang thought both of our results were way groovy.

I kept Bangs' photograph, and he kept mine. And the night of the garden party, I also got a comic book he made me. He signed it and everything.

Joe and Trevor and Ernie gave me a sweatshirt with a Doggy Life logo on it. "For Hawaiian winters," Joe said.

And then, suddenly, it's ten o'clock on Monday morning, the cars packed, and Mom and Dad and Nigel and Pepper pull away in the van, and Nate and I have promised we'll be right behind them in the hatchback, but Kelly won't stop crying, and Mike and Jeremy and Meghan and I stand by the hatchback, and don't say anything.

I wish I had a photograph of the last minutes: Mike's Venus Girl Trap t-shirt, and Jeremy with the light washing his face, and Meghan tucking her hair behind her ears. We already know the old stories, and can't tell the new ones yet. We've promised about letter writing, phone calls, Christmas.

I don't remember how long we stood there, waiting to part. I remember Kelly cried for a long time, and Nate wouldn't leave until she'd stopped. I remember Jeremy and Mike ran inside to help their mother with something, and Meghan stared at her shoes until they'd returned. I remember worrying Nate and I would get lost, and have to pay for our own hotel room. I remember the sentry saluted when we left the base.

♫ ♫ ♫

Nate and Nigel swear I didn't quit basketball until senior year. And

Jeremy claims he wrote the letter that got us back together—not Mike. He didn't make this claim until I admitted I didn't have the letter anymore.

When I talked the whole thing over with Meghan, she laughed, and said, "Oh, Cole, you know it wasn't like that at all. We had sex all the fucking time."

But that was later. She's thinking of later. The truth is it happened exactly like this. Every word.

About the Author

Jill Malone grew up in a military family, went to German kindergarten, and lived across from a bakery that made gummi bears the size of mice. She has lived on the East Coast and in Hawaii, and for the last fifteen years in Spokane with her son, two old dogs, and a lot of outdoor gear. She looks for any excuse to play guitar. Jill is married to a performance artist and addiction counselor who makes the best risotto on the planet. *Giraffe People* is her third novel.

Go to jillmalone.com to read her idiosyncratic and candid blog.

Bywater Books

LEAP

Z Egloff

"This is a talented writer."
— Carol Anshaw

Summer 1979. Rowan Marks is done with high school. Next comes college. And in between there's a yawning gulf—the last carefree summer vacation.

At least, it should be carefree. But Rowan's older brother Ben is smoking way too much pot. Her best friend Danny is in love with her. And Catherine, the new girl in their small Ohio town, rubs her the wrong way. Well, that's OK. Rowan can deal. She's got it all worked out.

Then everything turns on its head. Catherine steals her heart, Danny falls out with her, and Ben crashes the family car, ripping the family secrets bare.

All of a sudden, Rowan has a stark choice—is she going to grow up or give up?

Print ISBN 978-1-61294-023-6
Ebook ISBN 978-1-61294-024-3

Available at your local bookstore
or call 734-662-8815
or order online at www.bywaterbooks.com

Bywater Books

ART ON FIRE

Hilary Sloin

Winner of the Bywater Prize for Fiction

*"You need characters and plot and tension to drive the reader
through the pages. And* **Art on Fire** *has these things in spades.
Let this one seep into your mind and work its magic on you. It's
the superb craftmanship of a master storyteller at work. "*
—Out in Print

Art on Fire is the pseudo-biography of Francesca deSilva's
short but colorful life, interspersed with essays on her paintings by critics, academics, and psychologists. These razor-
sharp satires on art, lesbian life, and the academic world,
puncture pretentiousness with every paragraph.

*"Far from dull, these essays are hilarious, pointed
mini-satires on art criticism (complete with fake footnotes)
that illuminate the chapters of deSilva's life at the same time
they bring her fictional body of work to life. Sloin clearly sees
these paintings in her head, and her ability to convey that
to the reader is astounding."*
—Out in Print

Print ISBN 978-1-61294-031-1
Ebook ISBN 978-1-61294-032-8

Available at your local bookstore
or call 734-662-8815
or order online at www.bywaterbooks.com

At Bywater Books we love good books about lesbians just like you do, and we're committed to bringing the best of contemporary lesbian writing to our avid readers. Our editorial team is dedicated to finding and developing outstanding writers who create books you won't want to put down.

We sponsor the Bywater Prize for Fiction to help